**DO NOT REMOVE
CARDS FROM POCKET**

Camp

CAMP

Alan Saperstein

TICKNOR & FIELDS
New Haven and New York
1982

Camp Freedom, its specific location, and the names
and descriptions of all other places, events, and
characters in this book are completely fictitious.
Any resemblance to real persons and their professions
or organizations is unintentional.

* * *

Library of Congress Cataloging in Publication Data

Saperstein, Alan.
Camp.

I. Title.
PS3569.A58C3   813'.54   82–5811
ISBN 0–89919–094–4   AACR2

Printed in the United States of America

D 10 9 8 7 6 5 4 3 2 1

For Lynn

But this people, which dominated the ancient world, left nothing but stones, either singly, or in groups of three.

— *Gustave Flaubert*

PART 1

All our troubles go away for the summer

ONE

Ten long strong fingers probed the delicate disks along the little boy's tense spine. The fingers moved slowly, like snakes on hard, cracked ground, searching for the right opening, the familiar chink in the spinal armor.

A shiny black shoe stepped on a steel pedal; the middle of the table dropped away; from shoulders to hips nothing supported the slender torso of the little boy.

The fingers stopped, dug in gently, took hold, remained poised until the muscles of the little torso were lulled into an instant of relaxation, and then quickly the fingers pressed-pushed-pulled.

In a split second the little back cracked, and so did the wall that holds back pain.

"Don't scream," the huge, muscular man warned. "You'll scare away my patients." His voice was deep and slow.

The boy could not scream. His pain had tried to drive him out of his own body. It had strangled and paralyzed his efforts to speak and move.

The boy's mother paid the chiropractor in cash.

"I'm going to run a camp this summer," Dr. Stone droned as he pocketed the ten and five singles without counting them. "It would be good for Samuel," he said. "Yes. Special exercises. Special activities. A special program to strengthen a boy's spine. In more ways than one."

"I'll talk to my husband."

No, don't; please, Ma, don't send me; he hurts me; please don't, Ma, please don't.

An invisible tear trickled down the little boy's cheek.

"Tell him it would be good for Samuel. He'll know what I mean."

"Don't you say good-by?" the slightly unnerved mother prodded her son. She felt as if the strong arms of the chiropractor had just forced her around a dance floor.

Dr. Stone squeezed the boy where neck and shoulder meet.

It tingled.

It went numb.

II

"I have this awful feeling in my bones."

Dr. Paluka said nothing.

"It's like being lost. Or being at the edge of some terrible danger."

Dr. Paluka said nothing.

"I feel as if I'm going through a minefield. Or that there's a deep hole. Like in all those Tarzan movies. A deep hole covered over with leaves and twigs and grass."

Dr. Paluka said nothing.

Mona lit a cigarette with the butt of the one she was smoking. "Is it Homer?" she asked.

"Is it?" Dr. Paluka answered.

•

"We're taking a cruise. I always wanted to take a cruise. Everett gets three weeks off now. The cruise is ten days. Homer will be in camp."

•

"I canceled the cruise. I'm too afraid to go away. How can I take a cruise when I can barely get myself out of bed in the

4

morning? I took a taxi here today. It's only three blocks. I couldn't walk. Why is my heart pounding like this?"

·

"It is Homer, isn't it?"

·

"I dreamed that Homer drowned. But not in water. Do you think it has something to do with the hole? The one all covered over with leaves?"

Dr. Paluka said nothing.

"I do."

·

"Dr. Paluka? Is that you? I'm calling from the emergency room. I didn't know who else to call. They took me here because I fainted. I was buying some things for Homer."

"What things?"

"Camp things."

·

"Listen to me, Mona," Dr. Paluka began. She spoke softly and evenly. "In June and July this place is crawling with mothers who don't know why they're so depressed. Why they're so . . . lost. They feel guilty. They feel scared. They can't even face — let alone enjoy — the wonderful vacations they've planned for themselves. One woman came all the way back from New Zealand before her tour was half over, that's how miserable she was. And why? Same as you. She had packed her kid off to camp."

Mona closed her eyes.

"You feel that you're dumping Homer for the summer, and you're worried that Homer will feel rejected. That he'll hate you and never forgive you. But you have a life, too, Mona. And you have a responsibility to Homer. Remember this: one of the most important jobs of a mother, maybe the most important, is to make your child's life a source of happiness to *you*. You know what's good and bad. You know what's best for Homer.

5

Why shouldn't he go to camp? Push, Mona. Push, shove, discourage, cheer, yell, manipulate, do anything you can to make Homer make you happy. That way you'll be doing the best for him, too."

·

"I've decided not to send Homer to camp."
  Nothing.
  "He's only seven."
  Nothing.
  "I always had the feeling he didn't want to go anyway."
  Nothing.
  "Naturally he pretended he was disappointed."
  Dr. Paluka said nothing.

III

Harry Mix watched his wife choke on a bone.
  Her face turned blue. His turned white.
  A man at the next table stood her up, clasped his hands around her, and squeezed hard against her diaphragm.
  A burst of breath dislodged the bone and she spit it up into her mouth.
  The danger of choking to death passed. But her panicky gagging had ruptured blood vessels near the base of her brain. She would not regain consciousness. Harry phoned his mistress and then followed the ambulance in a taxi.
  "It probably would have happened anyway, Mr. Mix," the doctor said. "The choking brought it on, but it was only a matter of time. Other blood vessels in a much broader area of her brain show a dangerous deterioration. We're not sure why. Anyway, the choking didn't help the matter certainly."
  "Oh my God!" Harry shouted at himself. "I forgot all about Harry Jr."

·

Two days later Harry's wife was still in a coma. The prognosis was not optimistic. Harry and his son had an awkward talk about sickness, death, spiritual matters, and summer vacation.

"Is she crying?"

"She's sleeping. She doesn't feel anything. She's fast asleep."

"Why don't they wake her up?"

"They're trying to, but she won't get up."

"Is she going to die?"

"Maybe."

"I don't want her to die."

"I don't want her to die either."

"If an angel tells that he saw her then that means she's dead."

"It's also possible that she'll just sleep like she is for a long long time. A year. Two years."

"You mean on a machine, don't you?"

"Right. Like the lady on television. They can keep her alive for a long time and in the meanwhile maybe they'll figure out how to get her better."

There was a long silence during which wife and mother was imagined plugged into a tangle of tubes, wires, battery packs, and monitors as if the very essence of life were an electric current. Harry and Harry Jr. tried to be brave. The boy broke first.

"What'll we do without her?"

"Hey . . . you crying?"

"I want Mom."

"We'll have to figure out something. Even if she gets better, she'll be different. Not as . . . not the same as before. She'll need more rest. She'll be weaker. She may not be able to use her right arm and right leg. So whether she comes home or not, we have to make a plan."

·

She lay frighteningly still. Her eyes were closed. The eyelids were so translucent Harry had the feeling she was looking at him through her unreal sleep.

He touched her bare arm and thought he saw the beginning of a smile.

"We had a talk and we decided," Harry said, "that he'll go to camp for the summer. He'll be outdoors, having fun, with something to do and people to be with all day and all night. And we won't have to worry about him for eight weeks. Eight weeks, my love. My dear, dear, sweet love."

This time there was no mistaking his mistress's smile.

IV

From the moment he was born Jeffie clung to his mother for the dear life she had given him. He would wrap himself around her, stick to her like a leech, try to burrow his way back into the dark, protective insides of her body.

At six months it was cute. At two years it was still cute, but annoying. At four years it was a definite problem. At five it was Jeffie's teacher's problem, too. At six it was Jeffie's psychiatrist's problem. At seven Jeffie's father decided to "fuck everyone else's bullshit advice" and take matters into his own hands.

"Come over here," he commanded one morning.

Jeffie ran to his mother and wrapped himself around her leg. He was small and thin for seven and his mother still believed it was his undersize in addition to his overly sensitive nature that made Jeffie so frightened of the world.

"Leave him alone, Sid."

"Get him away from you or I'll take your goddamn leg off with him."

"What are you going to do?"

"I'm going to show this puny little goddamn scared shit fuck-up that he can get along without his goddamn mama!"

Sid lunged at his wife and son. He caught Jeffie by his hair and yanked him free. He turned the shrieking, shaking boy upside down, held him with one arm, and carried him out back where Mutt was already yipping wildly and leaping against the limit of his leash.

Sid's wife ran alongside. She punched at Sid's shoulder and back. She tried pulling Sid's arm off Jeffie. She kicked and sobbed and slapped at Sid's head, catching his eye with a fingernail. Sid turned suddenly and batted his wife away with Jeffie's flailing legs. They didn't hit her hard but they caught her off balance and knocked her down.

"Sid!" she wailed as he flung the boy to the ground just within Mutt's reach. The dog jumped crazily all over the boy, barking the same for Jeffie's desperate situation as he did for table scraps or at a stranger or when birds flew too low or squirrels ventured too near.

"Sid! No!" Jeffie's mother begged. "Please don't hurt him, Sid. Please don't hurt him, Sid. He's just a baby. He's just my little baby."

She sobbed, Mutt yipped, Jeffie howled, his father sputtered and cursed under his breath. Years of frustration and anger had boiled over and caused Sid to act blindly. He had no plan, but he knew he had better come up with one fast or never again expect his family to take his rage seriously.

"I ain't hurtin' nobody!" Sid spit. "I'm just going to show you two what a goddamn seven-year-old kid is capable of!"

Sid's wife didn't understand.

He reached down, grabbed her under her arms, and lifted her to her feet.

"Let's go!" he said. Sid closed his aching eye. It felt better when he squinted. He walked his wife back into the house. In the doorway he turned toward Jeffie.

"And you," Sid seethed, "you are going to stay out here all afternoon and all night. Do you hear me? You're going to see that a seven-year-old doesn't need his mama to hold his hand every goddamn minute. You'll get along fine, Jeffie. Just fine."

·

By late afternoon Jeffie's mother was beyond calming. She paced and ranted and threatened. Sid sat cooly ready to pounce on any attempted rescue. His eye ached now even when he squinted. But he was determined to keep it open all night if necessary.

His wife begged him to listen to reason. She tried to bargain with him. He would not even answer her.

By dinnertime she decided she absolutely had to test her husband's resolve. She made straight for the door.

"This is stupid, Sid. It's getting cold and dark. He has to eat, for God's sake, Sid."

He let her get as far as the door before he shoved her back.

By nightfall Jeffie's mother accepted the horror. She had no choice. She sat on the floor in a stupor. She stared through the door at an imaginary Jeffie who was warm and full and comfortably falling asleep.

Through the night she dozed on and off, an indomitable maternal instinct shaking her awake every time her weaker self was about to give in. Sid never moved. His scratched eye grew more and more painful, but his determination soothed him.

At daybreak Jeffie's mother regained her sense of outrage and urgency. Why hadn't Jeffie screamed? Or banged on the door? Or run to a neighbor's and telephoned for help? What had happened? How was he? Where was he? God!

"Can he come in now? It's morning, Sid. When can he come in? How long are you going to keep on with this stupidness?"

Sid stood up, walked to the door, threw it open. His wife tore out of the house into the backyard.

"Jeffie! Jeffie? Jeffie? Where are you? Jeffie? He's gone, Sid! Where is he, Sid?"

"I'm here, Ma." Jeffie's voice sounded far away.

Mutt crawled out of his doghouse and shook himself. His chain jangled in the dirt. He stretched long and happy.

"Jeffie! Where are you, Jeffie?"

Then Jeffie crawled out of the doghouse, his face white and scared, his hair sloppy with dirt and matted with dog slobber.

"This is just the beginning," Sid swore to himself.

V

James Alleman Alcock peered over his notebook, past his T-shirted blubber, beyond the spurge of crumpled poems, at what he liked to call his "spawntaneous combustion." That is how the poet regarded his young son, Stonehenge, who sat on the floor toying with an electronic war game.

Init nice how it's all worked out so pat, the poet thought without a mind at creation but suddenly inspiring himself to write the following lines to a new poem: *sonshine, manshine, beaming love / the child has just enough in him of the parent to guarantee respect and even unreasoning worship for him who shines above.*

Thank Apollo, he thought, that things are worked out so tidy.

Stonehenge wasn't quite sure he liked the way the war was going. He slammed the computer one shot — bap — against the floor; picked it up and slammed it back down.

Nevertheless, thought the poet, there's always a new ingredient, something added just for the fuckin' sake of individuality, something maddeningly unpredictable. Scares me. Scares the bloody heart and soul of me like a bully's fist twistin' up the inside of my chest as if it was my shirt front.

He filed the simile for future use and remembered touching Stonehenge's baby-fine hair. His hair was so thin and red, threads of silk flowing from a diaphanous whorl. And beneath it, below the soft pink skin, within the skeletal jail of the skull, was a denseness, a toughness, an indissoluble nugget of pain capable of rattling the bony bars of its cage until Stonehenge exploded.

Most recently it had happened at school. Stonehenge had worked long and hard on a map of the United States. When he showed it to his teacher, Mr. Maglie snorted. "Where's Tennessee? Where's West Virginia? What's Montana doing over there? This is all wrong." He tore it in half and in half again and let it flutter into the wastebasket.

Stonehenge saw white, not red. A blinding white, hot as a bar of molten ore behind his eyes. The pain rattled in his skull like a silver ball skittering against the spin of a roulette wheel. Where it will stop no one knows, the poet thought. Certainly Mr. Maglie didn't know.

Stonehenge overturned his desk; he flung his chair in several directions at once it seemed; he ran full speed into the blackboard, into Henry Bleir, into the globe, onto the floor; he kicked and screamed and shook and punched at his eyes and head to kill the pain; finally he lay in his blood and spit and sweat, whimpering like a dying animal, waiting for the rescue squad to strap him to a stretcher and speed him to a place, a room, a man, a tiny light aimed at the dim and dimmer light blessedly fading behind his eyes.

A psychomotor seizure, a doctor said. But the poet could only think of *White Heat,* could only picture the agonized wriggle of killer Cagney high atop a surreal tower in unreal black-and-white in the last reel of a psychopath's criminal dementia. "Top of the world, Ma," Cagney screamed.

She should not have left us, the poet mourned. *Dear wife / dear mother,* he scribbled.

The poet watched Stonehenge unhinge parts of the computer. The boy ripped out the wires under the pretense of jiggling them to test their connections. Then, fed up with the works, he hurled the game against the door.

No mother, the poet thought. As gentle as I am, I can't give him what a mother would.

Stonehenge slammed the door to his room behind him.

Summer soon, the poet wrote, *when the heat fries the brain and the man from the moon drives the son insane.*

I think, the poet mused, that one of these days that boy will kill me. He'll take me apart like a toy. My own son.

The poet got up and poured himself a drink.

"But not this summer you won't," he said to the door.

VI

One-hundred-fifty-two days, five hours, and sixteen minutes.

Mirriam dusted without realizing she was dusting.

She washed dishes unconsciously, never actually seeing any details through the glaze of her stare.

She smoked one cigarette after another.

She answered a phone that did not ring.

She picked out a magazine and read the same paragraph five times.

Her mind wandered backward and forward, unwinding down the stairs like a mummy's bandages, to the park, to all the rooftops and alleyways and stairwells and courtyards in the ten square blocks surrounding the park; to the bus station, the train station, the airports; to awful places out of movies and TV shows — haunted houses, condemned buildings, rat-infested basements, spidery attics, locked rooms, secret laboratories, underground cells, all the time her mind unraveling to bare bone and then raveling back again to the bound, blind flesh of a mummy.

·

One-hundred-fifty-eight days, four hours, and thirty minutes.

When Ezra came home from school he asked his mother if there was any news. From his expression, Mirriam thought, he might have been asking if there were any powdered doughnuts in the drawer.

·

One-hundred-sixty-three days, one hour, and fifteen minutes.

Detective Denby telephoned.

"Sorry, nothin," he said. "They busted up a kiddie porn ring in Harrison, New Jersey, last night. I checked it out this morning, but nothin'."

She hung up and thought about kiddie porn. If not this kiddie porn ring, then maybe another. She hadn't imagined anything like that before. She thought she had imagined everything.

·

One-hundred-seventy days, four hours, and five minutes.

Dora Beagle appeared. She was pink and plump. Her frazzled hair was thinning, showing a pink scalp. She had one huge dimple and she had watery eyes like Detective Denby. Mirriam did not recall her knock at the door. She did not recall letting Dora Beagle in, nor offering her coffee, which now the pink lady slurped crudely, nor did Mirriam recall the beginning of their conversation which had led to the most unfathomable and outrageous request she had ever heard.

"I hope you don't mind me pokin' my nose in your personal

13

business," she slurped, "but it's the only way. My gift, y'see, works like a bloodhound's. It won't take but a second. Just undo yer bloomers there and spread eagle for old Mrs. Beagle. One whiff and it's straight into a trance I go."

Mirriam was sure she was misunderstanding the instructions.

"Come, come, you don't want to be bashful where it's your own flesh-and-blood's safety at stake. That's the key, flesh and blood. I've put my nose in the royal box, you know, a cousin of the Queen of England, poor thing, nasty business in the end, but still I fell right to a trance and there was the royal grand-nephew or whatever you call him under the floorboards of this stationer's. Egham I think was his name, Peter Egham, the stationer, that is, not the boy. There was nine of 'em in the floor there, all young boys in short pants and long hair — but in the trance only the nephew appeared."

Dora Beagle blew her nose the way a musician might clean his instrument. She used three separate handkerchiefs and examined each one before and after.

"Here's my theory, dearie; when you're lost, you're dead, and when you're found, you're born again. So these gettin' born juices from the original womb are the ones I'm after. Unmistakable, don't ask me why. I tried it once with a missing boy's father, 'cause the mother was dead and buried. Didn't work at all, just terrible embarrassin' sniffin' around his privates like that, though he didn't seem to mind. Tried to talk him into exhumin' wifey's remains, but he wouldn't hear of it. It's the woman, the mother, who holds the key. See what I mean? So now what say lets pull 'em down and open 'em up and stick in my extra sense and deliver this boy of yours from evil?"

She gave one last snort to clear the instrument of her ESP when suddenly Mirriam burst into a fit of hysteria.

"I've come a long way to help you!" Dora Beagle insisted.

"Get out! Get out of here!" Mirriam screamed.

"For the love of God, I called you last week and what did you say? 'Anything, anything, I'll try anything!'"

·

One-hundred-seventy-six days, thirteen hours, and twenty minutes.

Mirriam's husband, Stanley, wanted to make love to her. He didn't want to ask. He hoped she would sense his longing.

They hadn't made love since the disappearance, although they talked every day about the strength of their love and how it helped keep them brave and hopeful. Unfortunately that was not enough to calm Stanley's erection.

Mirriam wanted to slap it away. She refused to talk to him all weekend.

"What did I do?" Stanley asked a colleague at the office.

"You let it happen."

"I let *what* happen?" Stanley said, half-cocked.

·

One-hundred-eighty days, one hour, and six minutes ago the little boy vanished. He was in the park. He was going up and down a small sliding board. His father was sitting on a bench solving the *New York Times* crossword puzzle. The next thing his father knew, the boy was gone. He had looked up from his paper, and a bolt of fear impaled his heart, although he fully expected that he'd find his son playing in the very next place he looked: on the swings; in the sandbox; on the merry-go-round; behind the fence, behind the bench; across the street — but the boy was not there! Not there! Not there! At ten o'clock in the morning, in the middle of a busy park, in the heart of Manhattan, a four-year-old boy had vanished.

·

Mirriam felt her other son, Ezra, was all she had left in the world, and she smothered him with overprotection. All she cared about was keeping him safe, not happy. He traveled to and from school with a patrolman. After school he was not allowed out of the apartment. He had to give up his friends, his games, his art and swimming classes at the Y. Mirriam moved his bed into the hallway so she could keep an eye on him from her bedroom.

Stanley sympathized with Ezra, but he gave in to Mirriam

because he mistrusted his own feelings. Right from the start he hadn't suffered his son's disappearance as acutely as Mirriam had, and Stanley worried that he didn't care as much as a normal father should. Then came the weekend when Mirriam refused to talk to Stanley. It had been almost six months since she had allowed Stanley any more intimacy than his arm around her shoulders. It wasn't natural.

·

One-hundred-ninety-two days and thirteen hours to the minute.

Ezra lay in his hallway bed listening to the muffled voices of his mother and father.

"-ill me, you migh- -swellki— me!"

"-on- be stup—!"

"You wou— dothi- to me? You would do this to me?!"

"Jesus Christ, Mirriam. Jesus Christ. It's only for eight weeks! He'll only be gone —"

"Put a knife in me, Stanley! Put a knife in me!"

TWO

Francis sat in the first row. Frances sat in the last row.

Francis leaned forward in his chair. Frances slouched in hers.

Francis was not aware of his body. Frances scratched itches, twirled strands of hair, bit nails, fidgeted, even caught herself blinking; her lungs ached for cigarette smoke.

Francis thought the man on the stage was speaking only to him.

Frances thought the man on the stage was speaking only to her.

The man on the stage spoke only to each of the two hundred members of his audience.

"Look at you! Look at what you have done to yourself! You have handed yourself over to death! You have given up! What are you after you let the world set fire to the twigs beneath your feet? What are you after you let the world toss you out for carrion? What are you after the flames and the flies divide you up? You are nothing! You are remains! You are dry and hollow bones! You are splinters and shards of the men and women you might have been! Might yet be! Will you let me help you?!"

The man on the stage shouted at his audience of two hundred who were roused to shout back in a single voice. "Will you let me help you?"

"YES!"

"I will restore flesh and sinew!"

"YES!"

"I will talk your gods into breathing life back into you!"

"YES!"

"I will resurrect your bones if you will be an army! If you will seize life! If you will listen to the beating of your heart! If you will use strength and sinew to stand tall! If you will use new flesh and breath to love yourself, to trust yourself, to find and hold and keep yourself forever!"

"YES! YES!"

"Here is life! Take it! Here is the noise and the shaking! Here are the bones that are life making! Here are fingers and a palm and an arm and a shoulder and a leg! Here is breath to leave this Valley of Death!"

The man leaped from his stage into his startled audience and pressed his hand to a shoulder, to a back, to an arm, a brow, a chest.

"Remember our Creation of the Universe Exercise. Remember that you are the source of the universe. You! Your brain and spirit are the spark and gas in a vast black void beyond all comprehension. In an instant that takes a billion trillion millenniums, your brain and spirit heat and freeze and expand and combust and explode and generate an unknown number of miracles that seem infinitely more complicated and powerful than their own miraculous source. But you can steal back that power by knowing that you are the source. Go outside tonight and look up at the moon. There hanging high over our heads is the object of our passion, the object of our love songs, the object of our space program. But without the sun, we would not even be able to see the moon.

"You are the sun! You are the supreme star of your own solar system. You light and heat and nourish your own universe. Just you! All else is reflection!

"Go out," he said, lifting first one and then another and another member of the audience from his or her chair and urging each one to leave the ballroom. "Go out into the world!" he screamed, "and be dangerous! Come back next week with blood on your hands!"

II

Francis should have been the girl and Frances the boy. They had come to the seminars to move more into the opposite direction, to take the long way around into each other's arms.

Too soft and giving, Francis wanted to take on a toughness. Too tough and demanding, Frances wanted to be softer and more giving.

"What did you think?" she asked him when at last she could speak about their experience in the ballroom.

"The idea is not to think," Francis said.

"Oh fuck you," Frances said.

III

They sat in an all-night diner and she watched him turn the objects on their table into an orchestra: the knife, the fork, the spoon, the rims of the unequally filled water glasses, the thick coffee mugs, the sugar packets, the pewter creamer with the additional clack of its hinged lid, the glass ashtray — before Frances had a chance to fill it up — the napkin dispenser, even the laminated menu. Francis banged, tapped, drummed, clashed, clacked, spun, and scraped.

"That's 'Happy Birthday,' " she marveled.

"You know," Francis said to no one in particular — a habit he had developed over years of teaching inattentive students, "there isn't an object on this earth that doesn't have a musical sound in it. You just have to tap it. I mean tap it in the sense that you tap a tree. You have to locate the source of its music and bring it out."

As systematic as the making of music might be, Francis's extraordinary talent for it was purely intuitive. It was his by birth, not by assiduous study. He could play almost any instrument after a few moments of "tapping," and he could play any tune after hearing it just once. It was a talent that immediately awed anyone who witnessed it, as it had the night Frances and Francis first met. They had both been guests at a party. Francis was playing the piano. Frances leaned against the piano, singing along, playing "Name That Tune," identifying TV theme songs and commercial jingles, and falling in love with the expression on Francis's face, an expression of such complete happiness, such mindless serenity, that the usually depressed and agitated Frances had to have it for her very own, had to solve its mystery, had to — in Francis's words — tap it.

"Of course, putting the sounds together, now that's something else entirely." Francis assumed the smug, tutorial air that Frances hated. "Melody and harmony and rhythm don't just float around in thin air waiting for someone to reach up and grab them," he laughed. Frances squashed a cigarette in the glass-ashtray section of Francis's orchestra.

"If you're so damned smart, why don't you just quit teaching and become a professional musician? What are you scared of? You hate teaching."

"I figure I'm about the highest paid babysitter in the world. All I really have to do is watch my students from nine to three. Of course, as a science teacher, I have some advantages. I can amuse them with smoking beakers. Or by letting them inhale helium."

"But you hate it."

"But there's my salary, my union benefits, my tenure, my retirement. So I lose a few hubcaps along the way."

The neighborhood in which Francis taught was a ghetto of truants, vagrants, thugs, junkies, winos, and hoods. The teachers' cars were frequently stripped and smashed, as were the teachers themselves. Suddenly Frances felt sorry for Francis. The thought of his walking from his parked car to the school frightened her. She was quiet for a moment.

"Look," Francis said, just to break the embarrassing silence. He indicated the price increases that had been sloppily written on his menu. "First a quarter, then thirty-five cents, then a half dollar, and now seventy-five cents; the economic history of the United States for the last three years right here on a Kwik Bite menu. And you're asking me to quit my job as a science teacher and become a musician."

IV

The Sermon in the Ballroom had had a strange series of effects. First Francis and Frances were stunned. That lasted all the way to the diner in the form of silence. Then they opened up a bit and talked about their lives without talking about the Seminar. That lasted until Frances began to mourn the absence of idealism she detected in Francis's pragmatic disdain of becoming a professional musician. She became sad and quiet and dropped her guard.

Ordinarily she was unashamedly demanding and pushy, good traits for an aspiring actress. Whenever one of her outrageous demands was called to her attention, she did not flinch. She behaved, in fact, opposite of the way she felt at such times, opposite of the way she wished she could allow herself to behave. Inside she was anxious and crying and eager to yield, but in her dealings with others, with men especially, something prevented honesty. A psychiatrist called that something "the fear of loss," which sounded much too serious to Frances. So she said, "Well, I ain't afraid of losing you," and then stood up and walked out and didn't come back for three weeks.

Frances had believed in her own pretenses and defenses for so long that her "something" — the real reason she was afraid to be herself — had achieved a position of almighty strength. It made her do things she never thought she would do. It made her neglect herself. Her teeth needed filling. She needed a new prescription for her eyeglasses, and a nagging, hacking, bronchial-busting cough barked a warning to her to quit smoking every few minutes.

But this was not the Frances who now sat putting all the instruments back in place on the table. Francis had been right, the idea was not to think, but to feel, and Frances felt open and loving for the first time in her memory.

V

After the third phase of the Sermon in the Ballroom, Francis and Frances found themselves in her warm, dark, messy apartment.

Neither of them had ever made love before. The new Frances lay back and waited to be undressed. The new Francis groped in the dark for her clothed breasts and crotch.

It did not go well.

She coughed and lit a cigarette.

He began straightening up the things she had left out of place in the room.

Their communion started to come apart like one of her smoke rings. It disintegrated but still hung over their heads.

The old Francis was mortified.

"I'm sorry. I'm sorry," he kept saying. "I'm not like that. I shouldn't have been so aggressive."

"Why the fuck not?" the old Frances answered.

The Sermon in the Ballroom had now entered its final phase.

"But I don't want you to be the enemy," said Francis.

" 'Come back with blood on your hands,' he said. What he meant was don't be afraid to be yourself. If you aren't afraid, 'they' will be," Frances exhaled.

"Who's 'they?' " Francis asked, draping a shirt over the back of a chair, picking a bit of lint from the sleeve.

"I don't know who yours are, Francis, but mine are smothering me. Agents, casting directors, shrinks, friends, parents. Relationships, Francis, 'they' are all the fucking people on the other end of my relationships, all the people I have to deal with because they're always showing up or calling me or running into me at a party or dropping me a line, all the people who just won't go away."

"I sense that you want to go away . . ."

"You sense right."

". . . but that you're afraid to leave them. Leaving them gives them power over you."

"Well, I will, Francis. I will. I'll look them straight in the eye and they'll fall apart. Blood, Francis. Don't back off, tell them what you want and stand there until they start to sweat and shake and cry and give you what's rightfully yours."

"And what is rightfully yours?"

"Attention."

"What else?"

"Respect."

Francis and Frances had slipped into a Seminar Training Exercise called The Catechism.

"What else?"

"A demilitarized zone."

"How is it measured?"

"By an arm's length."

"Whose arm?"

"The other person's."

"What if they trespass into the DMZ?"

"Stand my ground."

"What else?"

"Stare them down. Stare them back. Stare them into kingdom come."

They felt now the way they had felt immediately following the Sermon in the Ballroom, as if the man in the turtleneck shirt had shaken them physically.

"My problem — which is now your problem — is that I am too assertive in relationships as a cover up for being too dependent."

"My problem — which is now your problem — is that I'm too weak. I let people push me around and walk all over me. But I believe that I do that as a way of controlling people."

·

The next day Frances phoned Francis. He said hello and never had a chance to add another word to the conversation.

"Look, I haven't got a lot of time to talk right now, but I've

got the greatest idea in the world. We have to go out and be
dangerous, right? We have to come back with blood on our
hands, right? Well, I met someone this afternoon at an open
call and he told me he was sending his kid off to camp this
summer and that they needed a drama director at the camp
and would I be interested? And I thought to myself this could
be it. This could be just what we've been looking for. A chance
to get the hell away instead of sitting here all summer and rotting. A change of scenery. A change of people. The great outdoors, you know? So I ran over to this office on Forty-second
Street, and I had an interview, and I'm in. Just like that! I'm
going to camp, Francis. It worked, goddamn it! I went in there
determined to get what I wanted and I got it. I stood my ground,
Francis. I even told the guy that I was never even a camper
before, never mind a counselor or a drama director or anything,
but that I knew I could do it, and that I needed the 'distance'
and the 'difference' in my life right now — not that he knew
what the hell I was talking about — and that I needed the
money, too — he understood that. And I told him I had the
greatest goddamn musical director in the whole fucking world
for him, so get your ass over to Eighteen West Forty-second
Street, Francis, room number one-nine-five-seven, because the
guy's expecting you in one hour. Don't even think about it,
Francis, just do it."

Frances hung up.

Francis held on for a few moments. As soon as he hung up,
the phone rang again.

"I forgot to tell you, don't take less than five hundred dollars,
that's what I'm getting, and don't lose your cool when you
shake hands with the guy — he doesn't have a thumb."

THREE

Camp Freedom was located at the edge of Geoff Thomason's mind. Its boundaries were indistinct. Its flora and fauna were unknown. The site existed through tractless, primitive images in Geoff Thomason's creative process. It would remain at the edge until refracted by the mind's eye, until Geoff Thomason focused it in the cross hairs of his readers' vision, for the camp's true reality was in the brochure he had prepared, not in the overgrown confines of an ancient New Jersey forest.

Control. Geoff Thomason was manic or depressed depending on how much in control he felt. Sometimes his photographs were open to interpretation and he worried that the reality depicted in them might be a figment of his Nikon's imagination rather than his. For Geoff Thomason, the only true reality was the one he created. The only true Camp Freedom was in the brochure he had envisioned, designed, photographed, written, and printed with his own nine fingers.

.

The first time his missing thumb upset him was when he began making marks and colored shapes on pieces of paper. He found it contradictory and unbalancing to hold a crayon in his left hand. But his parents slapped his grotesque right hand every time they caught its imperfect fist wrapped around the crayon.

When he reached for the crayon, he reached first from deep within his right shoulder where an urgent twitch triggered his right-handed nature. But then quickly he reached with his left hand in a conscious, mechanical effort to avoid punishment.

Geoff Thomason knew that if he had had a right thumb he would have been permitted to indulge his natural right-handedness.

·

He thrust out his hand unashamedly. Francis took it and felt himself bristle at the grisly touch of thumbless flesh.

·

In nursery school, a freckle-faced classmate refused to hold Geoff Thomason's hand during a square dance. The boy's freckles were so thick it looked like he was wearing a mask. Outraged by such insensitivity on the part of one of her children, the teacher tried to turn the incident into a moral lesson by making every child come up to the front of the room to take Geoff Thomason's hand and press it to his or her cheek.

It may seem impossible for a four-year-old to know that he is experiencing the utmost intensity of an emotion, that this is the most painful anguish he will ever feel in his lifetime, but Geoff Thomason knew.

As each classmate took his hand — holding it with two fingers at the end of a stiff arm as though the disfigured hand were a smelly dead thing — the teacher had to repeat her instructions. "Go ahead, show Geoffrey that you don't care if he has no thumb. Come on now, put the hand on your cheek. Do as I say, give the hand a little love. You know what you're supposed to do; hold his hand against that cute little cheek of yours. Come on, no faces. Don't make me say it again."

One by one his classmates brought Geoff Thomason's obnoxious hand up to their faces. One threw it down quickly. Another shuddered at contact. A third was able to hold the hand amazingly close without its actually touching her cheek.

The freckle-faced boy refused to do as he was ordered. He stood eyeball to eyeball with Geoff Thomason and told the teacher, "You can't make me." Yet the masked boy with such unmasked hate in his eyes would not haunt Geoff Thomason, nor would the boys and girls whose squeamishness barely masked their similar, open hatred. The face he would always remember with agonizing shame belonged to a boy named Martin who was the youngest in the class. When it was Martin's turn, he took Geoff Thomason's hand in both his own, brought it up to his lips and pressed a kiss directly onto the discolored stump where once a thumb had been. The kiss was so unexpected, so innocent and sincere, it caused Geoff Thomason to gasp.

·

"Frances told me a lot about you. Apparently you have magic hands."

"I can play the piano, if that's what you mean," Francis answered.

"Yes, but without really knowing how."

"Without knowing that I know how."

·

In high school Geoff Thomason was predictably ashamed of his deformity. He knew that everyone who noticed it shivered. No girl would let it do to her what Geoff Thomason loved to let it do to himself under cover of night and ripe dreams. No boy would hold it high in the air to celebrate the victory of a completed bullet pass, a swished jumper, a peg to the plate.

One afternoon in the boys' bathroom three backs were conspiring in the corner by the sink. At the sound of Geoff Thomason's entrance, one back spun around impetuously. The stunned boy was holding his erect penis in his hand, the other two boys were trying to force theirs back into their pants.

"We're jerking off," the boy finally said. "Come on and do it with us. Everyone pays a buck to the first one who does it."

If only they knew how proficient, how awesome, how exotically erotic Geoff Thomason's masturbatory performances could be. The roseate slash of scar tissue between wrist and knuckle was a hotbed of fantasy as his engorged pseudo thumb replaced his absent thumb to manufacture prodigious ejaculations. But they must never know. He must never show his hand. Never slap them with it.

When Geoff Thomason hesitated to join, one of the boys said, "Maybe the fairy just wants to watch, huh?"

So Geoff Thomason unzipped and took it out in self-defense. They edged sideways to give him a piece of the sink and he squeezed in. Suddenly he was one of them which was as close as he had ever come to camaraderie. To protect his secret self and newfound acceptance, Geoff Thomason ignored the twitch deep within his right shoulder and grabbed his unprimed penis with his left hand. His performance was as bad as his penmanship, a blotchy gibberish of zigs, zags, and loops. His left hand moved like a bad dancer searching for the beat. U-up, no, u-u-down, updown, downup, upup, d-down, d-dup.

During these rough moments of his young life, while his inferiors outmasturbated him — two of them arguing over controversial evidence of victory, the third slapping his own ass jubilantly when at last and at least he leaked out a third-place finish — during the spastic, abysmal, coarse anguish of petering out, Geoff Thomason saw the awful handwriting on the wall: he could never be happy unless he was in complete control of himself.

•

"I myself have absolutely no musical ability whatsoever. I've always envied people like you who can play an instrument, who can make a dumb thing" — he said the word *thing* as if it symbolized or referred to nothing recognizable — "turn out a beautiful melody. You know, it's pretty much the same with photography. I'm a photographer and a writer; I free-lance; I create brochures, pamphlets, flyers; and in photography you take a mirror and film and turn out a beautiful harmony of images. You use notes, I use images."

•

Geoff Thomason tried to control the mutilated right-handed nature of his life by creating a mutilated persona. He began to favor not just his right hand, but the entire right side of his body. At school, at the dinner table, at grandmother's house, wherever he went, he pulled his right leg along after him, let his right arm hang limp, talked out of the left side of his mouth, even showed more animation in his left eye. There was no warmth in his right eye, only a surreal daub of color like the spot of rouge on a dead man's cheek.

The limper, lamer, less dexterous Geoff Thomason became, the happier he appeared. His parents would have liked to feel that as long as he seemed happy there was no need to worry. But a child's happiness is never enough camouflage to escape the radar of parental suspicion. They took him to a specialist to determine the cause of the dragging leg and drooping right side of his face and what his father ridiculed as "that damned limp dick of a right arm!" The visit would have been a complete waste of time, except for Dr. Billfox's x-ray machine.

"What are you doing?"

"Don't worry, it won't hurt. I'm just going to take a picture of you. This machine works like a regular camera, except the picture that comes out shows the inside of you instead of the outside."

It must have been a powerful camera, for Dr. Billfox hid himself in the next room while it was on. He peered through a window in the door, waiting for a red light to go off.

Geoff Thomason's left eye scanned the huge, smooth, beige exterior of the x-ray machine as its magical works exposed his interior. Before he had seen the results, he was captured by its promise. Although the developed x-rays were not what he had expected — he had expected the same glossy prints he was used to seeing in his mother's albums — they shocked him down to the very marrow of the translucent bones clipped onto the light box.

"The x-rays show good musculature, perfect bone structure, no superficial nervous disorder — see these spaces along the spine, they're disks and they don't show up in x-rays, but if there were any superficial damage or abnormality it would show up as a disproportionately big or little or crooked space. In other words,

I can't find a thing wrong with him. Nothing at all indicates further testing. I could give you the name of a good neurologist, but I'd have to say that it would be more for your benefit than Geoff's."

It was an amazement. An educated doctor, two skeptical, apprehensive parents, and a repressed patient had seen the truth. And accepted it without a word. They had even *not* seen something — invisible disks — and taken that to be a truth, too.

.

Room 1957 was small and bare, but Geoff Thomason acted as if it were his Oval Office. During one part of the interview, he looked out of the window for five minutes while Francis was expected to read through the Camp Freedom brochure.

"There's nothing that I can tell you or that Dr. Stone could tell you that isn't in there."

.

From the moment he saw Dr. Billfox's machine, photography consumed Geoff Thomason. He read everything he could find on the subject. With his savings, he bought himself a Nikon camera and began taking pictures of household objects that had nothing more in common than their appeal to Geoff Thomason's newfound eye. Whatever that appeal, whatever the objects evoked in him, the Nikon failed to reveal. The significance of the objects remained a mystery in the countless, uninteresting prints that began piling up in Geoff Thomason's room. But in each reproduction of reality, he had come closer to controlling his world. A vase filled with artificial tulips. A pastel print of pink flamingos feeding on the shores of Shangri-la. A set of thin books, dark blue, each spine bearing an embossed, off-white profile of the same lovely female face above a florid Roman numeral. Three small pieces of carnival glass. The driftwood base of a table lamp. A porcelain egg. The egg open. A section of intricately patterned fabric most likely from a sofa or formal chair. A row of cans, boxes, and cellophane packages on a pantry shelf. Salt and pepper shakers in the persons of two red-lipped, wide-eyed darkies, the man in a baker's white hat and suit, his roly-poly partner in an Aunt Jemima bandana and frock. A scan-lined still of President Johnson's Thanksgiving Day TV address. Various drawer pulls. A shaving kit. A bedroom reflected in a mirror, the photographer out of view. Tools, bowls, articles of clothing, matchbooks, fruit, an umbrella, clocks, the grain in an oak table, a sweating pipe, a thick black Bible. In every picture the point was not to flatter the subject, not to make more of it than life had, or less, but to depict it faithfully, to isolate and define it by transferring it from the world to film to paper.

The high cost of developing his many photographs prompted Geoff Thomason to convert a large closet into a darkroom. There he discovered that he did not have to print everything the camera exposed. He could print part of an exposure, a specific area that more clearly conveyed the reality he was trying to capture. Or he could create a reality simply by including or excluding certain information on the negative. He realized, too, that he could combine elements from different negatives, superimpose one on the other, juxtapose subjects that never stood side by side in real life and make them look perfectly natural together in the printing.

His father always rested his idle hand on the kitchen table when he sat there drinking his morning coffee and studying the front page of the newspaper. On the negative both hands were visible, the one at rest and the one about to lift the cup. A corner of the newspaper could be seen, too. But in the printing Geoff Thomason focused on the idle hand exclusively. He was able to eliminate the other elements and zero in on the center of his composition, cropping out the useless information and enlarging his vision. The pattern in the Formica veneer showed up like cracked concrete. His father's hand, soft and even a bit pink and puffy in real life, looked thin and gray. Geoff Thomason's eye had turned it into a claw on a parched moonscape.

·

"I was offered an extraordinary opportunity," Geoff Thomason said to the window. "I was interviewed by three different officers of the ship and was finally asked to sail on the Royal Vik ing Line and run the ship's newspaper. Write it, lay it out, take pictures of the passengers playing shuffleboard, dancing, what- ever, to do everything, really. I'd have gotten my bed and board and a salary. And, of course, I would have had the thrill of being at sea and putting in to exotic ports of call." He turned to Francis who felt like one of his own uninterested pupils. "It's not exactly like going out on a whaler, it's not exactly *Moby Dick* or *Heart of Darkness* or *Treasure Island*, but it is the sea," Geoff Thomason romanticized, "and it is working aboard a real sailing vessel."

"Too posh though? Francis anticipated. The teacher's grin was meant to show that he knew the derivation of the word *posh*: *p*ort *o*ut, *s*tarboard *h*ome.

"The reason I didn't accept," Geoff Thomason replied, "was because Dr. Stone needed me."

•

Geoff Thomason gained control of himself and his world. He didn't need friends, so the lack of them no longer disturbed him. He didn't need his thumb, so its absence went unnoticed more and more in the course of his photographic work. But his physical problems persisted. The armor he had worked so hard to develop began to weigh on him.

"Why don't you take me to a neurologist?"

"You heard what Billfox said, there's nothing wrong with you. Why don't you just make up your mind to quit limping around? I don't have thirty dollars to throw away on a doctor when you're okay. And don't work on your mother to take you either — the bills come to me!"

"You don't care what happens to me, do you?"

"I ought to break that goddamned useless arm for you, you talk to me like that!"

"Go ahead, beat me up, that's all you think being a father is anyway."

"You shut up, you sonofabitch! After what I've been through with you! All the trouble you've been to your mother and me! And now you're telling me I don't know how to be a father?

Who the hell do you think it was that taught you to use your goddamn left hand so you could write your name, you sonofabitch? A name I gave you, don't forget!"

"And who the hell was it that mutilated my right hand? Whose fault was that?"

"What?!"

"Ow!"

"What did you say?!"

"Unh!"

"What did you say?!"

"That's it, settle it with your goddamn hands!"

"You dare to say that to me?!"

"Ooph!"

"You dare . . ."

"Ungth!"

". . . accuse me . . ."

"Gaaa!"

". . . of doing that . . ."

"Ai!"

". . . to your hand?!"

"o."

"Get up you sonofabitch!"

"uh . . . uh . . . uh . . . uh."

"Now you got a reason to go to the doctor's."

·

Geoff Thomason and his mother waited between a man with whiplash and a woman with a migraine headache. Across from him a well-dressed businessman kept shifting position in his chair to relieve the obvious agony of his lower back. Another patient was a very round woman whose left leg was shorter than her right; it dangled out of her voluminous dress to within an inch of the carpeting, while the other leg was drawn back beneath her chair with length enough left over to allow her pudgy right foot to rest comfortably on its side. There were three more patients whose suffering was disclosed neither by unconscious pantomime nor the friendly words of commiseration that break up such waiting.

33

Geoff Thomason's bruises spoke for themselves. One followed the contour of his jawline and was in its most vibrant phase of eggplant purple. Another one glowed rash-red around his neck, like an Indian burn, and caused him to tilt his head oddly. Most of his injuries were hidden by his clothing and manifested themselves not only in the tentative way he moved his head, arms, and legs, but also in the determined way he did not move the aching torso that somehow kept him erect.

"Mr. Thompson?" a nursevoice called through a quick opening in the sliding wall window of thickly bubbled glass. By the time Geoff Thomason could turn his head, she was a cubist shadow again.

Like locomotive smoke and track clacks, Geoff Thomason let out a chain of chest rales and shallow breaths in ironic counterpoint to his inch-by-inch maneuvering toward the examination room. On the way he was derailed by a frail, white-haired black man who was too intent on deciphering an insurance claim form to watch where he was going.

"Watch out, mister," Geoff Thomason's mother warned too late.

"Ah is, ma'am; sorry, ma'am," the old man apologized.

When the old man looked up, Geoff Thomason could see that part of his neck and jaw had been eaten away by disease and then zigzaggedly autographed by a surgeon. He remembered the rack of pamphlets on the wall just above the twisted businessman's head — "Chiropractic and Your Kidneys," "Chiropractic and Your Heart," "The Sound and Vision of Health," "Spinal Relief of Migraine," "Adjusting for Menstruation," "The Sciatica," "When Medicine Fails," "The Disease No One Talks About," "The Big C Meets the Bigger C," "Stand Tall," "Anatomy of an M.D.," "Anaesthesia — the Greatest Killer," — and Geoff Thomason wondered whether the old man had the disease no one talked about, or the Big C, or if he had just been getting the kinks out of his tired old back.

·

"As I said, everything you need to know about Camp Freedom is right in that brochure. I put the whole thing together myself."

34

Francis glanced again at the handsome brochure, fanning the pages deferentially. The black-and-white photographs of boys and girls playing, working with crafts, studying nature, swimming, hiking, singing, dancing, laughing merged into the single image of camp life Francis had been carrying in his mind for as long as he could remember. It was an image that never changed, not even in the smallest detail, and yet it had no detail. It was indescribable; it just was, the way one's image of school just is, or of army life, or the business world, or a stay in the hospital, or of traveling abroad, marriage, old age, death, all images that time and instinct have printed onto our brains in braille, images we feel rather than see.

It took the skill, perhaps the genius, of a Geoff Thomason to actually describe such an image, to put it down on paper in black and white. The black-and-white photographs in the brochure described for Francis precisely what he felt about camp, as though the photos had been taken inside his head.

"Dr. Stone was so impressed, he asked me to recruit the staff and the campers for him. He really doesn't have the time himself. But he knows what he wants and he trusts me. I've been associated with him for a long time. I've done his pamphlets and press releases. This is the office of another one of his associates. Dr. Stone has a great many. That's why it says Dr. Richard Voehl on the door. The table's in there," Geoff Thomason said without pointing to the door behind his desk. "Have you ever been to a chiropractor?"

.

The table was all Geoff Thomason saw at first. It was the only equipment in the room.

A motor sounded.

Black leather and gleaming chrome arose.

As instructed, Geoff Thomason faced the upright table and placed first one foot and then the other on the two chrome side bars and brought the right side of his face toward the cushioned headrest. Attached to the headrest was a roll of thin, stiff paper. A new sheet had been pulled down onto the cushion, and Geoff Thomason pressed his face against it.

The table dropped down slowly, gliding to a gentle stop when Geoff Thomason was perfectly horizontal.

Hands touched his neck and back and legs; two hands that felt like one, that felt like four. They did not press hard. They probed for a sign only trained fingertips could recognize.

He held his breath in anticipation of sudden pain. But the hands worked in unpredictable patterns to make him breathe more easily, to relax the girdered tension of his body which his held breath and frozen nerves had erected and then riveted into place.

At last the hands-acting-as-one found the mark. They moved in a definite pattern. The area of the lower spine on which the hands moved started to tingle. The tingle darted down into a leg and fizzled. Stabs of pain near his neck became blunt and then disappeared. Numbness tingled and buzzed in his lower spine. Movement of hands mesmerized skin. Movement of hands mesmerized muscle. Movement of hands mesmerized synapse. Movement of hands mesmerized blood flow. Movement of hands mesmerized heartbeat. Movement of hands mesmerized mind.

•

Francis wanted to ask the following questions.
  How many kids will there be all together?
  What ages?
  What does a musical director do?
  Where does he sleep and eat?
  With the kids?
  With the other directors?
  How many other directors are there?
  What happened to your thumb?
  What did Frances do or say to get the job?
  Is five hundred dollars okay?
  When would I start?

•

The table whirred to its upright position. As he was instructed, Geoff Thomason stepped off, turned around, stepped backward onto the chrome footrests, and leaned against the table. When it was horizontal again, he was instructed to sit up and ease his legs over the side until they touched the floor.

This time the hands came at him menacingly. As arms and hands wrapped and braced and settled into the prescribed hold on Geoff Thomason's head and jaw and neck, he looked around the room in desperation, recording the alien scene of what might be his final consciousness.

He saw a door that was open an inch and a blur of nursewhite pass through the crack of light. He saw another door marked X-RAY. A drab curtain screened a stall where patients could undress. Next to it, tacked to the wall, was an anatomical chart beginning to curl at the corners. Two shelves displayed plastic models of vertebral sections that looked like lengths of a skinned reptile tail. Hanging from a coat hook on the back of the door Geoff Thomason had come through a few minutes earlier was the most frightening sight in the room: the complete skeleton of a small child. It flashed in and out of his vision like streaks of lightning as countless hands and arms gripped and twisted his neck and head.

"Owch!"

"You don't want to frighten the other patients, do you?"

In the flush aftermath of the violent manipulation, all of Geoff Thomason's aches and throbs were swallowed up by a single new core of pain. Then that began to fade.

He sat on the edge of the table and grew braver as he felt better. There was an overall discomfort, a soreness from head to toe, that Geoff Thomason much preferred to the more acute pain he had suffered at the hands of his father. Gradually, tentatively, he tested himself, rotating his head slightly and his left arm, stretching his left leg, twisting and bending from the waist, flexing the muscles of his chest and stomach, touching himself here and there, verifying — internally and externally — the miraculous improvement he felt at the hands of Dr. George Stone.

"Your right arm and leg have been hindered for a long time. The right side of your face droops. When you're feeling better, I can help."

37

The hands picked up Geoff Thomason's right hand and examined the slash of flesh where a thumb should have been. Geoff Thomason looked away. He stared at the skeleton of the child.

The hands probed Geoff Thomason's right wrist and arm and shoulder, tracing a secret neural path to its terminal in the spine. The hands asked him to lean back onto the horizontal table and helped him turn onto his left side. He felt a knee in the small of his back. A hand grabbed his ankle and pulled back his leg. Another hand pulled his right arm to full extension and then bent it back slightly so that his shoulder felt the pressure. Another hand pushed his head forward. Another hand relocated the spinal source of his hindered right arm. Another hand braced him at the hip, at the thigh, at the knee, across the chest. Another hand yanktwisted his right arm with such great force that for a moment Geoff Thomason went blind with pain.

"Rest."

The hands placed his right arm at his side.

"Don't move. Let's not try too much the first time."

Like the previous manipulation, this one left a feeling of soreness. But very quickly this soreness became more intense. It pulsed and tingled more and more unbearably, like the ache in a waking limb. But it was good.

His right arm had never been useless, but it had worked clumsily, as though it were artificial. Now he felt he could do anything with it. He dared not test it too soon, but he was sure that when the buzz and ache dissolved, his right arm would be cured! Healthy! Whole! Restored! Alive!

•

"It's a privilege to work for a man like Dr. Stone. He is a man of great intellectual and physical genius. Five minutes with him and you'll see why I turned down the Royal Viking Line."

"Does that mean I have the job?"

"Musical director," Geoff Thomason said as he wrote the two words on a blank sheet of paper. Then he wrote Francis's name. The movement of his hand was awkward, but the penmanship flowed naturally. The letters were so neatly formed that the name seemed imprisoned by them.

"Now, as for money," Geoff Thomason began.

"Oh, it doesn't matter," Francis interrupted, "whatever you're offering is fine."

FOUR

It rained from Manhattan to Colt Points Stream, a distance of one hundred miles. Ill wind and pregnant clouds forged a dark corridor through the bright gray day.

In the city the rain fell in huge slanting sheets. People ran for cover as though the plate-glass façades of the skyscrapers had blown loose and were slicing down like guillotine blades. Businessmen dashed back inside marble lobbies or out into the rainy-day miracle of an on-duty cab. Shoppers ducked under striped awnings and into stores they never intended to browse. A hot-dog vendor climbed up onto his portable steam table to get in under the big blue-and-yellow umbrella advertising his all-beef franks. A sidewalk evangelist stood his ground, using the storm to illustrate God's wrath and his own indestructible righteousness. A policeman was almost thrown by his rearing mount. Two black teenagers materialized on a corner with a cardboard box full of cheap umbrellas for sale. Traffic all around the bus terminal came to a honking halt.

"Sonofagoddamnfuckingbitch," Sid growled. The blurted curse seemed to come from a source far deeper than Sid's throat. From an ulcer perhaps.

His son, Jeffie, stared at the metronomic futility of the windshield wiper. Just when the sweep of the wiper delineated the blur of city, the hail of rain turned it into another dripping aquarelle of tail lights and traffic lights. Jeffie was at that stage of his terror when he wished for the worst to happen, so excruciating was the waiting; and yet he really did not want to know precisely where it would happen, precisely where in the blurry city he was going to be put out of the car and taken away to camp.

The three of them sat in the wide cockpit of the family Pontiac. Lighting the dims lit up the dash in electric green. Sid clenched his teeth and the steering wheel. Jeffie's mother sneaked her hand onto her only child's thigh and squeezed it and patted it and tried to make him know how helplessly on his side she was. The green dash and gentle idle transported Jeffie to the control panel of the spaceship *Enterprise* where he monitored the alien, uninhabitable planet Camp.

·

"If the wall breaks will all water come in and we'll drown?"

"It can't break," Samuel's father said in the artificial light and dark of the Lincoln Tunnel. For thirty minutes the tunnel traffic had been moving along like a meal in a python, inch by inch, short stop after quick start, a grueling peristalsis through the heat and the stink and the visible fumes of carbon monoxide. The long tenor bleat of a horn sounded frustration. Impatience was several short flat beeps. But if either bothered Samuel's father, he never let it show. He was a stoic at the wheel, not the least bit annoyed that he was driving Samuel from New Jersey to New York just to meet a bus that would then take Samuel back to New Jersey. His face was a perfect mask of classic impassivity; not a hair out of place, not a character line out of character. Jammed cars, flooded streets, the likelihood of missed connections, nothing dared fault the noble set of his jaw.

"But what if it does break?"

·

"What if I promise to make him go out on his own more? Maybe get a paper route?" Jeffie's mother squeezed her son's thigh. "Why does it have to be camp, Sid?"

·

41

Her face was white, her eyes were white, even her hair had turned white in Harry Jr.'s imagination. He was too young to visit his mother's hospital room, and none of the adults thought to describe her situation in comforting detail to her baffled son, leaving it instead for his uninformed and overworked imagination to unriddle. Fortunately she was in no pain in his thoughts. The whiteness, no doubt, stood for hospital, but it seemed, too, to be a beatific bath of sweet light, a silken, milky heaven in which his mother serenely floated. He did not mind going away for the summer when he thought of her at peace like that. In fact, he preferred being away from his father whose face had aged terribly in her absence and who looked as if he were going to cry whenever their eyes locked.

"Is this the stop, Dad?"

"No, it looks like we're going to be stuck here for a while. The rain's probably causing flooding somewhere in one of the tunnels. Damned subways never work when you're in a hurry."

"You're always in a hurry, Dad."

·

"I am very jealous, Stoney, of your upcoming little adventure. Walden Pond comes to mind, Jean Jacques Rousseau; the Romantic poets, of course, all the literary pigs, (not lions), the wallowers, smart ones who weren't afraid to squish a little mud between their toes. Make the best of it, Stoney. Learn to use your eyes, m'boy. The great outdoors ain't nothin' like any doors you ever been through before. Trust me, Stoney, Don't worry 'about *ball* either. *Ball* is just an excuse for grown men to play in the sun. You don't worry about that, you just go on out there and play in that sun, son. Poets and their offsprung little tykes don't need no *ball* for an excuse. If ya hit it, grand, run them bases to beat the band. But if you miss, Stoney, if you miss the goddamned *ball,* please don't hit yer goddamned head against the wall. Please, Stoney? They said they can handle it. They said they got trained people up there who can take care of you if you go out of yer head. But I know that you can control it, Stoney. I know it. Things get too tough, just set down in the

42

grass and talk to the creepers and hoppers. Make it go way, Stoney, like I seen ya do a hundred times before. And keep them eyes open!"

The meter t-t-t-t-t-ticked unmercifully.

"Why should that thing be alive when this cab is stopped dead in its tracks?" the poet asked his muse.

"You can get out any time you want," said the cabbie, shifting his gears and his attitude into neutral.

"Wwwhat m-makes it t-t-tick?"

"Same thing that makes you tick, Stoney. All them little cogs on yer brain."

.

"You know, Dr. Stone hurts me sometimes," Samuel finally said.

His father's mask didn't move.

"But, honey," Samuel's mother said through her husband's mask, "you always feel better afterward, don't you?"

.

The rain beat a lyric tattoo against the skylight, a round if you listened closely, a few simple notes round and round until the wind blew up harder and threw it off. Then when the wind calmed again, the round was back, clearer than before.

"Why do you have a skylight?"

"Does it bother you?"

"Everett took Homer to camp, you know."

"How does that make you feel?"

"Angry."

Dr. Paluka said nothing.

"And betrayed."

Nothing.

"And scared."

Nothing.

"They're at the bus station right now. I couldn't even go down there to see him off. I was afraid I'd faint or cry or become hysterical in front of his fellow campers. How would that have looked?"

"How do you think that would have made Homer feel?"

43

"Angry."
Dr. Paluka said nothing.
"And betrayed."
Nothing.
"And scared."
Nothing.
The wind blew the rain off the skylight.

·

"And whose little boy are you?"

Ezra had grabbed the wrong man's hand. He looked up at the strangeness and the tallness and was too shocked to speak or run. Stanley was standing a few feet away looking at a windowful of half-priced briefcases when he checked and saw his son holding the stranger's hand.

Father and son had been strolling the huge yet intimate Port Authority bus terminal for a half-hour. They had arrived early for Ezra's bus and taken the extra time to have a second breakfast at Walgreen's, to buy a paperback edition of *Mad Magazine* at a Book Barn, and to window shop while the rain raged against the terminal's windowless walls and distant ceiling. Oddballs, vagrants, and degenerates outnumbered the people who had legitimate business in the terminal three to one, it seemed to Stanley. To Ezra, the odds seemed even higher. "Your mother always hated this place," Stanley had said, referring to the street people the rain had driven inside. He had been speaking for himself, too, about an abstract disgust that turned into a visceral revulsion when a bum or a beggar or a junkie or a bag lady with black ankles got too close. The closeness of these characters felt like slime to Stanley, like the worst human ooze upon his skin; they made the hairs on the back of his neck and on his arms stand apart so that disgust could crawl over him like a nausea of the flesh.

It almost happened again, Stanley thought to himself: I looked away for only a second and he got my Ezra. Could Mirriam be right? Of course not. Look at him. He's got such a kind old face and with a checkered shirt and bow tie, too. What does he have

44

in that bag? Bread. He smells from fresh bread for God's sake, what could I be thinking? But the awful thought persisted: it's the kindly, fresh-bread-scented, bow-tie type who can charm the little boys away, woo them into a car or a bus or a back alley or a basement apartment full of religious articles. Though it would take a monster to hurt a child, would a child take the hand of a monster?

·

The brazen scent of marijuana drifted through the half-lit subway car. In his mind Harry lined up four possible culprits, all black, all young, all threatening because they were young and black and riding the subway unaccompanied by a parent who could keep his kid from starting trouble or getting into trouble. Harry found the one standing at the very end of the car guilty. What affronted Harry most was that the offender couldn't have been much older than Harry Jr. Harry Jr. smelled the marijuana, too, but he didn't know what it was. It smelled like an exotic spice from his mother's rack of pretty green and amber vials. The scent tickled the inside of his nose much the same way his mother's perfume did when she dabbed it behind her ears and on her wrists and down her blouse; and he was drawn into a reverie that took him out of the dingy subway car up, up, up into a floating whorl of white that worked on his senses like flour and flannel and a woman's breath.

·

"Cartoon rain, Stoney, look at it. Long black lines. Good rainbow weather. Used to love it when I was a lad like you, Stoney, my laddie. I'd be at the screen door to sit watch, and then when it thundered down I'd smell the smiling smell the wet let loose and I'd blow out plugs of weather from the green cross-hatchings. Pungent, Stoney, dear. Hypnotic, too. And then I'd go out walkin' in it like a dip in the ocean. Thought it was, too, Stoney, old boy. Thought the ocean got itself turned upside down somehow. The same roar, you know. Not here, of course, not now, not against concrete and vinyl. And then there'd be the fishskin

45

shimmer of a rainbow to boot. That made me imagine, Stoney. Loved to walk in it the whole lovely day long. Loved it back then. Loved it back when."

.

"I'm sorry, I'm not here right now. Actually I'm not sorry at all. I am deliriously happy to be away from this stinking sweltering, oppressive city for the summer. Believe it or not, I have gone off to camp. And you are probably one of the people whose stifling presence and constant telephoning drove me there. You helped send this girl to camp.

"If this is my mother calling to suggest another get-acquainted lunch, I'll be out God only knows where eating wild berries for the next six weeks. Drop by if you're in the neighborhood. You don't need a reservation.

"If this is Dr. Wulkan, I'm making a thousand dollars for the summer, so don't worry about the lousy four sessions I owe you for. You'll get your money.

"If this is Gary, the answer is no.

"If this is Karen, I do want to be your friend, but I don't want to feel responsible for you. And Jesus, please, please be careful if you're going to keep hanging out in those pick-up joints on Third Ave.

"If this is Bennett, I'm sorry but our plan will have to wait. Of course, there's nothing stopping you from going ahead and finding a loft and chairs and whatever else. Do what you think is best. Just don't count on me right now.

"If this is Gary, the answer is still no.

"If this is . . . oh shit, look at the time, I'm late and I'll never get a cab in this rain and I don't even know what the hell you're supposed to wear at a camp. I'm sure I'm forgetting something crucial. Shit.

"If this is Jiggs, my dear, wonderful, concerned manager, call-ing to try to convince me to change my name, I remain yours forever, Frances.

"At the beep, please 'beep' yourself. All of you."

.

"Let's talk about trust, Mona."

Dr. Paluka spoke without expression. Because she represented wisdom and help, her patients desperately sought her views. But because she wanted her patients to help themselves by realizing the subconscious wisdom of their own ways, she hid her views behind a blank face and a monotone.

Mona wondered if she trusted her husband who had overruled her in the matter of camp. Did she trust his motives? His ability to make a sound decision? Did she trust Homer to take care of himself? Could any seven-year-old really be trusted to take care of himself in a dangerous situation? And what about the owners of Camp Freedom? And the counselors? She had looked through the brochure quite carefully, and then her husband had handled all the subsequent forms and correspondence. But could she, even after the most scrupulous investigation, place full trust in strangers? And then there was the ticklish question of whether she could trust Dr. Paluka, who was willing to raise the question at the possible expense of Mona's confidence in her.

"Mona? Did you hear me? Shall we talk about trust?"

·

Geoff Thomason had bought a huge yellow bus and the services of a French-speaking bus driver. Albert knew a dozen words of English, all of them curse words. He was slovenly, too, and had a naturally lewd way of moving and smoking and smiling. But his previous experience as the driver of a tour bus in Western Europe more than qualified him to drive the campers from the Port Authority in Manhattan to Colt's Point Stream in the pinelands.

Though he thought he knew no French, somehow Geoff Thomason had made Albert understand what was expected of him. And Albert did not disappoint his employer, despite the heavy hint of irresponsibility in the young Frenchman's appearance and manner. He picked up Geoff Thomason promptly at his apartment and helped him load his several bags of photography equipment onto the bus. Then he drove off for the Port Authority Bus Terminal, maneuvering the huge yellow bus

47

through rain and traffic as smoothly as Geoff Thomason had ever driven through the city.

Everything had been going smoothly for Geoff Thomason since he had heard about Dr. Stone's acreage in the pinelands. A lawyer Dr. Stone knew had been peddling options on a dying client's holdings in order to improve the tax situation for the heirs. That was how the chiropractor came to control several acres along the northeastern border of New Jersey's Pine Barrens. From back copies of the *Wharton Warning Register,* Geoff Thomason discovered a scant but colorful history of Dr. Stone's property. During the Second World War, the dying man had given the Boy Scouts of America free use of his New Jersey acreage for a week-long fund-raising Vict-O-Ree. A just amount of the proceeds was to reimburse the BSA first for having cleared the grounds with hatchets and axes and tandem saws, and then for having purchased and erected several cabins to serve as kitchen, hospital, and barracks for the national leadership. The scouts themselves spent the week in tents. The donor spent the week in his mansion in Pittsburgh.

The Vict-O-Ree — a circus of kissing booths, marching bands, exhibits, propaganda, and games of chance — circled a wide stretch of Colt's Point Stream. A footbridge was built so the paying customers could cross. On the opening day the vice president of the United States stood on the footbridge and begged the crowd to buy war bonds. Three days later Gary Cooper stood on the same spot and made the same plea, only, of course, Gary Cooper did not beg. The Vict-O-Ree attracted fewer people than an average golf tournament would today, but the visitors spent their money freely once they were on the grounds. More than two hundred thousand tax-free dollars were raised for the war effort; the reimbursement was made to the BSA; Lieutenant General Baden-Powell's troops scattered; the Allies won the war; and thirty years later the chiropractor owned an option on scarred tree stumps, a risky footbridge, and the ramshackle remains of a dozen rotting cabins.

Geoff Thomason remembered how he had persuaded the chiropractor to open a camp on his pineland property. "You are a great man, Dr. Stone," he told the chiropractor. "You have wisdom in your hands. You have a powerful hold over people."

The elevated tone and diction Geoff Thomason used, almost an incantation, was inspired by the imposing stature and manner of the chiropractor who spoke and moved like a statue come to life. There was never a wasted word or motion, a habit no doubt rooted in the chiropractor's training which taught any attentive student that if there were correct moves that healed, there must also be incorrect moves that destroyed. The effect on Geoff Thomason was elevating and was reflected in his exalted speech. Each word reported like a bootstep on the stone floor of a large, empty temple, the few steps strung together till they reached the hydraulic altar of the chiropractor. As the chiropractor resembled a priest whose every prayer and sacred gesture has been historically prescribed, Geoff Thomason resembled a disciple whose awe and reverence made him stand taller and straighter and speak more profoundly. The chiropractor stared into Geoff Thomason's eyes. He was accustomed to measuring pain by studying a patient's eyes. There was no awkwardness as he stared, no embarrassment, though Geoff Thomason continued to praise the great man far beyond flattery.

"Why not use your special gift to strengthen the bodies and minds of children? You are the kind of man I myself needed as a child. What I might have been was sealed inside of me by my parents' smothering yet indifferent performance. And then I met you and I put myself in your hands. And it was at that moment, when your hands first touched me, that I felt finally that I had grown up. I felt my back broaden under your hands. I felt muscle forge itself from the base of my spine up through my neck. When I stood up I suspected that I was taller, and I was certain that I was stronger. This is what you can give to children."

They never met as businessmen. Even when Geoff Thomason had copy and layout for the chiropractor to approve, their business was conducted in the context of a doctor/patient relationship. The main business at hand was always a spinal realignment, after which the two men would talk — one thin and haggard and breathlessly recuperating from the echoing ache of his wrenching adjustment, the other smiling and exhilarated, his body pumping precious iron from a deep, dark well-being.

Geoff Thomason realized that the romantic history of Colt's Point could be put to good use, could be effectively woven into a pamphlet and perhaps innocently exaggerated. That Gary Cooper once strode the ground where an eight-year-old might soon bobble a bunt was no reason for the little third baseman's daddy to feel secure. But Geoff Thomason knew that he would. He proposed his idea to the chiropractor.

"Why not take the children and mold them, Dr. Stone? This summer. On your New Jersey acreage. A camp, Dr. Stone. Twelve . . . fifteen hundred dollars a child."

In the end Geoff Thomason would remain in the background, but it would be a glorious background painted in the persuasive strokes of his own misshapen but eloquent hand. Touch — that is what came back to him in the bus as Albert proceeded to the Port Authority. The touch, from beginning to end, of his mind and eyes and fingers and ears. Like a foul-shooter, he would not let the round ball of his creation go until it felt just right. Touch. Life a chef, a musician, a sculptor, the words and pictures, alone and together, had to taste, sound and feel just so. *Voilà!* say the French when they know they have it, and *Je ne sais quoi* when they try to explain exactly what it is that they have.

Do not ask how Geoff Thomason knew what to include when he wrote and when he cropped his photographs, for he never even asked himself. Certain things seemed right. On the shelf to the right of his drawing table he had gathered several volumes of history and romantic lore containing much questionably relevant but unarguably persuasive information about Lenapes, Iroquois, aquifers, forest fires, Dutch captains, Scottish settlers, mosquitoes, marsupials, snakes, and a reclusive society of time-warped woodsmen and women called pineys who were as thick-skinned, hearty, and underdeveloped as the pitch-pine forests standing between them and the twentieth century. Eccentric rather than savage, primitive rather than ignorant, defensive rather than dangerous, the pineys mainly farmed, sang songs, hunted, and drank great reservoirs of hooch in a routine that threatened only those outsiders obsessed with progress. Geoff Thomason hated what he had read about the pineys, but he loved what he had written about them.

Yes, Dr. Stone had been interested in Geoff Thomason's idea. Yes, he had made his New Jersey acreage available, and the inspired pamphleteer had peopled it with avuncular pineys, American Indians, and guest celebrities from great human theaters. He had also painted a richly textured backdrop of fauna and flora onto which he skillfully projected the probable adventures of the reader's seven-, eight-, nine-, ten-, eleven-, or twelve-year-old camper.

As Geoff Thomason sat in the tense stillness of a city caught in a rainstorm, he recalled many of the kinetic words he had chosen for the genesis of Camp Freedom: dart, mole, twitter, vole, flit, whisk, gray fox, red fox, whistle, flash, meadow mouse, pintail, cottontail, weevil, beetle, buck, honey bee, butterfly, sky, fly, greenshoot, blueberry, cranberry, moss, broom, mistletoe, laurel, pickerel, mudminnow, pine snake, tadpole, shortleaf, broadleaf, hop, wriggle, scoot, flip, flapjack, leapfrog, bedbunk, high jump, swing, sing, bloom — brrrroom . . . Albert found the leeway to shift gears and plow forward for half a block.

·

Francis banged on the door of the bus until Geoff Thomason noticed and gestured to Albert to let Francis inside. It was still early, and Francis was pleased to have been the first to arrive. Carefully, he selected two seats for himself and Frances. Before he realized that Albert could not understand him, Francis told the driver that the best seats were forward, away from the heat and noise of the engine, but behind the front wheels so that vibrations were minimized and bumps could be anticipated.

By the time Francis had realized that Albert spoke only French, Frances swept herself and her gear out of the rainstorm and into the huge yellow ark. Nevertheless, Francis said to Albert, "This is my friend. This is Frances." He pointed at himself and said, "Francis." Then he raised both hands chest high and palms out to signal that the first part of the lesson was over. He paused a moment and then pointed to Frances.

"Frances," Francis said conclusively. But there was no sparkle of comprehension in Albert's baggy eyes.

"What is he, retarded?" Frances mocked.

"He's French," Francis explained.

"Great," said Frances. "Thank him for letting me on the bus in this goddamn rain and let's sit down and go over these song-sheets. Where do you think I've been all morning? I've been Xeroxing camp songs at the goddamn library."

Half of Frances's baggage was papers, books, and other resources for Camp Freedom's dramatic program. Among the shorts, underwear, socks, T-shirts, and toiletries were skits, lyrics, jokes, and several paperbound copies of *The Sound of Music*, which was to be the grand finale after the less ambitious revues Frances planned to stage during the first five weeks of camp. The revues, though minor divertissments, would serve three purposes: rehearsals and performances would give the children experience, stage presence, and confidence; Frances would find out who was most talented and reliable so she would be better able to cast the more important roles of *The Sound of Music*; finally, the rest of the camp could look forward to five consecutive Saturday nights of entertainment before having to wait three weeks for everyone's favorite Broadway musical.

"She is Frances, too, Albert. Both our names are Frances," Francis said with a child's delight. His voice ascending two notes of the scale, "Francis," he said, pointing at himself, "and . . . Frances," pointing at her, his voice descending the two notes again.

"Here's what I have, Francis, I have songs and I have riddles, too; maybe we should do the riddles on the way up," Frances said, finding the riddles while still searching for the songsheets she knew she had packed in her suitcase.

Albert began to speak the universal language of men, which Francis understood. With his eyes Albert said, You're a good-looking woman. By licking his lips and rubbing his hands together, Albert said, I'd like to kiss you. I'd like to undress you. I particularly like the way your backside looks as you bend down over your suitcase. I would like to kiss you all over, but mostly along a line that would bisect you from the top of your head down to between your legs. I would stop between your legs for a long, strong inhalation of that exquisite feminine scent so like our finest cheeses, so perfect an hors d'oeuvre or dessert, a meal in and of itself, requiring nothing more to satisfy man's deepest hunger.

Francis did not like what he read on Albert's face. But he was mercifully diverted by Frances.

"I'll bet you don't know which takes longer: raising the flag to half-mast or raising it to full-mast?" Frances posed, her hands still madly shuffling through her gear.

Francis would not allow himself to answer incorrectly. Even if he had to guess, which in this case he did, first he had to construct a logical explanation for both possible answers so that if the one he guessed were wrong it would still be right. Francis no longer remembered if this involuntary need and ability to be right had been part of him always or if he had acquired it along with his teaching certificate.

"Don't tell me," Francis begged.

"Don't tell you what?"

"The answer."

"Oh shit, half-mast, half-mast, Francis. What the hell would I ask it for if the answer wasn't what you'd least expect? Half-mast, Francis, like everything else in my goddamn life. Where the hell are those songs?"

"I was going to say half-mast," Francis mumbled to himself, working now for the explanation since he had been given the answer.

·

"Look at the world from as far away as possible, Stoney. The smaller it gets, the bigger your ideas, don't you see? Do you think for one miserable minute that poor, far-sighted mankind ever would have come so damn far in his knowledge of the universe if he could see it close up? Never! The moon, Stoney! That's what man is after. And then onto the next far-fetched, faraway, far too mysterious challenge. The sun, of course, is an entirely different matter, son of mine. It's even made, I think, of entirely different matter. Even a poor far-sighted poet like meself can't make it out for all the pain you get trying to stare into the blinding center."

"You'd be better off walking this last block, perfesser. I could be stopped here all day," the cabbie recommended.

"See there, Stoney, there's the bus up ahead. Think of it now as a faraway object, a bar of busyellow gold in the dead-center of a vast field or a huge mountain plateau. Think of it, Stoney, as an Incan centerpiece surrounded by huge symbolic stones forming a message that can only be read from an impossible height. The Incans themselves, my little sun, could not read the very message they built, could only imagine, could only hope that some future far-off intelligence would be able one day to focus their eyes on the great eternal Incan vision. Sounds like something built by Sylvania, don't it, Stoney m'boy? Heh, we'll get out and walk, why not?"

The father and son took the block slowly, father dragging a small steamer, son dragging a duffel bag. The rain was like a hard shower aimed at their faces. Their hair straightened and clung, the tips of their noses poured off water, their mouths did most of the breathing. The father had to raise his voice above the storm.

"Picture this busyellow Incan gold rectangle on wheels — I said rect, not wrecked — as the omphalos, the black eye in a Susan, I don't care, just get some distance, boy. The hub of a wheel, if you like. And what are we? One spoke, Stoncy. Shhh . . ." he said suddenly, stopping, looking straight up into the rain. "One spoke, Stoney. *One voice spoke/One spoke in the wheel.* Ahh, Stoney," he said joyously, his right arm upraised. "Thank you, Stoney," said the arm. "A poem, Stoney!"

·

The bus was a former horse on the city line, a faded yellow bruiser with orangy leather upholstery installed before plastic became the municipal rage. There were no luggage holds along the yellow horse's muddied flanks, so the drenched and darkened assortment of duffels, valises, trunks, laundry bags, backpacks, and zippered totes had to be squeezed, jammed, squashed, and wedged into the overhead racks, any extra seats, and the fast disappearing aisle.

When all had arrived at the pick-up spot, the campers and their families had to find whatever shelter they could in the tumult of people and rain blowing in all directions outside the terminal. The broad marquee at the front of the terminal just around the corner from where the bus was parked offered some protection from the rain, but the storm was now slanted almost completely horizontally. For this reason, as well as for the obvious emotional reasons, the good-bys tended to be quick. Hadn't everything that needed to be said already been said twenty times a day every day since the first day the child realized he was being sent away to camp? "Don't worry, Jeffie, I'll write you every day and tell you what Daddy and I are doing and I'll telephone you whenever I can and we'll be seeing each other before you know it." "They have a good program, that's why you're going. Maybe they'll put a little muscle on that skeleton of a body of yours, Samuel." "What is there for you to do at home, Harry? I'll be working, Mom will — Mom is —." "Heh-heh, you're off, my little Apollo, because I'm afraid that whilst I'm sitting in my nest hatching a long-awaited flight of fancy you're liable to climb up my tree and sneak out onto my limb and grab me by my scrawny neck and squeeze until my feet stop twitchin'. Then you'll probably open me up to see what makes you t-t-t-t-tick." "If he asks you why you are sending him to camp, you can tell him that he has indicated a desire to go to camp by virtue of all the things he likes to do. He doesn't know about camp life, but if he did, he'd choose it for himself over any other kind of existence this summer. Being more experienced, you are able to know this about your son, Mona. You actually know more about Homer than Homer knows about himself." "I'm doing this, *we're* doing this, for everyone's good. Especially yours, Ez. What happened to your brother could have happened to anyone at any time in any place. Camp is no more dangerous than the street corner. In fact, it's a lot safer. You'll be out in the woods with boys your own age. That's freedom, Ez. That's what I was — what *we* were — trying to give you. Freedom. That's why I picked out this camp from all the other ones. In the ad and the brochure they seemed to really understand the importance of giving a young boy his freedom, a free hand; there's nothing stopping you from doing anything at all — except your own limitations."

"What's limitation?"

"It means that you can't do a certain thing. The size of your muscle, for example, limits how far you can throw a ball. But you'll never be able to throw it farther than a certain distance — whatever that distance is. Maybe it's two hundred feet in your case. The best you can do, Ez, is also your own personal limit."

Stanley thought about his wife and marriage and missing son and wondered for one quick aching moment if he weren't trying to do more than his best by sending Ezra away to camp. Was he trying to overstep the limits of his marriage? Of his fatherhood? Was he trying to take into his own hands the ultimate, intricate cat's-cradle he and his family had worked so long to develop, trying to undo and outdo the interdependent pattern of their lives?

Stanley squatted down to hug Ezra. Geoff Thomason had advised each parent that it was easier to leave the child at the bus than it was to drive the child to the campsite, which only prolonged the separation. It was best to start the children off equally. With the same apprehensions, the same chance to ally themselves early on against the communal unknown. Secretly knowing this, perhaps, Mirriam would not even go to the bus. She sat in her kitchen, stone-faced, beginning another count for another son.

FIVE

At the other end of the rainstorm, at Colt's Point Stream, stood Dr. George Stone, a biblical, mythological figure of a man. The nobility of his posture strained against gravity, giving the impression that he was an inch or two off the ground. His stance and upward glance and defiant chin in the face of the storm suggested that he had God's ear, or that he was himself a god. This prophet, this daemon, glowered at the thundering heavens, his hair curling into Romanesque ringlets, his clothes becoming transparent against the extraordinary definition of his body. Ribs and muscles seemed drawn onto his soaked, skintight T-shirt. Thick bulging braids of strength filled out the white trouser legs that would have been loose on another man of the same height and weight but lacking this man's brawny proportions.

The sound of the rain at Colt's Point reminded him of the sound of the rain in the narrow alleyway between two old apartment buildings where his father would drag the ashes of every tenant's garbage through the early-morning darkness. That narrow way had seemed dangerous to him after his father had sighted huge, mangy rats scuttling along the cracked cement of the small, concave courtyard to which the alleyway blindly led. It was in that courtyard that his father had witnessed a terrifying struggle. He had just shoveled the last bit of ashes into the tenth can and was hauling the can along the bumpy cement ramp leading from the furnace room to the courtyard where the cans remained until early the next morning when he would drag them out, one by one, in front of the apartment building to be collected, dumped, and carelessly thrown back onto the sidewalk, into the gutter, upside down, sideways, banged up, dented, scattered there like empty shells after a battle. In the center of the courtyard there was a small square grating for drainage. As the old superintendent dragged the can past the grating he heard an angry squeal. A rat was banging its snout into the grate, forcing it between the bars, dancing to the left and right on panicky hind legs. His father thought the rat was attacking, but all of a sudden the rat pulled back with a single, desperate effort, "and there," he told his wide-eyed son, "was the creepiest, crawliest, nastiest little alligator ever you wanted to meet just biting right onto that poor scabby rat's face." His father then went on to describe the fight in gruesome detail, explaining, between spurts of blood and frantic shrieks, how all of life is such a struggle and how each creature is equipped with certain advantages to help him get through.

The alligator, which was still thin enough to squeeze its head through the grating, was one of "hundreds, maybe thousands," living underground in the sewer system. "They come from Florida," his father had told him. The migration of college students to the Floridian warmth in the chill of the North's early spring always included a large contingent of jokers and jerks. They would mail the tiny alligators back home, enjoying at the point of purchase the uncontrollable belly laughter they would have to miss when Mom or Sis or Aunt So-and-So or Professor Such-and-Such greedily unwrapped the mysterious gift, opened the lid, and let out an unearthly scream. When the alligator-mailing fad finally came to the attention of the Post Office, the officials stopped it. But the damage had been done. What does one do with a six-inch-long alligator? Flush it down the toilet, of course. And where does that lead? To the sewer system, of course, where the amphibious alligators survived, flourished, and multiplied. It was one of the new breed of hardy sewer gators his father had found locked in deadly combat with the overmatched rat.

Never underestimate the power of even an infant alligator's bite, nor the ease with which it can wriggle out of danger.

This cold and slimy scene had been set and performed forevermore in George Stone's mind, the presence of his father, old and weak and unarmed, the moonlit darkness, the scratch and squeal of the tiny combatants resounding in the eerie acoustics of the courtyard, their fight to the death, the sweet stench of burnt garbage, the clatter of the ashcans, the open eyes of his father as two weeks later he lay on his back in the rain in the courtyard with a first can of ashes pulled over onto himself, tins and bones and other fire-resistant elements poking through the wet ash, the unsympathetic insistence of the rain, its luminous visibility in the moonlight, its "creepiest, crawliest, nastiest" feeling on flesh, the malodorous reaction of the rain upon the cinders and the powder — these had become the omens and the evidence of a murdered heart, of an attack, of his father's fight to the death with the trash.

This god, this superintendent's superman of a son, would not give in to the murderous rain. He clenched and unclenched his left fist, a habit. He took a single stride as if to chase the rain away, and, in his mind, it worked. In his mind, the downpour receded like a biblical plague in a Hollywood epic.

The power of this man's will was visible on his face. One could see his bravery, the transfusion of strength he stole from a storm that meant to reduce him to ashes, his willingness to confront and conquer the very elements that signaled the failing of his father's heart.

His hands flew up to his head. He staggered and reeled and fell to his knees. He tried to get up but fell back and rolled over in the mud. His hands remained at his head to soothe him, to "break a pain," as he termed a necessarily violent chiropractic adjustment. He seemed drunk or dizzy as again he attempted to stand up. This time he made it to his feet and spread his arms for equilibrium. The muscles of his arms and legs felt smaller. Nobility ran out of him like the air from a tire. Then, just as he succeeded in steadying himself, he tumbled into Colt's Point Stream.

II

The bus was about to leave for the campsite. Francis and Frances were the only hired help who chose to take advantage of the bus ride. The other counselors and directors, Geoff Thomason explained, were from New Jersey or Pennsylvania and had their own cars or would be arranging their own transportation.

Frances tried to rally the boys, but they were sullen and unresponsive. She approached Stonehenge Alcock first, drawn to his fiery red hair.

"What's your name? Mine's Frances."

For a moment the boy looked as if he wanted to speak, as if he were trying to, but couldn't. Then his face gave up the effort, and he hid his feelings and his stutter by acting hopelessly shy.

"Well, you'll tell me when you're ready," Frances cooed with syrupy understanding. She understood, too, that her habit of dominating a relationship as a cover-up for being overly dependent was quickly broken in the company of children. To them she gave everything she had.

"What about your riddle?" Francis chirped. "I'll bet these boys know the answer," he said slyly.

"Okay. I've got a whole bag full of riddles here," Frances announced. "What takes longer: raising the flag to half-mast or full-mast?"

No child's face looked as if it were working on the riddle. No star or white. No red or stripe. No blue in the eye of this child. Or this. Or this.

"Here's a clue. You don't *raise* the flag to half-mast, you *lower* it."

Her clue was a knife to Francis. The bloody answer trickled out of his wound. Too late. Too late. Francis stared out his window at the continuously washed-out view. The rain sounded like fat frying. The bus's engine droned in his head. He leaned against the vibrating window and tried to block out the clue by singing to himself.

> We are going down the valley
> Going down the valley

Going down the valley
One by one
One by one

"According to flag etiquette, you have to raise the flag to
full-mast first, and then you lower it to half-mast. So do you
see why it takes longer? You'd think it would take only half
the time to put the flag at half-mast. But you have to go all
the way up and then back down again."

III

Mirriam sat in a house that felt as empty as she was. She day-
dreamed that the house was a shell and that a huge finger put
a hole through the wall. Then the finger poked a hole through
Mirriam.

"Where are you," Mirriam said silently. There was always a
storm of voices, of sirens and telephone calls, of trash cans being
kicked aside so the police could storm a dark alleyway. In this
hail of noise, she heard only her own silent voice: Where are
you? Where are you? Mama wants to know where you are? Who
you're with? What's he making you do? If he's torturing you?
Or does he love you? Is that why? Does he love you so much
he can only prove it by hurting you? Tell me. Tell me, have
you eaten today? Did he make you cream of wheat and pancakes with powdered sugar and orange juice poured only up to
the second button of Ronald McDonald's vest on your favorite
glass? Did he let you dress yourself in stripes and checks? Does
he keep you tied up in a closet? Tell me he doesn't force drugs
down your throat or into your arm to keep you quiet. Tell me
he doesn't touch you you know where.

Mirriam felt as though she were falling through the cavernous
emptiness of her house. Her two sons were falling with her.
She tried to grab them so she could pull them to her, but they
were just beyond her reach.

Just a fraction of an inch beyond her reach.

IV

Colt's Point Stream was not so deep nor the bottom so treacherous that the fallen god had to worry himself or his one lone observer. George Stone flopped in the water like an adult in a kiddie's pool, the shock of his quick submergence failing to bring him to his senses, but managing to awaken those senses. Still disoriented, still suffering the benign blockage that upset — or offset — the workings of his brain, he nevertheless was encouraged by the starkly clear vision he had of himself crawling out of the stream. Instinctively, he knew this had to be done. His instincts for survival took over as he fought the storm and the agitated current and the bothersome shifting of silt, sand, clay, and bog-iron ore.

He got himself onto his stomach. Something told him he could propel himself forward in that position. His arms weighed heavily as he used them to keep his head above water and pull himself toward the nearest bank of Colt's Point Stream. First he cupped his hands. It was a reflex. He always cupped his hands when he was swimming. But as they hit bottom in the shallow stream, he found it more helpful to spread his fingers apart and dig them into the sandy floor.

He reached out of the stream and grabbed hold of mud. First one hand, then the other. Slowly, weakly, still unsure of any purpose other than survival, he dragged himself out of the stream into the storm.

He was on all fours. The strenuous effort of leaving the stream and bellying through the mud seemed to concentrate its wearing effect on his neck. His head hung down limply. It had been no small feat to struggle to his hands and knees. He needed rest. He could barely move. Because his head hung down, his face was protected from the rain by his arched back. He had created a crude incubator within his own form which sustained him while his rushing blood beat against the blockage to his brain.

Soon he was strong enough to push his hands off the ground. He was just on his knees now. His head began to clear. The more sensible he became, the more the storm menaced him. But he was determined to get to his feet, and he readied himself psychologically as well as physically. After flexing his muscles, taking several deep breaths, and making his eyes lock onto a rock that kept slipping in and out of focus, he stood at the very edge of standing and prepared to lift himself up as though he were the first of his species to stand erect upon the earth. The one lone observer was reminded of something but could not remember immediately, too compelling was the sight and might of the man beginning to raise himself up from the earth.

The one lone observer watched him pull himself up to his feet as though he weighed nothing at all. He was up. He was standing. He was laughing at the storm.

The one lone observer saw the remarkable similarity between the man's soaking-wet curly hair and the photographer's scraggly beard. He noticed such things. He himself wore a wig.

PART II

Going Down the Valley

SIX

In his mind, the one lone observer hears the voices of the children whispering like the pines. It's as if they're praying to him: Help us, Gus. Save us, Gus. Come back for us, Gus.

In his ears, Gus hears only his own breathing, nervous, irregular, too loud, and the breath of the woods, which sounds so faraway in comparison.

— We're all in the woods, Gus thinks. Me up here, them down there.

The spot Gus is in started out as a crow's nest. Now it's a birdcage. From high up on his bluff, he was able to see everything. Now he's afraid to poke his bald head up out of the brush. In the beginning the wind almost blew off his wig. Later he ran right out of it.

When he escaped the camp, Gus ran as fast as he could in as many different directions as possible in order to throw Stone off his trail. He ran scared, too, with held breath and on the tips of his toes so as not to wake up the thugs Stone said were out in the woods guarding against anyone who tried to make a run for it. But Gus ran anyway, he had to, he couldn't take any more of it down there; and, as he was zigzagging through the woods, his wig caught on a low branch, and he nearly broke his neck because the tape half held, and all Gus could do was rip off the rest of the wig, which he did in what was left of his stride.

— It's down there somewhere right now, Gus thinks, hanging from I don't know what branch of I don't know what tree.

II

Gus, the one lone observer, had observed Geoff Thomason in the spring when by chance Gus had been up on the bluff just as Geoff Thomason arrived at Colt's Point Stream to photograph the area for the Camp Freedom brochure. From that curious day, curiosity grew, keeping Gus coming back every day to watch for new developments. He had been in the middle of one of his binges, soaking up homemade corn whiskey and store-bought wine all day, all week, all month. All that drink never made him drunk, just happy and warm, especially the wine. His habit was to drink himself through to lunch, munch a handful of berries, and then wander through the woods, reading leaves, orating, stopping by Old Ex's place for some extemporaneous chitchat and another "tetch" of whiskey, or visiting the Kristal family who were all undersized and good dancers, or relaxing for an hour on Sister Victoria's porch while she played her box guitar and set to song the weather, the color of Gus's shirt, an animal that happened to scoot by, what Sister Victoria had for breakfast, what she was planning for dinner, and any other inspiration that popped into her melodious and poetic mind. Eventually he would wind up at Jeremiah's Store and sweep the floorboards or unpack crates or just spell Jeremiah for an hour in return for which Gus got a decent meal and his last drink of the day. Where Gus went after dark, everyone was too polite to ask.

When Gus saw Geoff Thomason, he quit his normal routine. He stayed in the vicinity of Colt's Point, which was not a main attraction, and no one missed him. Not Old Ex or the diminutive Kristals or Sister Victoria or the regulars at Jeremiah's Store. Nor did Gus himself miss the boozy sustenance of his friends and habits. His curiosity sustained him. Every day he nosed around Colt's Point Stream and environs, wondering why and who and what. Two months later he got his answers. That was the day of the storm. The day Dr. George Stone made his grand entrance.

Gus could not believe how the rain came blowing in so fiercely only to stop practically dead at the stand of pines below his own high-and-dry perch. From his perfect vantage, he saw Stone's reckless arrival, and Gus felt justified in having waited so many weeks, in having sniffed and poked and rooted and hypothesized in vain, but in having believed, nevertheless, the way a person awakened in the middle of the night by an unidentifiable noise believes that someone has broken into his home; and Gus had spent several sleepless weeks within glimpse and earshot awaiting the intruder's next footfall. He did not expect it to come crashing down a slippery hill in the person of Dr. George Stone behind the wheel of a U-Haul, plowing a narrow country lane wider, uprooting an infant tree, raveling wiry bush on a rear axle, and skidding, slipping, spinning to a lucky stop on a spongy bank of Colt's Point Stream.

Stone got out and slammed the door of the cab. Gus thought he was mad at the U-Haul for getting away from him; now he knew Stone had been mad at himself for having failed to manipulate the U-Haul appropriately. Stone looked as if he were thinking about grabbing the front fender and dragging the huge semitrailer off the bank with his bare hands. Instead, he considered the rain and traction, got back in, and drove the U-Haul to the cabin which was set farthest from the stream, closest to the wood. Stone backed the truck up to the door of the cabin, turned off the motor, jumped down on strong legs, went around back to open a padlock and release the tailgate, and then tried the door to the cabin. Rust had worn the hinges, and, when Stone pushed, the door swung open on the top hinge only, the bottom of the door scraping crazily and noisily along the pebbly floor.

Inside the truck were various supplies: canned goods, dry goods, paper products, plastic utensils, and a haphazard assortment of pots, pans, hardware, tools, bedclothes, soaps, linen, spray cans, medicines, bandages, crayons, clay, beads, balls, bats, and boxes whose contents Gus couldn't guess, plus two satchels and two trunks probably containing Stone's personal property. Each box or bag or carton or tin played a different song when the rain beat on it for the moment or two it took Stone to rush it from truck to cabin. In all, it looked like the makings for one grand outing, a huge Fourth of July picnic perhaps, or a weekend jamboree, certainly not the entire store for eight weeks of summer camp.

Stone loaded everything but the satchels and trunks into the cabin. Those he carried through the mud to an adjacent cabin and put inside. Then he started up the U-Haul, drove it far enough forward to reverse back to the adjacent cabin, shut off the motor, and disappeared inside the semitrailer for several minutes. Gus looked on as though Stone were a magician preparing his next trick. The arrival and unloading had Gus hypnotized. Months might have sped by as he lay still and unblinking up on his bluff watching the drama of the trick unfold. And when Stone finally reappeared, it had been well worth Gus's anticipation.

First the tip of something large slid a foot or two past the tailgate so that it stuck out of the truck just enough to be wrestled the rest of the way out, but not nearly enough to cause it to crash to the ground by its own momentum. Stone then jumped down and grabbed hold of the large object, which, as he struggled to pull it out of the truck, slowly revealed itself to be a long wooden crate that resembled a coffin.

Using all his considerable strength, Stone grappled with the crate and finally eased it onto the head or feet of the "corpse." There it stood, Stone steadying it with one arm and with the other mopping rain from his brow. Gus realized that if the crate were a coffin, it was deep enough for three medium-size bodies, one on top of the other, or four or five Kristals all jammed in anywhichway.

Stone saw that he would have to carry the crate inside. He concentrated strength in his legs and arms and lifted the crate

off the ground, and then he pushed on, taking baby steps, pausing, using up his strength and not being able to replenish it
fully, losing his hold, feeling the roughness of the wood afflict
his fingers with a similar roughness, making them feel raw, feeling his body beginning to break, his muscles beginning to tear
like expensive silk, until finally Stone had no other choice. He
dropped the crate to the ground, splitting the wood and cracking one section loose, which revealed an odd combination of
chrome and black leather inside.

Gus was at the edge of his excitement at the edge of the cliff.
He was sure that the photographer he had seen in the spring
was connected in some way to the strong man and his still unidentifiable shiny-chrome-and-black-leather mystery. Whatever
the mystery was, Stone was desperate to protect it. First he tried
refitting the shattered pieces of wood. When that didn't work,
he threw his own body over the exposed area to keep the rain
from damaging his precious chrome and leather. This he did
long enough to come up with a more practical idea; he leaped
up into the truck and jumped out with a length of canvas which
quickly he draped over the broken crate. Then he spread the
canvas carefully, making sure it covered those areas most vulnerable to the storm.

What happened next was unpredictable, illogical, and believable only because the extraordinary had become commonplace
in Colt's Point.

Stone began to reel. He grabbed at his head and eyes and
stumbled through the storm without any sense of his whereabouts. It seemed as if suddenly he'd been struck blind and
that the blindness itself was terribly painful because he was
grimacing and clawing at his forehead and eyes as if to stop
intolerable pain. Eventually he plunged into the stream, which
was swollen but still shallow and safe. He flopped around in
the water for a while and then managed to drag himself out
of the stream. It appeared that the pain in his head had subsided. He got to his hands and knees. Then to his feet. Then,
as suddenly as it had come over him, the seizure went away.
It had lasted several minutes, causing Stone to act drunk, des-

perate, comical, weak, near death. Gus was not surprised when Stone was theatrical in the triumph of recovery. Stone raised his fist at the heavens and dared the storm above him and within him to cripple him again.

III

— I'm hungry, Gus thinks. I feel raw. It's been three days. That's not the longest I've ever gone without food, but I'm an old man now.

He searches his knowledge of the woods for scraps of food he can reach without moving. He's afraid to move. He's been afraid of something ever since he set eyes on Geoff Thomason.

Gus came back to settle in these woods because his tired life needed gentle surprises. Here you can round the most familiar corner and discover a path, a clearing, a bog, a cabin, a family, a whole stream of life you never knew existed.

But the minute he saw Geoff Thomason's two-tone green Chevrolet pull up that day to Colt's Point Stream like a deer coming for a lick of water, Gus expected trouble.

Geoff Thomason was not a lost camper or a runaway convict or a hooched-up hillbilly. He was a man on the offensive, a chessboard knight moving three squares at once along the crooked angle of his own devious strategy.

He got out of the car quickly, tired of sitting, it looked like, and he ordered the children out like a schoolteacher.

"Let's go," he said. "Let's go. Only a few hours of good light left. You want your mothers to get a good report, then let's go."

He had to send that threat up over the trunk of the Chevrolet, which he opened and emptied and closed, one, two, three. He did everything in a hurry; talked fast, walked fast, looked like he had sped through his twenty-five years or so in half that time.

Even that first day, before Gus got to know him, he could see from all the way up on his bluff down through the oaks' spotty spring array that Geoff Thomason was concerned about making a fool of himself. He didn't mind, or wasn't aware of, his tangled hair and beard, the scarlet scab of a shaving mishap on his Adam's apple, the stooped shoulders, the nine dirty nails, the flapping shirt tails, unpressed pants, falling socks, scuffed shoes. He cared only about what was going on inside his head. His mind raced way ahead of his ability to express what was on it. He already had looked up and ascertained the condition of the daylight and calculated exactly how many good shots he'd be able to take and in what order he would take them based on the position of the sun, certain lengthening shadows, distant clouds, the speed and quality of his film, the complexions, coloring, and temperaments of the kids, the set-ups, the props, the sense light and dark and shades of both would make in this or that scene, and then all that brainwork came out as, "Let's go. Only a few hours of good light left."

Geoff Thomason had curly hair and a tight curly beard and a curl of an upper lip trying to hide an overbite that slashed its way through to your attention like a machete. If you were looking right at him, which those strange children were not, his teeth added a nastiness, a harshness to whatever he said, even if none was intended.

— How many times, Gus thinks, during our "philosophical" chats he said to me, "I love you, Gus," and it sounded like he was insulting my mother. We philosophized about those five little humanoids that had been squeezed into the back of the Chevy along with their designer suitcases and their duffel bags made out of Dayglo-colored parachute silk from France.

There were three boys and two girls, all approximately the same age and exactly the same size. They climbed out of the car like movie stars at a Hollywood premiere, careful not to lean too much of their slight weight on the backrest of the front passenger seat which Geoff Thomason had collapsed protectively on top of his most expensive and fragile photography equipment.

"What you fail to understand, Gus, is that people need to see and hear and touch perfection right here on earth," Geoff Thomason said that night Gus accused his models of being inhuman. "They're not inhuman," Geoff Thomason countered, "they're superhuman."

"Superhuman, my ass," Gus said, scratching it and ending the discussion by walking away. "They're supercute is all. And too damned super grown-up for their own good."

"Gus, I love you."

— All you have to do, Gus thinks, is line up those kids who were in the brochure next to the kids who are down there in the camp and you can see the awful difference. To look at those five models even from way uptop the cliff made my skin jump the way it does looking at animals that are slimy. Or spiny. Or dead and unburied bluefly food. Of course, there was nothing disgusting about those kids, nothing physically repulsive, just the opposite. And that was what was so disgusting. Not a flaw anywhere on 'em. They were absolutely perfect specimens of the human race, I'll give Geoff Thomason that.

To speak about one, boy or girl, described them all: clean, silken, soft, wavy, honey-hued hair that falls perfectly in or out of place, that curls and whorls over dainty pink-and-white sea-shell ears, that rings a rosy fair face of smoothest off-white; good shading everywhere, too, the lights and darks, good shadow-black hollows each side of the thin white sapling of a neck, good dots of darkish dimples on the elbows and knees and just a quick wink of one on each cheek.

— Even far off, Gus remembers, the eyes looked night-owl big but pale and blue as a fine French sky, and I swear that from a hundred feet away I could feel myself see myself in those eyes as if I were staring into my own disbelief that any eyes so big and so light could be human.

One by one the humanoids took their orders from Geoff Thomason. While he talked he led them down to the least dilapidated cabin. He piled his gear at the doorstep and then retraced his quick steps to fetch another two armfuls of props and equipment from the front seat and from the ground behind the emptied trunk, the ducklings following him back and forth, back and forth, from cabin to Chevy, Chevy to cabin. Even the ones who had received their instructions remained on Geoff Thomason's shuttle until he brought everything down and began setting up the first shot. Then, with only his subtle nod as their reminder, the two boys Geoff Thomason had cast for the first shot produced the required outfits from their bags and changed into bathing suits on the spot.

They stripped down to their underpants in almost perfect synchronization, the blonder boy just a beat or two behind because he was wearing a belt. Then they took off their underpants, too, and no one — not the naked boys and not the blasé girls — batted an eye.

— Is that human? Gus asks himself. Two red-blooded boys dangling full naked and not a drop of that red blood pumping into their cheeks? Two sophisticated little women of nine without so much as a blush or a "tut tut" or the tiniest titter of excitation? I didn't know who to be more embarrassed for.

Immodesty was nothing new, Gus understood. After all, it was one of the earliest conditions of mankind, a natural characteristic of Adam and Eve when all they did was walk around this wood naked and neutral. And there's the vestigial immodesty all humans feel whenever their forbidden apples are strained for them — when they're babies, or old and infirm, or when they're sick as the devil. But for boys and girls at such a crucial age of discovery and peer evaluation to be so unshy and so uninterested was a revelation to Gus.

— If I hadn't seen the boys' goods with my own eyes, he thinks, and then the girls', too, I'd have bet someone a bog of berries all five were drugged and neutered on the way up in the Chevy.

The best Gus could do was make himself believe he had walked in on the middle of a movie so he could give the shocking scene the benefit of some doubtfully moral explanation. For all he knew, those kids could have been cousins, and Gus missed finding it out because he came in late. Or maybe the man with the camera was some sort of back-to-nature guru. It had always been Gus's nature not to interfere. He reserves judgment for as long as possible. The jury's still out on many of the things he has seen in his time. But after comparing the reality of Camp Freedom to the Camp Freedom brochure, Gus had a verdict all ready for Thomason. Guilty! Guilty for knowingly distorting the facts, although Thomason would defend his side of it — that people need perfection here on earth — with an indignation equal to Gus's. According to Thomason, perfection was the distortion of reality; so the knowing distortion of the facts was not only desirable, it was artistic, and damn well essential to the well-being of a society.

— Whew, Gus thinks. He sure can keep a body off balance with his talk. Stone just grabs the body and ties it in a knot if he has to, but Thomason unravels your brain and lets you hang yourself in your own loopy ideas. I've peed and shit up here, although not lately without food, and I've wiped my ass with that damned brochure Geoff Thomason always showed so proudly. I wiped myself on those perfect little humanoids looking just like everyone thinks kids look, and doing everything everyone thinks kids do at camp. Disgustingly clean pictures I call them, because not one was real. If I had known then what was going to happen to real live normal flesh-and-blood kids because of how believable his lies would look in a brochure, I might have interfered. That was the time to interfere. That was the beginning.

Geoff Thomason motioned for the two boys to get into the stream, which they did with smooth obedience. The temperature was only in the fifties that day, and the boys had no way of knowing how deep or unfriendly the water might be. Yet in they splashed without delay, trusting him with their lives.

— One hundred dollars a day, Gus marvels, that's what they trusted. Or something in that grotesque vicinity. Money. Lots of it. All for getting their pictures taken by someone who was able to pay.

The two boys swam, floated, laughed, whooped it up, laughed some more, belly-flopped, doggie-paddled, batted an inflatable ball, peered through goggles, showed flippered feet, stood on one another's shoulders, cavorted, romped, splashed, skipped like little stones across the surface of the stream, smiled wrap-around smiles, while Geoff Thomason waded into the stream with his Nikon and stooped, craned, bent, squatted, dropped to his knees, clickety-clickety, his camera going like mad, clicking like the ticking of a wild man's pulse. He kept shouting directions at the boys, "Now you," "The other way," "Smile," "Look up," "Move an inch back," "Switch places," "Brush the hair out of your eyes," "Stop squinting," "Squint" — and those little ducks took his directions like they took to the water. They were professional, no doubt about that. But what was so damned unholy about their rollicking, frolicking fun was that Colt's Point Stream was not really the place for it. The water was too cool, too shallow, the bottom too irregular, the banks too much like mucus with their clayey goo and hairy ferns that are green to the touch. It was Homer who said, after he yanked himself out of the stream by tufts of fern, "Hey, this green comes off on your hands," referring to the slimy film of algae that can make even a grown man shiver.

— A week ago I saw real kids trying to have real fun in Colt's Point Stream, Gus remembers. They had to bring shakers of salt down to the water in case leeches stuck to their little arms and legs to suck out their blood. "When you pour salt on a leech," Dr. Stone told them, "it shrivels up." All the little eyes widened in inverse proportion to the imagined shriveling of the leech. "Then you just flick it off your skin like a scab that's hanging by one last thread of blood."

The little girl humanoids were even more disturbing to Gus than the little boys. He is still disturbed.

— Girls are more grown up at that age anyway, Gus thinks, and Thomason's girls were like miniature fashion models, the kind that stare out at you from billboards and magazines as though their brains had been cut back to make room for more teeth. I guess that's especially unsettling to me here in the thick of the pinelands where maybe there are fifty, sixty teeth in a whole town. I guess I've grown to love the hard-working, hard-looking women of the woods.

One of Thomason's little girl models got into a tutu and slowly twirled around while Thomason shot her from every angle. The picture had such impact he wanted to give it a whole page in the brochure, but Stone wanted it out altogether. And Stone was paying.

Stone also removed any of the other pictures that featured the girls too prominently, setting Thomason back several days in preparing the brochure for the printers. Photos of the girls cooking, sewing, playing instruments, dancing, painting, or even engaged in activities that are usually done alone, like reading a book or writing a letter home, had to include boys in Thomason's cropped version or else Stone struck it from its proposed place in the brochure with a thick X.

Thomason thought the photo of the girl in the tutu was significant. It tempered the rougher elements of camp life. It added a reassuring touch of civilization to the woods. It suggested that the counselors were not only competent to teach so difficult an art as ballet, but were sensitive and intelligent souls who were eager to do more than sit around and toast marshmallows. All of this Thomason would have argued had he not been so much in awe of Stone.

Gus still doesn't dismiss those X's so easily. To him they mark the beginning of a subtle and terrible realization. I don't want little girls in my camp, those X's said, and if I don't want little girls in my camp, all I have to do is cross them out.

Although, ultimately, he permitted brief glimpses of girls in the brochure, Stone wound up not permitting them at all in his camp. Thomason hurried the first proof of the printed brochure to Stone's office for final approval, and Stone told him that he was disturbed by the presence of girls in the photos, but that he would not hold up the presses. Then he told Thomason to tell any parents who tried to enroll a daughter in Camp Freedom that it was an all-boys camp.

"But what if they've seen the girls in the brochure and start asking questions?" Thomason worried.

"Then tell them," Stone ordered, "that there's no more room for girls, there are no more beds available in the girls' cabins."

"There was lying going on right from the start," Gus said to Thomason when he showed Gus the brochure. "You deceived people who were willing to give you the benefit of any doubt because they wanted so much to believe in you and to think you were smart and good and on their side."

"I only showed people what they wanted to see, Gus."

"You showed them what you wanted them to see. Lies."

"Back in the spring when I was taking all these pictures I never knew how it would turn out, whether or not anyone would enroll in the camp. But I knew for sure that if I had photographed real life, Camp Freedom would have died on the drawing board."

Gus knows what Thomason meant by real life. He meant Jeffie's having to be carried into the water, Stoney's sawing open a bird's neck, Homer's throwing up at every meal, Sammy's carrying his wet bedclothes down to Colt's Point Stream in the jeering light of morning.

"I didn't lie, Gus. All the others lied to themselves."

IV

When the storm was over, Stone removed the canvas from the broken crate. It was evident that dropping the crate had upset Stone, and he was growing increasingly nervous for fear that uncovering the contents of the crate might uncover damage as well.

Not until the wooden crate had been removed completely did Gus have even a guess at what he was looking at. He saw that it was some sort of table, but it was also a contraption, part hospital bed, part circus apparatus, part ultramodern furniture. The table revealed was an even greater mystery than it had been concealed.

Satisfied that it was intact, Stone slid the strange table inside the cabin. A few moments later he returned to the truck to unload a large generator. Perhaps, Gus guessed, the table swivels or rises up like an hydraulic lift, or vibrates, or blasts off, or does some other fool thing that doesn't make any sense at all out here. Here of all places. But it made sense soon enough.

V

The big yellow bus rumbled down the lane that Stone's U-Haul had widened an hour earlier. It stopped short of the skid marks, however, for the storm had not washed away the broad, stippled crescents leading to the bank, preserving them, perhaps, as a warning to Albert, the bus driver.

The door hissed open and Geoff Thomason got out. He walked quickly to Stone. They talked briefly, looked around, pointed, and then Thomason ran back to the bus. Albert pulled the bus up to the cabin Thomason indicated and kept the bus at an idle while the children flew down the steps. The trip had taken more than the hour and a half the ad and brochure for Camp Freedom had promised; the boys were exhausted and raced around the clearing to refresh themselves. But Stone would have none of it. He blew a whistle that hurt Gus's ears from one hundred feet away, and the children stopped what they were doing at once, as though they had been in the middle of playing a game of Statues. Whoever was left on the bus was told to come out. Then, when the last boy was off the last step, Thomason signaled for them all to crowd around the front of the cabin in which Stone had put his strange table.

A young man with visible nervous energy and a young woman reeking of annoyance were also waved over to the huddle by Thomason, as was Albert after he parked the big yellow bus at the edge of the woods.

Gus could hardly contain his curiosity. He was too far away to hear what was being said, so he decided to risk moving closer. Slowly and silently he descended the bluff. He even jettisoned an unfinished pint of wine that was making a sloshing noise in his back pocket as he descended the sheerest face of the cliff, the face that kept him safely out of the groups' view. He slid down closer to the group, and could begin to make out assorted words and phrases being delivered in a deep, resonant baritone.

"Doctor." "Freedom." "Thomason here." "The power that ..." "... is the power that ..." "Natural causes, natural cures." "Happiness."

It was a voice that could soothe or frighten, depending on the aria.

"How many of you boys wear a wig?" the voice asked.

The boys giggled. Finally Gus reached a point where he could hear every word.

"You're laughing, but it's not funny. Why would a person wear a wig? To hide his baldness. But why hide it? Because baldness is an embarrassment. A weakness. And people are ashamed of their weaknesses. They try to cover up weakness instead of curing it."

The boys liked Stone until they understood where his lecture was leading. They began shifting their feet.

"I'll bet each one of you has a weakness you're trying to cover up."

Each boy made sure to look at another boy.

"I'll bet one of you wets his bed."

Stone's accusation hung in the air like a damp sheet.

"I'll bet one of you has a headache right now, and you're afraid to say anything because you think it's a sign of weakness."

By now the children were squirming and looking at one another with suspicion. Since Stone wasn't talking about him, he must have been talking about the others — that's what each boy secretly thought.

"As I look out at you boys, I see poor posture, indigestion, nervousness, constipation, stomach ache, headache, poor eyesight, poor hearing, coughs, rashes, fever, lack of concentration."

Gus remembers seeing Stoney daydreaming.

— He almost saw me, too, Gus thinks. He was looking right at the scrub oaks where I was hiding. I should have warned him to turn around and pay attention.

"I said lack of concentration, young man!" Stone's words worked like a good shaking, and Stonehenge Alcock faced around immediately, paying sheepish but agitated attention to what Stone said next.

"You're not here for my benefit, boys. You're here for your own benefit. You might as well understand that right now. All of you might as well understand that you can't keep your secret weaknesses from me either. Or from your counselors. Or from Mr. Thomason here. We can see your weaknesses because we are adults. And we can cure your weaknesses because we know the truth about health and healing."

Geoff Thomason was proud to be included in Stone's rhetoric. Francis and Frances were not so sure.

81

"Nature wants you boys to be healthy. What is normal is healthful, and what can be more normal than Nature?"

The big, thick man bent down and plucked a tiny weed from the ground. He held up the weed and told the nervously attentive campers how, in Nature's vast Eden, plant life is virtually unbothered by disease, infection, and parasites as long as the soil is rich with nutrients.

"Except for sunlight and water, everything this plant needs to survive is in the soil, feeding this fragile stalk, which, in turn, nourishes these even more fragile leaves and shoots. But it is the stalk that is all important. Just as in our bodies it is the spinal cord that is all important. It starts in your brain, boys, and branches off into every single square inch of your body. It delivers health, strength, and life. And it masterminds one of the most complex systems known to man: your own nervous system; your own system of health. But it is a system that can be easily short-circuited by the spinal cord, just as these leaves would wither and die if I were to break the stalk."

Stone walked among the boys as he continued what turned out to be the invocation to Camp Freedom.

"Have you ever fallen down? Bumped into something? Been hit on the neck or back? Stopped short in your parents' car? Slid a little too hard into second base? Jumped a little too high going for a rebound? Pulled a muscle wrestling with Dad or the dog? Ever land wrong when you leaped from a high building to save Lois Lane? Well, I know that life is full of bumps and bruises. But I also know that these innocent beatings you give your body can lead to terrible problems. They can take their toll. They can shock the spinal cord, twist it, misalign it, disrupt it, prevent it from delivering healthful nourishment to your head. To your face. To your throat. To your heart." Stone's speech amputated each unreachable part of the body and spit it at a different boy. "To your lungs. To your stomach. To your liver. To your gall bladder. To your kidneys. To your bowels. Your appendix. To your bladder. To your balls, too, boys. Do you know that your spinal cord could be the reason you can't pee or shit or eat or sleep? Did you know that a damaged spinal cord can be the reason you sneeze, or cough, or itch, or stutter, or wet your bed, or even hiccup? I'm not here to scare you, but you need to know the truth about your bodies. And the truth, boys, is in my hands."

Stone held up the biggest hands the boys had ever seen. Except for Samuel, who had felt Stone's hands on his frail back, the boys thought or hoped Stone was being figurative.

"These hands are more important to you than anything else you will find here at Camp Freedom. You will swim and play sports and learn songs and make things out of clay — but all of that is just a way to pass the summer. The adjustments you will receive by these hands will stay with you all your lives. They will have a positive and permanent effect on your health and happiness."

Only Samuel understood the excruciating pain associated with the word *adjustment*. But the other boys suspected the worst. They stopped believing Stone had referred to his hands in a figurative sense and began plotting ways to prove that they were strong and healthy and in no need of any tampering with their stalks.

"I want you each to see something. I want you to come into this cabin with me one at a time and let me show you the only thing I will use — besides my hands — to make better, stronger, healthier, happier men out of you. I want you to get to know what's inside this cabin, to touch it, to operate it, to feel comfortable when you have to lie down on it. I want you to understand that it's only leather and chrome. It isn't a giant capsule, or a bitter elixir, or a surgeon's scalpel, or a hypodermic needle. It won't hurt you. It isn't painful. What I want to show you will help me repair your body so that it can function the way nature intended, because all that is ever needed for a healthy life is inside your body from the start. The power that made the body can heal the body."

Stone took the first boy into the cabin. The other boys buzzed with fearful anticipation. It was as if they were in line for a frightening ride at an amusement park. They knew they would survive the ride, but they were not sure they could survive the suspense. It was this attitude that set the tone for the rest of each boy's stay at Camp Freedom, except for Stonehenge Alcock whose behavior was not always subject to his or anyone else's control. But even Stoney, when he was not in the grip of one of his burning headaches, behaved and believed as the other boys. All were apprehensive about the whole of camp life, and so no one aspect troubled them any more than another. Having taken a collective deep breath when their parents kissed them good-by, they arrived at the campsite prepared for anything. Nothing could surprise them in a context that was itself totally surprising. Each boy believed he was safe, that his mother and father would never have sent him away to danger. No matter how frightening anything seemed, lurking beneath the fright was the secure trust that all would be well, that all was for the much promised benefit of the camper's physical, emotional, intellectual, and social development.

VI

"Oh shit," says Gus. He sees a squirrel.

— It's not moving a muscle. Gus thinks. The two of us are frozen. I don't want to move in case Stone's men are really up here waiting to grab me and bring me back down to that devil so he can crush my back or break my neck or paralyze me like he did to poor Jeffie. But I'm so hungry I might not care. Is it any better to die from your insides banging together? It's been four days since I've had a scrap of decent food. I've been nibbling the grass. Ordinarily I'm not a big eater. I can get along on berries, spring water, and a small animal of one kind or another now and then which usually I can stretch out into one good meal every day. Birds are my favorite, when I can get one. Nice-size birds that cook up quick and give six good gulps after the gristle's gone. Six is plenty. Except now. I'm beyond a bird now. I keep hearing the crackle of coon or muskrat or possum or squirrel, and keep smelling the pungent mixture of bark smoke and scorched flesh and seeing the freshness of the kill

and the fire juicing out of each torn bite, and tasting the gamy
insides of a raggedy strip of hot flank. I guess my ears and nose
and eyes and tongue are all hallucinating in some stage of star-
vation. It's been several minutes since that squirrel moved. I've
been watching. Maybe if I'm quiet, I can ease over on my belly
without arousing suspicion. If I can get my hands around the
squirrel's neck I should be able to crack it quick. A little twitching in the bush is all anyone would hear. Maybe Stone was lying
anyway, despite the gunshots. And even if there are gunmen
and they are staking out the woods, chances are they're not *from*
the woods. Old Ex told me once how a boy who was raised in
the woods, like himself, couldn't even see what an Injun could.
"Ask any Injun ex-actly what he sees when he looks out there
into the ex-treme black wood," Old Ex said to me. "An Injun
would look out there at the night wood and see the world from
ex-traordinary beginning to ex-traordinary end. Think that's
easy? Well, try imaginin' your own two eyes so ex-tra sharp
they can pin a water mocassin to a ripple; they can catch a polli-
wog wriggle his ex-cited self into a full-growed toad; they can
pick up the beginning blight on the bark of a birch in time
to reincarnate that dead wood into an ex-cellent canoe or two.
Now that's eyes, Gus. Ex-pert eyes that can ex-pose them thousand and one eyes starin' back, too, even in the dead of a night
like this one. Coon's eyes. Rattler's eyes. Ex-otic eyes. Ex-trater-
restrial eyes, too, like flirty blinky little bird brain eyes shootin'
theyselves through the trees like they's stars." According to Old
Ex, even a natural-born piney didn't have the acumen of an
Injun. So why don't I test his judgment right now and go on
after that frozen squirrel?

— Its head is peeking out of a crevice formed by the rotted
trunks of two saplings that must have fallen in a storm, Gus
thinks. It appears that the squirrel has made its nest there, otherwise why would it be so content to stay put with my presence
no more than thirty feet away? I'm surprised I never heard or
saw the squirrel come and go before now. Possibly it isn't the
nest after all, but just some comfortable, dark, dry, safe haven
the poor squirrel is partial to. And maybe it isn't moving be-

cause it's afraid I'm close enough to nab it. Animals have so
much more patience than humans. I know it can outwait me.
It can sit there still as a tree stump until I'm almost on top of
it and then scamper away like a shot. But I'm too hungry to let
it get away. I've got to try to catch it. But I can't think straight.
My mind keeps shuffling thoughts like a deck of cards. There's
the Ace of Stones, the Geoff of Thomason holding a lance in a
four-fingered fist, Frankie and Frannie in crowns and robes —
an upside-down King and Queen. And remember those children's card games? Tiny little cards with colorful illustrations
of animals on them? First time you ever saw a racoon's mask,
or a fox's bushy tail, or a rooster's comb. Remember? All I can
see, every other flipping card, is Mr. Squirrel, still as a stuffed
lamp base, not even his nose twitching. What I need to do is get
onto my belly. Quietly though. I wouldn't want to scare away that
squirrel. Or is it me who's scared. I wouldn't want to give away
my position to Stone's henchmen. If they're really here, of course.
On one hip now. How slow and strained every move is reminds
me of the way Stone struggled when he fell into the stream that day
and whenever else he got one of his attacks. When Stoney's head
went haywire, so did Stoney, running all over the place, fighting,
flailing, screaming, his eyes going all marbly like a cat's. But
when Stone's head acted up, the big man fell down weak as a
kitten, his head and arms and legs fluttering like a crying baby's
— but Stone never cried. It looked like an invisible boulder was
crushing him to the ground. Slowly and without coordination,
he'd try to push it off his chest and get to his feet. And now
here I am, too scared to extend my coordination to the fullest,
holding back natural movement like a case of the shivers, slowly
trying to get onto a belly that'd crawl over to that squirrel on
its own if I let it.

VII

As each boy came out of the cabin, he was told to go back to
the bus.

"Find your things on the bus, and then Albert will help you take your belongings to your assigned cabin. Mr. Thomason, will you tell Albert, please?"

The bearded young man took it upon himself to meet the boys at the door of the cabin as they exited, escort each one to the bus, and, while Albert helped haul the boy's gear off the bus, assign a cabin. Thus it was impossible for the uninitiated to ask questions or even read the faces of the boys who had seen Stone's mystery. The apparent well-being of the boys who had been in the cabin gave some relief, but apprehension intensified as one's turn came closer and closer.

When it was Stoney's turn to enter the hut with Stone, the boy was already on the way to one of his seizures. It was normal for Stoney not to anticipate a seizure; it sneaked up on him in ways that were undetectable or seemingly unrelated to the full-fledged attack. He might bite his lip, but he might not. His stomach might churn, but he might be so intent upon who or what was agitating him that he wouldn't be aware of the condition of his stomach. He might breathe heavily one time and shallowly the next, shake on one occasion and stand paralyzed on another. Except for a brief loss of consciousness immediately before the onset of a seizure, the signals were always unpredictable; the triggers, however, always could be easily identified by a veteran observer. Frustration, fear, anguish, and embarrassment were sure-fire causes. And as Stoney moved slowly toward Stone, at least two of these triggers — the embarrassment he felt when Stone yelled at him for not paying attention and fear of the mysterious chrome and leather — were cocked inside Stoney's head.

"If you pay attention, young man, you will learn everything. If you drift and dream, you will learn nothing more than what you arrived with. Are you listening to me now?"

Stoney stared up at the gray space in which Stone's face was half resolved. He tried to fine-tune the image. He wanted to say that he was listening, but he could not keep the words from jumping. The *y* of yes jumped ahead of his answer and batted against the back of Stoney's teeth. His tongue and teeth threw the *y* back and forth like two adults tossing a ball out of the frustrated reach of a small boy. Instead of the quick, short, decisive answer he wanted to give Stone, Stoney involuntarily repeated a sad, breathy grunt of noise, an inhuman whimpering that expressed exactly the opposite of his clear desire.

His father, who was a poet, who drifted and dreamed in print, took Stoney's seizures as the conquest of the boy's maddening stutter over rational desire. In a broader, more philosophic, rather revolutionary thought, he saw in his son's affliction the eternal conquest of feeling over expression. The boy himself felt only his rational mind banging against a blank wall until everything went blank; and the banging, the mayhem, the terrible jumpy energy of the fit became — in a poem his father called "Stonehenge Unhinged" — *Your physical stutter / My metaphysical shudder!*

The stuck record of Stoney's *y* infuriated Stone and frustrated Stoney, cocking still another sure-fire trigger in the boy's head.

"Spit it out, boy. What's your name?"

"St-St-St-St-"

He wanted to spit it out. His name had become cruelly linked to his stutter. In school he was called St-St-St-Stoney the St-St-St-Stutterer behind his back.

He wanted to say "yes" and "Stoney" obediently. Contrary to what many strangers and a few acquaintances believed, Stoney had no desire to disobey, to wreak havoc, to break rules and hearts and vases. Like the other boys — even those whose abiding hatred of going away from dear home to dread camp had generated bitter vow after vow of revenge — Stoney only wanted to do what was asked of him, to do it well, and to survive with honor, and honors, and the respect of the authorities as well as his peers.

"You mean you stutter?" Stone diagnosed almost gleefully. He moved his foot without looking, and it landed on the mark. Stone depressed the floor pedal at the foot of the table, and, once again, the boys outside heard the faint whir of the chiropractic table as it rose in mottled darkness. Through the open door of the cabin a spray of dreary daylight entered, reflecting flatly off the chrome, eerily framing the sleek leather which towered over Stoney's trembling little body like a door to blacker darkness, like a trapdoor to a black hell about to come crashing, crushing down.

Stoney's last flashes of consciousness made nightmarish sense: the sound of a dentist's chair, the threat of his forceps, the paralyzing fear of an oncoming steamroller, the dread of night, the banging of rational desire against a blank wall, against black leather, against the leering blur of Stone's unfocused face, Stoney's stutter ticking off the seconds, Stone's "tsk-tsk-tsk" providing a wickedly offspeed drumroll as the huge man clamped a huge hand on the little boy's collarbone, turning the little boy away from the table and into the flimsy light which blinded him nevertheless, which made the pupils of his eyes contract, which countermanded the hellish dark and flooded Stoney's throbbing head with white unconsciousness.

"There are a number of possibilities, a number of approaches we can take. The first, second, and third vertebrae are the likeliest suspects, but we can't ignore the others. This one way down here controls the hiccuping," Stone said as two powerful fingers isolated the thoracic vertebra he was referring to. "You've got a pinched nerve somewhere, young man, and it's making you stutter. This little demonstration is not going to be lost on you. This will be your first adjustment. This will be the beginning of the end of your stuttering."

Stone misinterpreted the brief, limp loss of consciousness that always characterized the onset of one of Stoney's seizures — *His mindless swan dive into boiling water,* as Stoney's father had written. Believing the boy had given in to his forceful, therapeutic touch, the chiropractor began confidently. In fact, Stoney was oblivious.

Stone positioned the boy against the table and, by depressing the release pedal, caused the table to recline to the desired angle, the one at which Stone could work most easily and Stoney could rest on his side without sliding off.

"My fingers are so sensitive to a misalignment or a blockage or an inflammation," Stone said as he proceeded to crack Stoney's safe, "that I don't need to take a single x-ray. I'll be able to feel the trouble."

What Stone felt were Stoney's small muscles rippling beneath the skin near the base of the neck, where humans normally lack such muscular articulation; the rippling reminded Stone of a horse twitching a fly off its flank. Then the veins in Stoney's temples became engorged with blood, making the boy's forehead swell before Stone's eyes. Then came an unearthly scream.

Stoney took the swan dive into the boiling water. The shock awakened unbearable pain. The little boy felt he was drowning in consciousness and swam desperately to an ever receding surface, flailing his arms within Stone's sphere, slapping at the startled chiropractor, kicking at him, thrashing and screaming with such reckless fury that Stone had to let his patient go, Stone's nostrils flaring, his mouth open, his chest heaving, his eyes as seeing as Stoney's were purblind, his fingers itching for three or four or more pinched nerves, for a knotty tangle of ganglia, for dislocated disks, for a broken, blighted stalk.

— No one knows for sure exactly what happened in the cabin, Gus recalls. I watched Stoney go in, nervous, slow, but no more nervous, no slower than any of the other boys, his right hand slapping time against his thigh, the toes of his sneakers kicking up wet sandy mud that splattered onto his cuffs, and then all of us hearing the screaming and the ruckus and Stoney shooting out the door, bowling over Thomason. That one good look at his eyes still scares me. What was it like? It was like all the wires going from his brain to his eyes were crossed. Like an animal's face. Racing blind on a steamy savanna. Prehistoric eyes.

In retrospect, Gus blamed everything on that first confrontation between George Stone and Stonehenge Alcock, on those two flinty stones whose clash threw sparks through Camp Freedom, sputtering, frantic sparks that caught, spread, lit tempers, fired madness, and exploded into blazing chaos.

— Stone must have pulled Stoney's trigger, Gus thinks, and then the poor boy blasted out into the remaining group of boys and he savaged them, tearing at their skin and clothes as he raced around, fell, tumbled, crawled, spun, punched, and clawed through their terrified ranks. I saw him running right at me, and I had to hold myself still or else Stone might have discovered me; it was hard not to jump around and shout when you were watching the kind of soccer match Stoney put on. And then, when Stone ran out of the cabin and started chasing Stoney, I nearly gave myself away rooting for the poor boy to escape. But I could see that he wasn't going to escape. He was running too blind, circling wildly, and all Stone had to do was just cut across one of the boy's crazy circles and wait for him. Twice Stoney ran right into Stone's arms, but, big and strong as Stone was, he hadn't braced himself, and Stoney broke through. The other boys were scattered and trembling. Geoff Thomason was stunned. So were Frankie and Frannie. Albert was laughing and shouting in French; he was hysterical, doubled over, slapping his thighs, acting like some rube who thinks a greased pig squirting out of a farmer's arms is the funniest sight on earth. Everyone was out of the way then, and nothing was going to stop Stoney except a tree, or the stream, or possibly Stone. I knew Stone wasn't going to let him get away again. This was not a game to Stone. The difference in their eyes told the story. Stoney's were marbles, wide open but blind, looking like little globes of the world, a blotch of blue and brown for ocean and land, and spinning like pinwheels, the pupils dilating and contracting as if they were reacting to what was going on inside the boy's head, as if blinding white light and perfect darkness were alternating inside his head and causing his pupils to get bigger and smaller, while Stone's eyes were narrow and clear, and his squint was squeezing Stoney more sharply into his sights, the jet-black pupils looking almost telescopic, three-dimensional, like the gleaming tips of twin bullets pointed right at the back of Stoney's head, one for each hemisphere of Stoney's brain. When the two of them collided in front of me, out of the quick tangle of bodies, out of the screaming and scolding, all I could see were their eyes.

Not more than fifty feet from Gus's hiding place Stone caught the boy. He easily wrestled Stoney to the ground, but then faced the continuing difficulty of trying to still a wriggling fish so he could gut it. Finally Stone pinned the twitching boy face down in the mud with a knee digging into the boy's calves and a forearm pressed against the back of the boy's neck.

"Quiet!" Stone outscreamed the wailing boy to no avail. Stoney was as deaf to reason or authority as he was blind.

"I said shut up!" Stone shouted. "Don't scream," he warned, "you'll scare away my patients."

All the time Stone had Stoney pinned and was reprimanding him, he probed the little boy's spinal column with his huge hand. When finally Stone's long, strong fingers found what they were searching for, the chiropractor pressed down lightly. In a reflex action, the boy's head snapped back, held there as if by an invisible thread tied to Stone's fingers. For a long, tense thirty seconds, the screaming and twitching stopped. Keeping his hand firmly in place, Stone cautioned Stoney against further tantrums.

"When I take my hand away, I want you to lie there quietly. Take a few deep breaths, relax, then stand up and walk back to the cabin. I'll be right behind you. You have set a terrible example, and now you have to behave perfectly to show the other boys that you were wrong."

Although Stoney was quiet, he still could not hear the voice of authority. His body was quiet only because Stone held it in a suspended state of tension. In Stoney's head, pain still rattled and roared and would have found physical and vocal outlets if Stone's fingers were not temporarily short-circuiting the boy's nervous system. As soon as Stone relaxed his fingers, Stoney's head fell forward, his body rippled and twitched, and blind, unreasoning, relentless pain wound out of his throat like a siren. Stone had no choice. He could not allow Stoney's disobedience to inspire the others. Again his fingers found the mark. Again he pressed down, harder than before, as hard as necessary to suppress insubordination, mutiny, revolution. Stone's fingers yanked the invisible thread. Stoney's head shot back and then immediately fell limp. The fish had fought too long out of water.

VIII

— Why won't it move? Gus wonders. Is it dead? Is it real? The squirrel just peeks its head out from between the two saplings and doesn't bat an eye. It's frozen the way human beings are frozen right before they die. When I was a bombardier soaring the sky in the nose of my B-29 Superfortress, I had to get my target in the crosshairs of the bombsight and then feed in my speed and altitude and the direction of the wind and the condition of the atmosphere and the motion of the target so that all the right compensations could be calculated. Then the bomb would be released automatically. If we were lucky, it hit within a thousand feet of the target. And always right before it hit, all of the world stood stone still, and the music stopped, and the human beings down there in their haylofts and barber shops and front-yard gardens looked up at me like photos in an album. Now I've got the squirrel in the squint of my eye, in the crosshairs of a blind hunger that can see out through a Norden telescope and make that small, furry head look as big and tasty as a Thanksgiving Day turkey.

— Over onto my belly. But it hurts, Gus realizes. My belly's already aching with hunger. The pain is trying to make me gasp out loud, and I'm afraid I won't be able to keep from screaming and scaring the squirrel and giving myself away. So I'm using my arms and I'm rolling over onto my side. The squirrel still hasn't moved. I don't know why. I'm pulling myself over to the furry little lifesaver as inconspicuously as I can. I don't even want to blink. An inch toward the squirrel and then a moment to let the woods settle down as a result. Another inch, another moment. And again. And again. I fear that one of my tiny advances is going to shake loose the whole bluff and an avalanche will deposit rocks and clods and bushes and trees and a wake of slime and dust, me in the middle, at the wide-open stance of Dr. George Stone, his feet spread apart like the Colossus of Rhodes', me run aground on his toe like the wreck of an Aegean hurricane.

— But I've got to keep going.

— I think it may be irony that's beginning to ache in my belly. Last week at this time I was the official cook of Camp Freedom, the Pooh Bah of breakfast, lunch, dinner, and after-curfew snacks, the flapjack man, the pontiff of peanut butter and jelly, the lord high lama of leftovers. Stone stuck a spatula in my hand and I took it — not that I wanted the job — but I did the best I could for as long as I could. Last week I was friend and confederate and provider, and today I'm a starved renegade who's gone from stirring the soup to being in it.

— At last. An ear is twitching. A lid is flickering. The squirrel is alive.

IX

When Stoney regained consciousness, his seizure had passed and he remembered nothing of what had happened.

Frances had been given the job of staying with the boy until he recovered. When she tried to express her outrage to Stone, the chiropractor stared her down.

"Didn't you see him run out of the cabin like someone possessed? What should I have done, let him run wild until his heart gave out, or until he ran into a tree or into the stream or into one of the other boys and knocked them both unconscious? Just do what I tell you. When I tell you."

"What is this, a jail or something?" Frances protested.

Stone stared at her, Stoney's limp body in his arms. The chiropractor stood perfectly still, but it seemed to Frances that he had taken a step toward her. It seemed that he was within an arm's length of her, his arm's length, and had clearly trespassed into the demilitarized zone between them. He said nothing more to her, only stared into her eyes. Frances tried to stare back, to stare him down, to stare Stone into kingdom come, but he never cracked. His face was like a wooden Indian's; the angry features were exaggerated, unflinching, carved and painted onto the mighty tree trunk that stood before Frances. Everything about him served to repeat the order he had given her to stand by the boy until the chiropractic adjustment wore off. Everything: the unblinking eyes, the set jaw, the thick neck, the broad shoulders, the massive chest, the lifeless body of the boy in Stone's solid arms.

Frances took stock. Francis did not come forward, nor did she expect him to. She could not appeal to Geoff Thomason, for he was Stone's man. And Albert was probably still trying to translate into French the Grand Guignol that had just been played. Of course, there was always the possibility, too, that she might be overreacting, that Stone might have been justified in what he did to Stoney.

Finally she knew she would give in, but not without saving face. Unwilling to surrender completely, but also unwilling to risk a confrontation between herself and Stone on the very first day of camp, Frances said, "Maybe you're right. Anyway, what can I do about it?"

Frances began to turn away and then turned back.

"But this place probably isn't deserted, Dr. Stone," she said. "Maybe someone in the woods heard all the noise and saw what happened and is going for the sheriff or whoever they have in charge around here to come and check things out. I'll believe you if you say you had to do that to Stoney — that's his name, by the way, it only took me an hour on the bus to get him to tell it to me — but I sure hope you're right. And I sure hope the sheriff buys it."

Frances turned away, and Stone took the boy to one of the cabins, calling to Geoff Thomason to tell Albert to fetch a bed-roll for Stoney to lie on.

"Thanks for your help," Frances said to Francis as she passed by him on the way to her assigned vigil.

Inside the cabin, after Stoney was stretched out on the bedding and Stone left Frances to watch over him, she soothed the boy's forehead with her hand. Stoney's forehead was on fire. At one temple, beneath a wisp of muddied red hair, Frances felt the unmistakable stickiness of blood.

X

— I don't want to think about the way it's going to taste, Gus thinks, or whether or not I'll be able to stand the freshness of the flesh and blood. Once I was at a wrestling match with my third wife who always got us ringside seats so we could hear the wrestlers snort and curse and they could hear her scream instructions and insults. "Get him! Rip him! Kill him!" The hulk in the tigerskin outfit and the flabby Mongolian crashed together in the middle of the ring and quickly knotted themselves into a mythological monster with abdominal arms and cervical legs and two snarling, spitting, bellowing heads. When tigerskin summoned all his strength for an attack and managed to maneuver around slightly so he could grab the Mongolian's ear with his teeth, my wife saw his advantage, stood up on her two-dollar ringside seat, raised her arms and eyes to the cigarette smoky heavens, and pleaded, "Bite it off! Bite it off!" All I can see is a small, even frail-looking woman screaming for blood as a twitching ear is savagely ripped away by flashing teeth. All I can see is a spurt of blood shoot out from a mythological monster that is half man, half squirrel.

Halfway, and it hasn't moved its body. But the squirrel's head is cocked. It's seen me. I know it sees me now. I'm halfway there, the squirrel knows I'm coming. Another inch, another moment. What I can't understand is why the squirrel doesn't scoot away. It can. I'm not nearly close enough to pounce on it. Its cocked head is looking right at me now. The squirrel could be relieving itself. There's a very natural faraway look in those staring eyes. Maybe it's sick. Or trapped. It's possible that the squirrel is caught between the saplings instead of using the crevice formed by the saplings for safety or shelter. Except there doesn't seem to be a sign of struggle or frustration in the eyes or in the fur. I hope I have the courage to stand what I will do to the squirrel if I get my hands on it. I'll use a rock if there's a big one or a sharp one handy, otherwise I'll just have to make do with my bare hands. If it is sick or trapped, that'll make it easier, but I'm not counting on it. I'm not counting on anything.

XI

Against his will, against his unshakable faith in the absolute correctness and sanctity of his life's calling, Dr. George Stone worried about the theoretical spy in the woods Frances had conjured. Certainly the establishment — the American Medical As-

Sadler Barry

Author: _____

Title: _____

CALL NUMBER

LOCATION

Staff use:

sociation, the hospitals, the insurance companies, the scientific community, even the popular press — had waged an insidious campaign against chiropractic physicians and their methods. The manipulation of a spine was always suspect. And the farther one got from liberal big cities, the deeper one went into the woods, the greater the suspicion.

Stone walked the grounds of Camp Freedom, vaguely realizing that he was searching for the spy. In the backwoods, he thought, the more unorthodox the crime, the more unorthodox the punishment. If they misunderstood and thought he had hurt a little boy, they might do anything for revenge. The fact that Stone might be right wouldn't matter.

Gradually he talked himself into a decision to defend what he had done and the future of Camp Freedom by whatever means were necessary. No one must be allowed in. No one must be allowed out. He traversed and circled the grounds. Francis was watching him closely, as was Gus who was afraid to climb back up to his better hiding place, and neither of them could follow Stone's every move. The chiropractor would disappear behind one of the cabins and reappear moments later from behind a different one. In the sparse stand of pines between the stream and the compound, he'd steal in and around the chalky green trunks with an illusionist's finesse. Gus narrowed his eyes to see more clearly, but Stone ducked or passed behind a leafy bough or in some other way caused his observer to resight and refocus.

At one point Stone crossed over the creaky footbridge and disappeared into the woods beyond Colt's Point Stream for what seemed an eternity. Gus barely allowed himself to breathe all the while his eyes scanned the distant wood. Although he was constantly ready to give up, Gus was certain that if he turned away for just a second he'd miss Stone's reemergence. So he stayed where he was, his heart pounding, his forehead dripping with sweat, his tired eyes straining to read the landscape.

XII

— A whistle! Stone's. Three short blasts. One of the boys is in for it. It's amazing how quickly and permanently those terrifying whistle blasts become a part of your life. I don't even know who's left down there. Or what more could be done to those poor boys. Louder. Three more blasts and louder. One of the henchmen maybe. Three more. Oh, heart, stop pounding like that. Three more. Louder still. There's a nervous rustling everywhere now. Birds are flitting, there goes a deer, you can hear every animal making its fear noise, and all the sounds blend into one: the arousal of a trespassed wood.

— A moment, Gus counts. Several moments. It may be over. It sounds like it's over. No more whistle blasts. The blasts were never that close; I never heard human footsteps. Now the blasts have stopped, but not before the whole forest was aroused. Except for the squirrel. The squirrel hasn't budged. It looks as though it wants to cry. Cry if you want, squirrel, but both of us aren't going to make it, and I'll never have a better chance than I do right now. Whatever that search-and-destroy mission accomplished, it's over now, there's a lull down there now. This is the time for me to make my move. I'm hungry. The forest is still calming down. I'm only a few feet away now. If you're going to run, you better do it quick, squirrel. I'm getting too close. Another inch, another inch, another inch. I can taste your little legs. I can smell the sweet meat of your breast. You can hear my stomach growling at you, can't you? Oh, that's better, you're snarling at me. You're alive after all. But not for long, squirrel. I've got my hand poised right over your head. You can probably leap up and nip me, I'm sure of it. But you haven't moved yet, not all this time, not even when those whistle blasts scared the whole damned forest half to death. And I'm moving so slow. So slow. And I'm so hungry. Don't look up, squirrel. Keep snarling at my face. You can probably feel my hot breath on your whiskers. Don't look up at my hand. I've got a nice pointy rock in my hand. It'll all be over in a second. You won't know what hit you. I don't know why you ain't running, but I sure ain't complaining. I figured it would be a lot tougher. I thought it would be impossible, if you really want to know. You squirrels are so skittish. Why aren't you scampering away? Why are you making it sooo easy? Soooo simple? Sooo . . .

"Hengh! Hengh! Hengh! Hengh!"

— Oh shit. Oh shit, Gus keeps himself from saying out loud. So that's why. Oh look. Oh shit, look what I killed. I got her smack in the middle. That's why she never moved. I got her smack in the middle of squeezin' out a litter.

XIII

Gus never heard Stone's footsteps. He felt a huge hand on his shoulder and wheeled around and reeled backwards, falling, looking up at the angry man who stood over him.

Stone clenched and unclenched his left hand. "You sonofabitch," he said.

"What do you want? What did I do? I didn't do anything," Gus pleaded.

"You've been spying, you sonofabitch. I caught you. You've been sneaking around here trying to spy on me."

"I ain't. I'm just a bum. I'm just a boozy old bum, mister," Gus swore, feeling for the pint of proof in his back pocket and remembering that he had scuttled it while sneaking down the cliff to spy on Stone. "You can ask anyone around here. You can ask the Kristals. I don't get involved in anything. You can ask at the store. I don't even know who the president of the United States is. Everyone'll tell you the same — I'm just a harmless old boozer."

"Not any more," Stone decreed. He grabbed Gus by his shirt and lifted the old man onto rubbery legs. "Congratulations!"

Stone spun Gus around and shoved him out from the cover of the scrub oaks into the fringe of the open compound. The old man landed in the mud.

"You're the head cook of Camp Freedom," Stone shouted down at him.

SEVEN

Stone helped me up out of the mud puddle in his rough manner and proceeded to kick me across the spongy ground like a tin can, pushing and prodding me ahead of him through the ranks of the boys who had been scattered like tenpins by Stoney, and up to the door of the largest cabin.

"Okay," he started to say. "Uh, what's your name?" he interrupted himself.

"Gus," I told him.

"Gus what?"

"Jus' Gus," I said honestly. I hadn't used a surname for years.

"Okay, Jus' Gus." Stone smirked. "Hop to it. Dinner. In an hour. These boys are really hungry, aren't you, boys?"

A few of them shouted out their agreement. But they did so only because their fear of Stone manifested itself in blind, over-anxious, transparently insincere obedience. Even when Stone was solicitous and tried to win the confidence of the campers, as he had tried with his opening remarks, his deep voice, huge form, and slow, menacing movements tyrannized everyone in his sway.

Stone opened the door. Before he pushed me inside, I realized for the first time that although it was midafternoon and the sun was still high, darkness seemed imminent. It had stormed earlier, but the sky had recovered; why then did it seem so dark?

Now I realize that the darkness — I don't know what else to call it, a sinister presence of darkness — constantly threatened Camp Freedom. Before dusk, it wasn't a physical phenomenon so much as a feeling, a scent in the breeze, a flash of a thought, the lack of a glimmer in a little boy's eyes. So many of the boys were afraid of this dark from the moment they opened their eyes in the morning. And the dark that came at night provoked an even greater fear. With no electricity and no windows onto anything but the woods, nothing could fight or forestall the sudden fall of night.

If there is a theme to Camp Freedom, a motif that insinuates itself into little boy's nightmares through the ragged timbers and shattered windows of their cabins, an eerie air that lurks in the woods and leaks out into their daydreams like a poisonous gas, it is darkness. Thirty-three boys had come to a dark place in their lives.

Camp Freedom was a travesty. In one quick glance, before being shoved inside the cabin, I could see that the camp — now that I knew it was a camp — failed to measure up to the general standards a camper or a parent had the right to expect. Danger reared like an unbroken horse at the rickety footbridge and the collapsing cabins; it slithered like a snake along the slippery banks of Colt's Point Stream and at the edge of the maze of woods. The compound consisted of the beat-up cabins, the unsafe bridge, and a clearing barely large enough for Little League. No infield. No outfield. Just the raw area. Nor was there a tennis court, a bridle path, a theater, a science lab. There were none of the features you'd expect after reading the ad and looking through the brochure. Camp Freedom was inadequately developed, designed, equipped, staffed, supervised, and managed, although none of it had been planned as a deception. Thomason simply made the best of a bad scene when he portrayed the camp in the brochure. And Stone saw little use in anything beyond a spine made straight by his magician's hands. As so often happens to a man obsessed, he no longer felt the world spinning forward beneath his feet; all modern discoveries, conveniences, and amenities were pointless intrusions; the only state of the art worth improving was his own. Who needed a ballfield or Bunsen burners or kleig lights at Camp Freedom? They needed to be advertised, Thomason knew; and the young disciple also believed that they would have their place at the camp, even if only in verbal lessons, or, in practice, during the campers' free time, of which there would be plenty. "Let them organize their own games," I heard Stone say more than once, "and watch how their adjustments will improve their reflexes, their eye-hand coordination, their strength, their strategy, even their sportsmanship."

But too many years of defending his life's work had made Stone suspicious, inflexible, and desperate.

"Imagine," Thomason told me one night in the kitchen when he wanted a snack, "here is a man who takes into his hands a two-hundred-pound adult suffering from stomach pains and general fatigue. After several difficult sessions, the patient is cured. No more stomach pains, and his tiredness has vanished completely. With just his two bare hands, he has been able to accomplish what no medical doctor has. But, 'It has to be a miracle,' says the AMA. Or 'something new in the patient's diet' that did the trick. Or 'the ailment was about to run its course anyway' and happened to coincide with the charlatan's worthless manipulations. In other words, there is not the slightest concession that the adjustments could have been responsible for the recovery. Now take this isolated incident and multiply it a thousand times. Ten thousand times. For every cure, an M.D. who says 'Impossible!' For every relieved ache and stopped infection and revived natural function, there is an article or a professor or a TV commentator or a congressional finding that denies the accomplishment he himself has witnessed. They cheat him out of his success and slap the very hand they should shake. And what if the patient attempts to corroborate the success? He is only a layman, what can he possibly know compared to the tomes and years and incontestable knowledge stored in the heads of our most esteemed practitioners of a science, mind you, that not too long ago was itself considered to be ritual and superstition? Well, what is there left for a man faced with such relentless condemnation of his beliefs? For his art, his practice, his healing and strengthening, he is ridiculed and reviled just short of legal sentencing. To be allowed a legal place in society and then treated like a criminal can lead a man only one of two ways: either he hates himself, extinguishing the flame of his belief by deserting his practice for something more acceptable and honorable such as the job of physical therapist for a professional football team, or else he stands firm, his spine unbent, his head unbowed, and throws himself heart and soul into the fires of his obsession. Dr. George Stone has made his decision."

That speech, flowing as it did through mouthful after mouthful of crackers, eloquently explained not only Stone's actions but Thomason's as well. There was no cruel ambition, no lust for money, no secret depravity to be found in their characters, only the relentless desire of the one to save the world and of the other to spread the gospel. And that was even more terrifying than pure and simple malevolence.

Stone pushed me into the kitchen. There was a wood-burning stove with a pipe chimney that had been bent out through a previously broken windowpane. In another corner was a huge barbecue with several large sacks of coals stacked nearby on the floor. I envisioned myself grilling an endless succession of hot dogs and hamburgers, the sweat dripping out from under my wig. I never planned to disclose the secret of my wig and no one ever suspected that it was not my own natural growth, but it gave me something to trade with Thomason when he was reluctant to talk about his missing finger.

In addition to the grill and the stove, Stone had provided plenty of pots and pans, and a big black kettle — more like a cauldron — which might be used for saving or boiling water, or for washing dishes. There was a supply of plastic utensils, paper plates and cups, and a large store of dry goods, cases of fruit juice, cartons marked HANDLE WITH CARE, filled with eggs, I guessed, and there were several hundred pounds of assorted fruits and vegetables.

I asked Stone what we could do to keep things from spoiling.

"We can keep what we can in the stream," he said. Then he added, "I'll send Albert for dry ice tomorrow."

But Stone's tone of voice suggested that I had better not hold my breath waiting for him to let Albert, or me, or anyone else out of his sight. Let the fresh food rot, there was plenty of flour, pasta, cereal, jelly, peanut butter, breads, spreads, snack food, and the like to put flesh, mere flesh, on the all important, all powerful spine.

Stone slammed the door behind me as he left, shutting out the sun almost completely. The cabin filled with a grainy light of such palpable texture I thought I could grab it in my hand; like a cloud conforming to all four corners of the room, a billowing grayness veiled everything.

After a few minutes, I heard a quiet, fearful tapping at the window. Squinting to see who it was, I saw no one, but again I heard the faint tap-tap. Then I heard another sound. It might have been a wounded animal. Cautiously I went to the window which still had its wooden bars dividing the frame into four smaller panes. The top right quadrant was filled with the pipe chimney. The bottom two still held jagged pieces of glass. That left the top left quadrant for me to look through; it was empty, and I didn't want to call attention by breaking more glass or forcing the window.

I stood up on my toes and moved my face closer and closer to the opening, nervous as a mouse anticipating the cat. Who knew what creature might be waiting to spring up at my face, claws out, fangs bared?

It was Jeffie, clinging to the wall and whimpering like the wounded animal I had imagined.

He gasped when he saw my face at the window.

"Shhh." I didn't know what else to say or do.

The poor little boy had disturbed my cloud of depression, my shock, the personal ineptitude I felt at having been caught spying and sentenced to the overwhelming job of head cook by the sly and judicial Stone. The little whimperer was siphoning off my self-pity and mortification. In his face I saw my own fears, my own impotence. What was I to do? Kick him away? Turn him over to Stone? Ignore him? Such wretchedness was unusual in a face so young. And the longer I took to decide on a course of action, the more agonized his expression became, as if my indecision were another lash by the whip of time, another heartbeat stolen from his life's allotment. How could such a little boy know the profound anguish and despair that showed through his eyes and convulsed his pitiful little body?

I took the one chance I saw. Binding my hand in a handkerchief, I attempted to remove the zigzags of glass in the bottom two quadrants. To my surprise, the glass surrendered easily, each in a single piece, and I laid them down on the floor without a sound. Then I tried the vertical wooden bar and found that it would splinter apart. Finally the window was clear enough for me to lower my hands, get hold of the sobbing boy, and lift him up into the kitchen. I could feel him trembling like a bird, and I hugged him tightly to try to calm him.

"Why did you sneak off? They'll find you," I said, at the same time warning myself that such a plan was foolish.

"I wa-as sca-hare-ed," came his reply. Every word shook. "Th-at b-b-boy . . ."

It was Stoney's seizure that had upset him, and Stone's handling of it, of course.

"Why did you come here? Why to me? What can I do?"

I waited for him to catch his breath. Then he looked up at me with his sorrowful eyes and said. "Because you're in it like us. You got caught."

Stroking his soft, damp cheek left the ghost of a touch on my own face, for I was in it like him, I realized; we had been caught.

·

I had never been devoted to cooking. In the air force I had pulled occasional KP. My first wife had cheated on me so often that for that marriage I had fallen into the routine of providing my own dinners; however, I prepared simple meals only — a bowl of cereal, a sandwich, soup from a can, nothing too elaborate in the making or the cleaning up. Nothing in my experience had prepared me for this job. And yet, as my eyes adjusted to the new light, the sense of human superiority that had always separated me from things that are dumb — rocks, clods, spuds, roots — dissolved, and I saw myself clearly as the cook, the provider, the stirrer of the primal soup for thirty-three hungry kids waiting for a first taste of happiness at Camp Freedom.

I I

The first supper consisted of peanut-butter-and-jelly sandwiches — forty-five — each one on a paper plate, garnished with an apple, and accompanied by a paper cup filled halfway with lukewarm grape juice.

In the half-light of the kitchen, I set crates on end to make a work surface and covered the rough and dirty wood with a paper tablecloth. Jeffie helped me by laying out ninety slices of bread, putting a jellied slice against a peanut-buttered slice, and then putting the sandwich on a plate. He also helped distribute the apples, and he separated the paper cups from the stacks they came packed in so I could pour the juice.

Jeffie was willing to do anything as long as he could stay close to me. Like a cat, he kept within the warm aura of my body: I could feel his head at my elbow, his shoulder against my hip, his sneaker on the edge of my sole.

To my surprise, no one came looking for him. He had been assigned to one of the cabins and then forgotten in the hour before dinner while Stone walked around blowing his whistle and barking orders, and the campers tried settling in on their own, or with the tentative assistance of two equally confused counselors. There was still no sign of the other seven who were scheduled to arrive at any time in two cars that had left from New Jersey and Pennsylvania.

Stone had set up six large folding tables; their aluminum legs sunk an inch into the mud. Each camper was told to come around to the front door of the kitchen where Jeffie and I could hand him his plate and cup, and then he was to find a place at the table which was numbered to correspond to his cabin number. He couldn't sit at the table, just put his meal down, and some of the boys left their plates and strolled about, sandwich in one

106

hand, juice in the other, apple tucked under an arm or perched in the top of a too small pocket.

Suddenly there was excitement near one of the several tree stumps that stood as tombstones in the forestal graveyard. Two boys were disputing each other's claim to the stump/seat with their fists. One boy was bigger and stronger, and he kept connecting with straight, hard blows to the head while easily dodging, deflecting, or absorbing the weaker boy's helter-skelter roundhouses.

Everyone crowded around to get a good show before it was stopped. The two counselors who had come up on the bus shouted at the boys to stop fighting. Frances, who was tall and sensually overweight, shouted for the bigger boy to lay off. Francis, who was thin and intense, pleaded with the weaker boy to surrender by not fighting back. Neither intervened. Albert was right there, too, and he seemed to enjoy the uneven row more than anyone. Although they couldn't understand his French, the boys seemed to respond to his loud cries and broad gestures by intensifying the action. Albert threw targetless punches along the sidelines as if he were the cornerman for both fighters, delivering a barrage of punches to the right, and then an answer to the left. Thomason watched Stone's face, waiting for a sign.

By the time I made my way through the crowd, the weaker boy's face was covered with his own blood. He would have been better off if his opponent had knocked him out, but unfortunately the stronger boy was only good enough to win on points. His limited repertoire still lacked a knockout punch, and, as a result, the weaker boy had to take a terrible beating.

When I moved to break it up, Stone shouted for me to leave them alone in a gruff, frightening, definitive tone.

No one was willing to go against Stone. We all had to stand by until somehow the fight ended. Eventually the fighters grew weary. Their arms were too heavy to lift, their legs too numb to keep them propped up, and they clinched and fell into the mud. The stronger boy held an advantage for another minute or two. He got on top and kept punching the defeated boy's face. They were feeble blows with hardly any sting to them, but they were hitting into open cuts and raw skin, and the downed boy's whole body winced at each pat-a-cake punch.

Finally the last breath of stamina wheezed out of their angry, muddy embrace, and the boys rolled to a stop. They loosened their grips and let their bodies go slack. The bigger boy got to his feet first to prove he was the winner. He staggered over to the disputed stump, sat down heavily, and nursed the few minor scrapes he had picked up in the bout. The other boy lay on the ground with his eyes too puffy to close. The purple sky seemed to spin him around, and he gagged on a sudden wave of nausea.

I realized that Jeffie was clinging to my leg. I could feel his little fingers digging into my flesh.

Frances, meanwhile, was propping up the loser and promising that if he ate his peanut-butter-and-jelly sandwich he'd feel a lot better. The poor little boy's mouth was a crooked, clotted, swollen gape, the soft, veiny insides of his lips squishing out through blood-caked split skin as if it all had been overcooked on a spit. She put the sandwich up to the gape and urged her patient to take a bite, "One bite, that's all, you'll see how much better you'll feel."

Powerless to disobey, the boy tried to take a bite. He bit off what he could and almost immediately started coughing and grabbing at his neck as though he were choking on a bone. Frances slapped his back and bent his head forward. The little boy spit up a small wad of brown-and-purple goo and cried out loud, the wad seeming to have unplugged his throat. Still coughing, crying, and spitting, the little loser kept bringing his hands up to his mouth and pulling them back quickly when they got too close to a tender spot. No one but Francis heard himself say, "You made him spit his teeth right out of his mouth. That bully loosened them, and the peanut butter did the rest."

"The winner," Stone announced, placing his huge hand on the victor's small shoulder, "is the man who has the most spine." He squeezed the shoulder, and the victorious boy crumpled before everyone's eyes. His mouth opened, but not a sound came out, as his body collapsed under the pressure of Stone's effortless hold. "And I am the man who has the most spine," he reminded everyone.

The boy's mouth remained open, emitting a long, silent cry for help.

III

"Don't throw that away."

Stone's voice surprised me. For a man as big as he was, he got around like a ghost; I never heard him come into the kitchen.

"This is just what the boys left over . . . crusts and apple cores mostly."

"Save it."

"What for?"

"Just save it."

IV

Although I had lived in the pinelands for a long time, I had never before noticed the nightfall. I had never closely observed the dramatic change of colors, the quickness, the eerie invisibility of towering trees and rushing water and your own five fingers in front of your face, and then the subtle revenge of the eye as blinking lashes repaint everything more vividly in a contrast of night colors only the morning sun can fade. These observations were inspired by the fears of the children who were without their luminous beagles, radiant rockets, glowing basketballs, or any of the countless toys-as-lamps that lit a safe path from the edge of daylight to the precipice of sleep.

The first nightfall found several of us behind the kitchen, which was separated from the thick woods only by the sparse edge of the woods. Whereas the compound itself — the dozen cabins between wood and stream — had been cleared of trees by saw and ax, the perimeter looked merely pruned, a scattering of scrawny blackjack oaks venturing out from the dense pine forest.

There was a before-and-after quality to our huddle. Before nightfall, we sat in the warm and glowing descent of the sun.

Everyone retained a certain optimism. Still in a state of grace from Jeffie's earlier illumination, I was undaunted by my dismal kitchen facilities, by the impractical equipment and lack of space and by the already festering problem of food spoilage. I hid whatever concerns I had in communal chitchat which also hid the others' confusion about the methods and possible madness of Stone, their grave doubt about how trustworthy Thomason and Albert were, their thumping fear of an unpredictable attack by a bear, or a lion, their goose-pimply dread of bedding down in a filthy cabin, all their secret worries about food and shelter and personal safety.

"First thing we have to do is something about these names of yours. We can't go around calling the both of you Francis," I said to Francis. "Ain't that right, Frances?" I asked Frances.

To keep from talking about anything more disturbing, it was decided that Frances would be called Frannie and Francis would be called Frankie by everyone other than themselves. But uneasiness ran through us all like our blood, and as the sun got set to disappear and the night animals began filling the forest with sinister sounds and Stone and Thomason started rounding up stray campers and ordering them to their cabins, our little group grew fearful.

"Have you ever been a counselor before, Frannie?" I asked in the direction of her cigarette-lit face. She was not about to let herself fall apart.

"No." She exhaled, not wanting to elaborate.

"I was never a counselor before either," Frankie volunteered, "but I went to camp for three summers."

Frankie's remark seemed to be a signal for the black hood of night to be thrown over the boys' heads. The sun was gone. Our faces went black, then blue, then gray, and the harder we tried to hold on to images, the easier it was to lose sight completely. The boys stared intently at the slightly darker space where Frankie's apprehensive expression had last been seen, and all they saw was what they heard him say. "But it wasn't like this camp. We had clean, decent cabins with bathrooms and showers and shelves for your clothes and a place for your toothbrush and a washcloth, and there were spring cots with three-inch mattresses and woolen blankets if you needed them at night, and those cabins were a lot bigger, too; there were at least a dozen boys in each one — and lights, we had a bright light over every other bunk that the counselor switched off at curfew; but for an hour before curfew, while it was pitch dark like this, you could get ready for bed, or read a book, or you could write a letter home to your mother."

"Hey, Francis, what are you scaring the kiddies for? That was that camp. This is a different one. This is rougher. It's a lot more . . . this is like the pioneers lived," Frannie said enthusiastically.

Homer, Samuel, Harry Jr., Ezra, and, of course, Jeffie, all turned toward Frannie's surprise attack, hoping Frankie would go on to explain in what other awful, evil ways Camp Freedom differed from the camp he had attended.

"There is a difference," Frankie continued, "between roughing it, which is in the very nature of every camp, and the unnecessary, inhuman hardships which this camp seems to specialize in."

I could not believe how close Frankie's words came to expressing my exact feelings. It was almost as if I had written his speech; and in the darkness I could feel his eyes on me, acknowledging my amazement while trying also to reassure me that it was simply a case of our combined common sense and not some mysterious transference of thought.

"What about toilets?" he asked Frannie. "Do you enjoy going into the woods and digging a hole? Does it make you feel like a pioneer to eat standing up in mud? And what about you, Gus? Do you agree with Frances that poor provisions and terrible sleeping conditions and no medical facilities and no telephones or electricity and a man who acts more like camp dictator than camp director are all just typical pioneer phenomena?"

Except for Jeffie, the little boys still were not certain exactly who the enemy was, and they were reluctant to ask questions, suspecting that the answers might be more frightening than the doubts they might dispel. As for me, I was content to let Frankie anticipate and speak my every thought. It was uncanny. I felt that every word he spoke originated in my own head and was formed and released through my closed mouth. Once again I came to realize that we were all "in it" the same as Jeffie and Frankie and the others. It was as if a divine hand had sorted all the world's victims from the victimizers and cast the miserable lot of us into the black hole of Camp Freedom. A bond formed between the eight of us, partly because we had found each other when we were looking for any port in Stone's storm, and partly because together we had observed the rite of first nightfall.

"We'll all feel a lot better after breakfast," I said.

V

The next morning when I awoke it was fairly dark outside and almost completely dark inside. I thought I must have been the first one awake, but while I was still clearing my head and my eyes, Stone threw open the door to the kitchen.

Even in the semidarkness of the hour and of my consciousness, Stone stood in the open doorway looking emphatically refreshed as people do only after a morning shower, shave, and cup of coffee. His damp curls were perfectly distributed over his broad head, like a Roman emperor's, and his freshly shaved face shone like a smooth stone. Even his clothes looked freshly scrubbed and ironed, and his athletic shoes were so white they had to be fresh out of the box.

I stayed on the floor, where I had slept, and would have landed down there anyway after hearing what Stone had come to say.

"Efficiency. That's the secret. No unnecessary movement. No unnecessary waste."

His tone was the same as when he had delivered his lecture on the spinal column; he reserved that effective mix of professorial wisdom and evangelical fervor for talking about the spine as God and the chiropractor as Priest.

"That's my secret as a chiropractor. And that's going to be your secret as a cook," he explained. "Suppose you were suffering severe gastric pain." Stone indicated the exact location of the hypothetical pain on his own stomach. "What does a medical doctor do? If he's a general practitioner, he may not do anything. He may refer you to a specialist. Time spent. Pain suffered." Stone became more animated. Like a passionate priest who bangs and shakes and drapes himself over his lectern, Stone was able to produce the effect of great movement without, in fact, ever moving out of the frame of the door. The width of the threshold was his lectern, his stage, another example, no doubt, of efficiency.

"If you are lucky enough to get a quick appointment," Stone continued, "this specialist will then have to perform a battery of tests, for what first makes him a specialist in one area is his ability to rule out every other area. This pain," Stone grabbed at his gut dramatically "might be a gallstone, an ulcer, heartburn, a kidney problem, who knows? It might be anything from a slight case of indigestion to a malignant tumor. Only after x-rays and a GI series and blood tests and a look at your bone marrow and a look at your stool and urine and the inspection of everything else that can be extracted or probed or palpated or given a biopsy will the specialist be ready to make his diagnosis. Meanwhile, of course, there has been the further waste of time and your further suffering of not only the original pain, but the added discomfort of needles, tubes, barium, IV hook-ups, and, worst of all, medicine. Pills! Capsules! Tonic! Serum!" At the mention of these words Stone's eyes bulged more and more. "Medicine to calm you! Medicine to stimulate you! Medicine to strengthen you for the tests that will show what kind of medicine you will have to take! Medicine instead of food! Medicine instead of sleep! Medicine in preparation for more medicine! And then medicine to remedy the ill effects of the previous medicine! And then — if none of these miracle pills and elixirs should happen to work — surgery! A slice here, a slice there — until the scalpel has destroyed whatever the medicine managed to miss."

Then Stone changed up like a fastball pitcher going to a slow curve. "But suppose," he said quietly, "you came to a chiropractor with your gastric pain . . . to a man who has been trained to read the human body like the blind read braille. He can touch you and understand your pain. He doesn't care if it's a gallstone or an ulcer or a rotting colon or a swollen liver or an inflamed appendix — he only cares about stopping the pain by correcting the misalignment that is causing the pain. With only his hands to guide him, he knows that a pain right here, exactly here, a pain whose dimensions and intensity he can actually feel, requires a correction right here, exactly here," Stone pointed in the air as if to a specific part of the spine on a hanging model of a human skeleton, "where an inflamed or pinched or damaged nerve is blocking your body's own incomparable healing power. No delay, for delay is the best friend of disease. And no drugs, for only what is naturally made in the laboratory of the body can lead the body back to natural health." With these two chiropractic slogans, Stone ended the first part of his lecture. He began again almost immediately.

"Just as chiropractic efficiency means going directly to the source of a pain in the stomach rather than going round about through the mouth, or the rectum, or the skin, so should efficiency in cooking go directly to what is apparent. No unnecessary movement. No unnecessary waste." He stopped. To see if I had any questions, perhaps. Then he started again.

"This morning we want pancakes for breakfast. So let's talk about the batter." Stone entered the kitchen and sat on the corner of a crate I had stood on end. "You need milk and flour and eggs. We have the flour, we have the eggs, and we have condensed milk you can mix with water from the stream. We also have something else," and there he paused to crane his neck this way and that, looking for whatever he was talking about. "We have, we have . . ." still looking, and then, "aha!" finally spotting a large black garbage bag in the corner. "We have this!" Stone walked to the bag and lifted it in one of his huge hands. Then he walked back to me and held the bag over my head while he finished his lecture on efficiency.

But halfway into the lecture the sun burst upon us and stirred Jeffie who had been obliviously curled up behind the large stove where Frannie and I had agreed to let him sleep the night. When it had come time to disperse and bed down in the appropriate cabins, Jeffie had latched on to my leg as he had done at the sight of the two boys fighting over the stump. Since no one had been counting heads, and the campers had been forming cliques and settling into any cabin they pleased, we had decided that Jeffie could sleep with me in the kitchen, but that eventually he would join the others in our group. The others, meanwhile, had groped through night and cobwebs to retrieve their belongings from previously assigned cabins so that together they could move into the first empty cabin they found.

"You buggering the little boys already!" Stone seethed. "Can't I trust you damned hillbillies for one lousy night!"

I was speechless. Jeffie, now wide awake and terrified that Stone had come to get him, flew out of his corner behind the stove to cower within the quick shelter my arms formed, even though it meant running directly under Stone's towering, threatening presence.

"He's scared, that's all," I said at last, my hand patting Jeffie's back as fast as his little heart was beating. "He's sort of my helper anyway," I risked, avoiding Stone's eyes. Whatever was going to happen, I decided, would happen to me first. And I gathered Jeffie deeper into my protection.

"Then both of you should hear this," Stone said, and he went on with his amazing lecture as though Jeffie had never interrupted. But something in his expression and tone of voice told me that it was just not efficient for him to deal with Jeffie at that moment.

VI

The most efficient moment for dealing with Jeffie came soon afterward. Stone had finished his lecture and left Jeffie and me to prepare the pancake batter. But he told us not to begin the actual cooking until he blew his whistle four quick blasts.

While the two of us dumped ingredients into the biggest bowls we could find, we began hearing the crisp sounds of little boys waking up. Every thirty seconds or so Geoff Thomason's voice rang out. There was a rapping, a shout of no more than two or three words such as, "Let's go!" "Wake up!" "Rise and shine!" followed by the slamming of a door as Thomason roused each cabin.

The high-pitched hum of young voices grew louder as more of the boys woke up and came outside. When all were accounted for, Stone addressed them. I opened the door to the kitchen, and we were able to hear him very clearly.

"Good morning, boys. We're lucky to have a good one. And we are going to take full advantage of it. But first, I have a few words to say about hygiene. I'm sure you have noticed that these cabins do not have any toilets or sinks or showers. But that does not mean we can't go to the toilet, that we can't brush our teeth, and that we can't keep ourselves clean. We'll just have to go about it in a different way."

Stone was not derelict in his duties as director of Camp Freedom. He had odd but resourceful ideas and he implemented them forcefully. No one, so far, could accuse him of shirking his duties or of cheating anyone or of mistreating the campers beyond the physical inconvenience of inadequate facilities. But even there, Stone tried to make the best out of what he had to work with. And with what others had to work with, too; he suggested I use coals to heat the burners of the stove instead of firewood, and that four small frying pans all going at once would yield more pancakes than the two large frying pans which would extend out beyond the smaller burners and less efficiently distribute heat.

"Last night, while you were all sleeping, I dug three long, deep ditches out in the woods. Those will be our toilets. In that last cabin over there, the one no one was assigned to, closest to the stream, you will find plastic wash basins. All you have to do is wait your turn, rinse out an available basin in the stream, fill it with fresh stream water, and use it for brushing your teeth, washing your face and hands, and so on. As for showering, there's nothing we can do. In the late afternoon you can bathe downstream where the current will move the suds out quickly; and no more than five of you at a time."

"Keep stirring, Jeffie," I said. I'll get this pan going."

"Now when the weather is good, as it is this morning, we're going to start off with a swim before breakfast. I want you all to do what you have to out in the ditches, and then brush your teeth, and then get into your swimming suits, and line up right here again. When you hear my whistle three times, that means you should be finished and back." He blew the whistle three times. "And if you're not, you're responsible for holding up everyone else. If that's you, or you, or you, or you, any one of you, the rest of the boys will hold you up. Literally. In their hands. Over their heads. And they'll march you around until they decide where to throw you. In the stream. In a ditch. It's up to them. So move it!" And he blew his whistle one blast to send them on their way.

"That's not us," I said. "He told us four blasts and we can start cooking."

The ditches were fifty yards into the woods on a direct line with the kitchen. We could look through the window and see the campers stomping in and out of the trees. Back-lit by the brilliant sunlight, their bodies seemed to catch fire around the edges.

"Do you have to go?" I asked Jeffie when I noticed him looking at the others gathering at the ditches. But I guessed that he wouldn't budge without me. He'd sooner hold it in than leave my side.

Three whistle blasts. There was a lot of scrambling and shouting, as the boys hurried to get back in place. A few were still at the ditch when the whistle blew, and now they were in a life-and-death race to beat each other to the finish, for no one wanted to suffer the psychological and physical humiliation of being thrown into the lake, or the ditch, or anywhere else by speedier peers. What made the punishment so clever was that Stone did not have to dirty his own hands. The whistle was judge, and the boys carried out the sentence. Stone, in fact, could place himself in the estimable position of saving a guilty boy from too harsh a fate at the hands of the rabble. Even more clever was his suspension of punishment for the first offense.

117

"You, boy, what's your name?"

I couldn't hear who the boy was, but his small, frightened voice told me that he feared for his life.

"You held everybody up, Homer."

Jeffie clutched at my leg when Stone identified poor Homer. I tightened my grip on a wooden spoon.

"Step up here, Homer."

The two of us inched over to the door and peeked through the crack. Homer was walking up to Stone with his head held low. Each step was a labor, and twice he rubbed a tear from his cheek with his tiny fist. Jeffie, too, was crying.

"Turn around, Homer, and face the boys you've let down," Stone ordered our pathetic soulmate. And Homer turned around to face the other boys who were as apprehensive as he was.

"Homer has held you boys up," Stone's voice boomed. "He has kept you all waiting. All of you managed to finish and get back here in the allotted time. None of you abused the generous time that was given. Except Homer. He's not even in his swimsuit yet. What were you doing, Homer? Where have you been, Homer?"

Stone's voice was so deep, so powerful, that he sounded more menacing than he might have intended. As he measured and detonated each sentence, the boys' anger rose. When Stone complimented them, they were indignant, and when he condemned Homer, they were outraged; in effect, the boys turned on Homer as one, until — at the end of Stone's condemnation — the few boys who knew what had delayed Homer could not keep from tittering.

"We can't hear you, Homer," Stone prodded.

"Oh, leave the poor boy alone," I said to myself, careful not to let Jeffie overhear. Then Homer said something into his own chest that no one could hear, and some of the boys shouted at him.

"We can't hear you, Homer!"

"Whadja say?!"

"Where were you, Homer?"

"Crybaby Homer!"

"Rotten Egg Homer!"

The nastiness was so contagious, I began worrying more about the mob of boys than about Stone. The pancake batter began to congeal and lump.

One of the boys yelled out, "He was going doo-doo in the ditch!" and all the boys laughed out loud. But, as I said, Stone was clever. More clever than I had imagined. After working the boys to a dangerous pitch, he pulled the carpet Homer had been called up on out from under them all. Stone let out one long deafening blast. I pictured the little ball inside the whistle dancing frantically inside my eardrum. Everyone hushed.

"This group is a single body. One boy out of joint with the rest of the boys is like one bone being out of joint. It weakens the entire body. Homer was out of line. The body was weakened. But I am here to set things right. Get back in line, Homer. This is the first time, so we'll let it go. But remember the lesson."

Homer walked back into the group at once, head still down, lower than before, it seemed, and the boys moved out of his path contemptuously. Stone had worked them like an actor works his audience and brilliantly left them begging for more. They felt cheated. They felt teased. And, most important, they no longer felt incapable of revenge.

I stayed at the door and watched Stone parade back and forth as he presented his rules for swimming at Camp Freedom.

"I don't believe in the buddy system," he began. "I believe it's up to each boy to know his own strengths and limitations and to be responsible for his own conduct and safety in the water. Someone will always be there to help in an emergency." He glanced at Albert who had stripped to his underpants and who acknowledged Stone's nod by running several steps in place and then touching his toes several times as though he were preparing to swim an important race. "So don't worry about hurting yourself on the rocks, or being swept off by the current, or getting a cramp in your leg, or going under, or any other problems that can be handled by a lifeguard. Albert has volunteered to stand by this morning, and I'll be there, too, just in case."

119

How quickly the mood could change within a group of young children. Moments ago they had been screaming for Homer's blood, and now they were quiet, subdued, as edgy as the running, ragged edge of the stream they feared. Even those who were not afraid of water were concerned, for they were used to neighborhood pools, YMCAs, perfectly still lakes, even the gentle surf of the ocean, not the hectic babble and flow of a rocky stream.

"But there is one thing that you *will* have to worry about, boys," Stone warned.

Just then, for no apparent reason, my eyes leaped from Stone to Stoney. His red hair stood out like fire, even from the towheads, and I thought to myself how perfectly his hair matches his temperament. What struck me most was that Stoney appeared to have completely forgiven Stone for what he had done to him. He seemed neither bitter nor apprehensive, neither angry nor afraid.

"There is one thing, boys, that is more of an annoyance than anything else." Stone got my attention back.

"Leeches," Stone said.

Cartoon gasps hung in the air; you could almost see the word disintegrate over each boy's head.

"How many of you know what a leech is?" Stone asked. And without waiting for an answer he told the boys. "The kind you find around here look like black worms. They're flat and slimy and an inch, two inches, three inches long at the most. They live by sticking to your flesh and sucking out your blood," he said matter-of-factly. I thought some of the boys were going to faint. The blood drained from their faces as if Stone's description of a leech were actually clinging to them.

"Doctors used to cure sick people with leeches." Stone smiled. "Believe it or not, for a hundred years the infallible science of medicine prescribed leeching as the most advanced treatment known to mankind. The good doctors would come in their frock coats and high hats carrying their special breed of leech — the dragon leech was the one they used — and if you had a fever, they'd put a dragon leech in your ear to suck out the disease. They'd put leeches on your back, on your legs, on your arms, on your neck — wherever the malady struck they stuck a leech. Little did they realize," here Stone mused to himself before getting back to his frightening description, "how close they were to the right idea of simple cause, simple effect, simple cure. It took them a century to get off the right track. These damned know-it-all doctors today in their golf clothes instead of frock coats don't even tolerate their own predecessors."

Stone never went off on a tangent for more than a few seconds. "The dragon leech, boys, was the miracle drug of its day," he continued. "Each leech could be counted on to suck up three times its own weight in diseased blood, and each patient needed several of these tiny bloodsuckers on the affected part of his body. So businessmen started leech farms which turned the lakes and ponds and streams into factories." The boys had never paid such close attention to a history lesson. Stone knew it, too. "This was in Europe," he explained. "There were no leeches in this part of the United States. But there were doctors here who wanted to suck the blood of their patients, and arrangements were made to ship great numbers of dragon leeches across the Atlantic where American businessmen could start their own farms in our lakes and streams. Who knows — a hundred years ago Colt's Point Stream may have been one of those farms." End of the history lesson. Start of the psychology lesson.

"These leeches are not painful. They won't hurt you when they bite and start sucking your blood. But they're ugly. And they're stubborn. If you try to shake one off, it won't let go. If you try to flick it off like this," Stone shot an imaginary marble off his forearm, "you may get only its tail loose and it'll still be dangling by its mouth."

Some of the boys actually took a step backward as if Stone were dangling a dragon leech between his two fingers and menacing them with it. Never had I seen such an identical pallor on the face of everyone in a group, not even in my old combat days when the enemy dangled bombs and bullets and bayonets; there were always a few whose blind bravery flushed their cheeks with red-blooded American valor no matter what peril was upon us nor what gruesome consequence their sanguine Christian onwardness was bound to provoke. But, to a boy, the campers' faces were white and nervous, as were the spindly legs their swimming suits revealed.

"You boys thinking of running away?" Stone asked, his mighty forearm still up in the air to demonstrate where the half-flicked dragon leech might be dangling by its teeth. He put the arm down suddenly and glanced our way. I ducked my head back, but Stone's eyes and mine met anyway, and I was angry that I'd been caught. To teach myself a lesson, I returned to my pot of batter and tried stirring it back to its former useful consistency.

"Don't run away, boys. I'm not telling you this to *scare* you; I'm telling you this to *prepare* you." He made an adage out of the sentence.

"There is a way to deal with these leeches. It's very simple. I'm going to show you how to get a leech off without any trouble at all." Stone's voice seemed to be getting louder.

"I need two things." And louder.

"I need a volunteer to go into the stream and attract a few leeches —"

I could hear the boys making quick, desperate noises that meant "not me."

"— and I need —"

Stone's voice was on top of us. For the second time that morning the door to the kitchen swung open and Stone was standing in the doorway.

"— salt," he said.

He didn't see me at all, he saw only Jeffie. Stone approached me as if I were a tree Jeffie was hiding behind.

"Let him alone," I said. But Stone didn't hear me either. He reached around behind me and put his powerful hand on the back of Jeffie's neck. The poor boy wailed like an animal caught in a steel trap. The efficient moment for dealing with Jeffie had arrived.

"Come on, son," Stone said as kindly as his grip was deadly. "The boys are waiting. You didn't come to Camp Freedom to sweat over a hot stove. You came here to swim."

What could I say? Stone was right. Although the camp was not what it might have been, and although Stone was far too heavy-handed in his leadership and the boy was somewhere between convulsive panic and unconsciousness, the facts of the situation were indisputable. Jeffie had been sent to Camp Freedom not only to embrace and be embraced by the great outdoors, but also — mainly — to grow toward manhood in one incredibly accelerated spurt. Unobstructed exposure to the elements and to the company of men were all the water and sunshine necessary to make a timid, insecure, clinging Jeffie mature. Whether the boy clung to his parents or to me was unimportant. It was the clinging itself that had to be stopped. And like him or not, agree with his methods or disapprove, Dr. George Stone was the world's foremost claw hammer. If anyone could pry Jeffie loose and hammer home the straight-and-narrow rules of self-reliance and independence, it was the man who picked Jeffie up and threw him over his shoulder like one of the sacks of vegetables leaning against the wall. At first Jeffie wriggled gamely, then he stopped, then he struggled again, wriggling and flailing and sobbing. He struggled until he was exhausted, nearly fell unconscious, recovered, and began the cycle again.

Stone ignored him. One huge hand clamped Jeffie to Stone's shoulder while the chiropractor searched the kitchen for a shaker of salt.

"Where is it?" he yelled over the hiccuping whimpering weight on his shoulder.

"Where's what?" I dared raise my voice, wishing I had said Where's your decency, or Where's your humanity? or Where's your compassion for your fellow man? But I remembered that Stone was right. Damn it!

"Where's the salt!" he screamed back at me over the screeching cries of the now frantic wriggler. He held the boy fast. For all his struggling, Jeffie never got a fraction of an inch closer to his freedom.

What happened next haunts me still. Once Stone found the salt, he went from speeded-up motion to slow motion. With Jeffie struggling on his shoulder, he walked out of the kitchen, ducking to avoid the top of the doorway, and returned to the anxious campers. For a few the spell of the dragon leech had been interrupted and they were playing in place, elbowing one another, examining the damp ground where they stood, comparing muscles, rock-throwing abilities, swimming stories. But even these boys snapped to attention when Stone reappeared. It was the bizarre yet plausible combination of panic and calm, frantic wriggling and deliberate movement, the scream of hysteria and the voice of reason that hypnotized everyone.

"This is ordinary salt," Stone told his audience. His voice and demeanor had the equanimity of a newscaster's. Not for one moment did he acknowledge Jeffie's squirms and cries.

"When you go down to the stream, you should make sure you take a shaker of salt along. One shaker for every four boys should be enough." Sometimes Jeffie kicked as hard as he could and caught Stone just under the rib cage, forcing his captor to grunt. But Stone ignored his own grunt; he glided past it with no more or less concern than he might have given a small, airy burp.

"Salt," Stone said emphatically, "is your best protection against a leech. It works like fire, only it won't burn you."

Turning and heading for Colt's Point Stream with slow, determined steps, Stone said, "Follow me!"

The two of them looked like a single mythic creature, a modern, distant cousin to a griffin, half-strongman/half-birdboy, a fierce lionlike monster heading toward the stream of leeches, an avian fear flapping and squawking like the lion's half-eaten prey.

As the great beast walked, it spoke of the leech and of the fire which did not burn. As the great beast walked, its panicky head screeched and choked to underscore each terrifying revelation.

"You'll feel something. A bite."

"AAIII!"

"But you may not know you've been bitten until you see the leech stuck onto your skin."

"PLEEEEE . . ."

"You should come out of the water. Come up onto the bank and get your salt shaker."

"Hhuh-uh. Hhuh-uh. Hhuh-uh."

"When I dip Jeffie's leg in —"

"NOOOOOOOO!"

"— you'll see how the leech attaches itself and starts sucking up the blood. If we're lucky."

"Hhuh-uh. Hhuh-uh."

"You can try to pull it off if you want, but it takes a pretty good yank, and it's awful slimy so it's hard to get a good hold."

"Uh-pleee . . . uh-pleeee . . ."

"It's best to use the salt. Just sprinkle some right on the leech and you can watch it shrivel up as though it were on fire."

Jeffie tried to keep himself still and quiet so he could gather every last bit of strength for one final effort to escape.

"I don't know why it works or how it works, but it does. When you pour salt on a leech, it shrivels up. It still won't fall off, you'll still have to flick it or brush it or pull it away — but it'll be easy. You just flick it off your skin like a scab that's hanging by one last thread of blood."

The creature stopped at the edge of the stream. With one awesome arm he unstuck his other half and dangled him effortlessly over the leech-infested water. There was a tumultuous flurry of everything the boy had: shoulders, elbows, arms, hands, fingers, nails, head, spit, shriek, gurgle, feet, knees, chest, lungs — everything! The energy and intensity were so wild as to appear pathetically silly, but in the end the laughable gave way to profound sadness. Jeffie had lost.

"How is a leech going to get through these pants? How are the boys going to learn their lesson? How are you going to learn *your* lesson?" Stone said, while his terrible arm unbuckled Jeffie's belt and unbuttoned his pants and pulled them down, catching his underpants, too, pulling both his pants and his underpants down over his tiny, muddy sneakers and tossing the clothes at the crowd of campers who leaped back and gasped as one. Then he pulled the tiny sneakers off, too, and the tiny socks.

Jeffie hung. Swung. From Stone's fist. Except for his shirt

which was gathered up into a substantial part of the scruff that Stone held in his tireless fist, Jeffie was naked.

Stone held the boy up, extended his arm over the waters of Colt's Point, and moved the limp body just an inch or two toward the limp crowd of campers, counselors, Thomason, Albert, and one compassionate but helpless cook. Stone held Jeffie up to show us the pitiful futility of rebellion.

No one spoke. Not even Stone. Then slowly, slowly Stone lowered his arm. As if the terrible dragon leeches which Stone had described were not enough for the imagination to confront, we imagined other monsters gathering at the surface of the water to devour poor Jeffie. These had the hairy, scaly, phlegm-eyed heads of the ugliest fishes we could find in the brain coral of our minds; they were deformed, engorged, skeletal, they were grotesque mutants taking the horribly combined form of turtle and shark, crayfish and crocodile, burbot and squid. Our own naked bodies shivered and shrunk as the monstrous fishes snapped their razor teeth bloodthirstily at Jeffie's toes and thighs and — most vulnerable, most awful to contemplate, most frightening for boys — . But just then Jeffie broke the silence, broke the surface, broke the tension. The poor boy's pee squirted into the stream. Leeches and other monstrosities awaiting, Stone dropped his arm suddenly. Everyone made some sort of noise as Jeffie's bare feet splashed into the terrifying waters. But at the same moment Stone staggered backward, his locked fist dragging Jeffie up out of the water and along with him. It was a primordial sight: a hulking, apelike figure lumbering aimlessly, as though having been struck on the head by an enemy, and carrying his hard-won prey in a fist made so tight that it no longer functioned as part of his arm and body and primitive brain, but acted on its own. Jeffie bumped and sprawled and twisted behind Stone's staggering bulk. Finally the stupefied primate stopped, teetered, and fell back stiffly, crashing to the ground like an axed tree. Still he had Jeffie — and our stunned attention — in his grip.

Stone stirred, rolling to one side and then the other, looking more dazed than hurt. With his free hand he tried rubbing his eyes the way a sleepy man would, but what had befallen him was not so easily rubbed away. As I myself had witnessed only a day earlier — not even one full day by the clock — Stone's sudden, disabling stupor had to run its own course. He fought back, but any success was directly proportionate to how much the invisible fist that gripped Stone happened to relax.

Jeffie was nothing more than a rag doll. He had escaped the dread leeches only to be dragged about and nearly trampled by a delirious giant. The other boys had no logical response to this. They could imagine how it must have felt to be lowered into the threatening waters of Colt's Point Stream, but they did not understand nor know how to respond to Stone's delirium and its consequences. In exasperation, the campers began to laugh. Someone tittered, another joined in, a few more giggled, and soon they were all laughing nervously. They might have been laughing at any one of several things: Jeffie's bare ass, his fall, Stone's drunken staggering, his fall, Jeffie's marionette movements, Stone's turtle-on-its-back struggle to regain control.

Goaded by their laughter, Stone fought to get to one knee. He screamed something unintelligible, and the image flashed through my mind of a slimy foal struggling to its wobbly legs but not being able to escape a suffocating membrane enveloping its frantic head, a snorting whinny trying to burst through, but the foal's gagging muzzle sucking up this natal membrane.

Stone flared his nostrils and glowered at the laughers. Whatever he saw, whatever he heard, whatever he felt or thought, Stone reacted like an animal. He flexed every muscle in his body at once, barreling out his chest, stretching every sinew to the limit, squeezing, clenching, bearing down, grunting, groaning, extending, exerting, and then emerging triumphant from the suffocating membrane, simultaneously breaking out and coming to his senses, a man reborn.

Everyone stared at Stone and cowered, for he stood there looking more powerful than ever. Only I noticed the body of the small boy on the ground beside him.

VII

All laughter was drowned out by Stone's deafening bellow. He had sunk as low as possible in front of us all, and then, with his bellowing and barreling, had astounded us by surviving whatever it was that had struck his body and soul. He walked through the crowd, which parted only too obligingly, and never turned back as he made for his cabin.

I was at Jeffie's side before Stone closed the door behind him. I had to open the boy's eyelids with my thumb. When I shook him violently, Jeffie managed a groggy moan; his head rolled and his mouth hung open. Frankie helped me lift the boy and carry him to the kitchen where I had noticed a box of first-aid supplies in among the boxes of food. I found smelling salts and passed the open bottle under Jeffie's nose until his eyes opened and began to fill with tears.

"It's all right," I kept saying. But when Jeffie tried to reach his hand up to his cheek to wipe away his tears, he could not move his arm. His left arm moved easily, but his right arm was stone dead.

VIII

Suddenly my obligations seemed clear. In my capacity as cook, I would keep the boys fed and strong; with the first-aid materials I had access to, I would keep them fairly healthy if nothing too serious presented itself. Jeffie's paralytic right side, though, was beyond any healing I could perform. I did not know then that this paralysis was temporary and would soon disappear. Instructions to Frankie were pragmatic; I told him to take Jeffie to his hut and make him as comfortable as possible, and that on the way he might ask for Frannie's help, too, since I believed Jeffie craved the maternal touch Frannie could provide.

I placed several pieces of dry wood and plenty of coal inside the huge black belly of the stove, squirted kerosene liberally, tossed in a lit match, and blew through the grate to questionable avail while waiting for all the wood to catch and the fire to spread and roar evenly, which happened sooner than I expected. The openings of the top burners could be regulated, and I allowed the flames to shoot through to the bottom of the frying pans.

"Albert!" I yelled out, surprising myself by my boldness.

"Albert," I yelled again, "come in here!"

The bossy edge to my voice reminded me of the crotchety old chuckwagon cook in the movies who was always named Cookie and whose toothless, harmless banter no one ever took seriously but everyone made sure to acknowledge lest there'd be no vittles in his tin plate come sundown.

"I'm going to need help, Albert! Set up the tables! Put out the plates!"

I met Albert at the door and pointed to the folded tables, the paper plates, the plastic forks, and the flapjacks so he would understand what I wanted him to do. At first he was indignant. But when he smelled the flapjacks and saw them cooking, he melted like the chunk of shortening I chucked into the next empty pan. The language barrier melted, too, as we communicated in a kitchen language that was a lumpy mixture of pantomime, facial expressions, and intonation.

Every time Albert set down a few plates on the table next to the stove, he came and stood by my elbow to watch the batter turn into golden brown cakes. His eyes fixed themselves so intently on the cakes that one almost felt the heat that was cooking them was actually being beamed directly from Albert's coal-black pupils.

The spooky first night of fitful sleep and the malevolent morning gave my humble pancakes a special importance; each boy's first bite was his first taste of anything normal and pleasant since his arrival at Camp Freedom.

I watched the boys' faces, testing Stone's theory of efficiency, of no unnecessary movement, no waste. Certainly the pancakes did not taste bad, despite what Stone had made me put in the batter.

Everyone ate so greedily, whether wolfing or savoring, that

the happy little symphony of children's teeth clacking and children's lips smacking drowned out the shrill note of skepticism that had been ringing inside me. Begrudgingly, I realized that Stone had been right once again, and I dug into my own breakfast as greedily as the campers.

But in the midst of our happy feasting one of the boys began gagging and coughing so hoarsely he sounded like an old man. I could see immediately that the boy was in no real danger, that his coughing was only a dramatic protest. Apparently he had come upon something extremely distasteful and was in the noisy process of engulfing his find in as much spit and phlegm as he could muster before sharing it with all of us who were crowding around his amazing performance. But as I rushed to the boy, my skepticism returned; the slightly unorthodox taste of the pancakes became vile, and the accomplice in me began to magnify every terrible possibility. Before I could get to him, the victim spit out the half-chewed contents of his mouth and probed it with his plastic fork until he uncovered a small, hard white object resembling a stone.

"Oh, it's only your tooth," said one of the boys.

Another boy made a bored face and waved his hand at the gagger pitilessly.

"Your tooth fell out. You're okay," the first boy said.

"I wonder how the tooth fairy will find you way out here," a third boy half joked.

But the boy who had spit up the tooth would not be consoled. He began crying and rolling his eyes and shaking his head. He pointed accusingly at the tiny white tooth while he tried — unsuccessfully — to compose himself long enough to utter the words that would convince us his suffering was real. But we grew impatient with the speed of his recovery. One of the boys who knew him called him by name.

"Come on, Jason," he said, spitting out the words with as much disgust as Jason had spit out my pancakes. "It's only a tooth, Jason. Look at the size of it."

Jason caught his breath and stopped gagging just long enough to shut the boy up.

"But it's not mine," he cried, "it's not mine."

EIGHT

Stone had made me dump the remains of the last night's dinner into the pancake batter. The bits of crust and bread and gobs of peanut butter and jelly were reusable, Stone had insisted. They could be mixed together with less than the usual amounts of flour and eggs and milk, blending lumpily into the batter, cooking up smoothly, and adding economical bulk to the first breakfast served at Camp Freedom. No unnecessary movement. No waste. The sweetness of the ingredients and of the final product was disguise enough. The boys would never know that secreted within their golden pancakes was the staff of another life, last night's, undetectable, sterilized by the red flames raging through the four open burners. Never would they know, unless a fragment were to be found, a remain, a fossil of imperishable bone. From such a fossil one could draw certain conclusions. Jason had nearly swallowed a tooth that had been lost in battle. The boy who had fought to sit on a stump at last night's dinner had had it knocked loose and then lost it in the gooey grip of his unfinished sandwich. No bigger than a small kernel of corn, it was never noticed in the batter; it might even have gone down smoothly when Jason swallowed. Yet the tiny white relic rose to the surface and with it arose fear and courage. The possibilities of choking on someone else's tooth, of being paralyzed by the strong arm of the chiropractor, of having one's veins sucked dry by leeches, of being thrown into a ditch full of human waste were all threatening. But the lack of evil intent on the part of Stone or Thomason or Albert made these terrible possibilities seem less like threats and more like the ordinary problems of life at camp. It was going to be rough at Camp Freedom. It was going to be dangerous. But we would do what we had to in order to survive our rugged new world.

After breakfast, the campers broke into one large group, several smaller ones, and a few twosomes, the remaining loners scattering to read, explore, or play alone. The large group tried to organize itself into a softball game. The smaller ones wrestled, tossed a ball, played tag, ran, romped, burned energy spontaneously. Budding friendships succeeded when two boys had mutual interests in comic books, movies, TV shows, superheroes, miniature car collections but died on the vine if the boys couldn't find something in common right away. The loners, whose ranks were increased by the failed twosomes, were a problem for Geoff Thomason, who put himself in charge of keeping track of all the campers. Frankie and Frannie were still the only counselors at Camp Freedom, and though they made themselves available to any camper who needed them, they spent most of their time with "Frannie's boys" as our group from the night before came to be known.

"Frannie's boys" included Harry, who was content most of the time to amuse himself with a tape recorder that he borrowed from Stoney, and who always looked as though something much more troubling than Camp Freedom was on his mind.

There was Ezra, the oldest, who was enthusiastic about camp. He was willing to endure the hardships and discipline for the chance to play any game with anyone who was willing. No one was more appreciative than Ezra of the little freedom available at Camp Freedom.

Sammy took on the slightly tarnished sheen of a veteran when he told the others that he'd been going to Dr. Stone for adjustments for more than a year.

"Boy do they hurt," he bragged.

But his mettle had to be tested in Stone's forge at Camp Freedom before the others would respect Sammy's past visits to the chiropractor.

Stoney was one of "Frannie's boys," too, even though he had slept while the rest of us had observed the rite of the first night. But no one had been in our thoughts more than Stoney, for what had happened to him earlier helped us define the dark dread nightfall had brought upon us. And we were happy the next day that Stoney seemed to suffer no ill effects either from his seizure or from Stone's therapy.

We could not yet say the same for Jeffie, who dozed and whimpered and complained that his paralyzed right arm tingled "like when your foot falls asleep."

When I stopped by the cabin to see Jeffie, Frankie pulled me in and insisted that I confirm his opinion that if Jeffie's arm tingled, it couldn't possibly be paralyzed.

"Fuck you, Francis," Frannie yelled. "He can't move his goddamn arm. You think he's pretending?"

"I didn't say he was pretending. Of course he's not pretending. But it isn't paralyzed. Is it, Gus?" Frankie said, smiling at me and by that smile including me in the humoring of someone as unscientific as Frannie.

With a single swift, smooth motion, Frannie found her pack of cigarettes, removed one, lit it, inhaled deeply, and blew a cone of smoke at Frankie. "What the hell do you know about it?" she said. "Why aren't you out there with the boys? I'll take care of Jeffie."

Unless you were to include Frankie, Homer was the last of "Frannie's boys." He was also the bravest.

"GET OUT OF THERE, HOMER!" Frankie yelled across the compound. "GET OFF THERE!"

Homer was at the center of the footbridge. He had climbed over the railing and was standing on the outer edge of the bridge, the rail at his back, his hands holding on to the rail to enable him to lean out forward without falling. If he let go, he'd fall for sure.

"DON'T DO IT!" Frankie was yelling.

"JUMP! JUMP!" some of the other boys hollered when they saw Homer swaying on the edge of the bridge.

Geoff Thomason ran down and started taking pictures. Stone never came out of his cabin. Frannie wouldn't leave Jeffie but kept yelling for information. "What is it? What's going on? What happened? Francis! Gus! Will somebody tell me what's happening!?"

Homer ignored all the excitement he was causing. He watched the energetic figure of a man swimming below him in the leech-infested waters of Colt's Point Stream.

"Come in," the man's hand motioned to Homer, "jump in." But Homer could not let go. He leaned out over the waters and looked as though he were gauging the length of the plunge, a distance of about six feet. But then he pulled himself back to the railing again. The man in the stream was gliding just under the surface of the water, propelling himself with broad strokes and quick kicks, barely raising his head to take in air. Soon all eyes were on the energetic swimmer as he splashed, wriggled, glided, and finally made for the bank. When he was forced to stand up, we were shocked at how shallow the stream was, though not as shocked as we were at the ghostly white sight of the swimmer's nearly bare body. There was not a single trace of a leech on Albert's dripping arms and legs and hairless, heaving chest.

II

Of all of us, Frannie was the least patient and the most disgruntled. She cursed Stone for what he had done to Stoney the day before and to Jeffie that morning. She condemned Geoff Thomason for deceiving parents, campers, and counselors with his dishonest brochure and false bill of goods. She assailed Stone and Thomason in particular and chiropractic and advertising in general. But she did not confront the chiropractor or the photographer. Frannie's courage to say out loud what all of us were feeling or wondering may have come from the fact that she didn't think Stone or Thomason or Albert would lay a hand on a woman. But the fact that she would not confront them directly bespoke the same doubt we all had: dare we provoke people we do not understand?

When she wasn't complaining or condemning, Frannie kept asking questions none of us could answer. "Is that guy Stone crazy?" "What the hell is going on here?" "Where are all the other counselors?" "That prick didn't hire any other counselors, did he?" "I can take care of my boys, but who's going to watch out for the rest of 'em? Thomason? That fuckin' weirdo Frenchman?" "Why the hell doesn't that weirdo Frenchman put on his goddamn pants?"

In the continuing absence of the other counselors, it fell to Geoff Thomason and Albert to keep the campers from straying out of the compound. Albert patrolled his side like the lifeguard he didn't get the chance to be earlier that morning. He swaggered, strutted, stopped to squint into the sun while scanning the entire compound for an emergency that might need his swift attention. Instead of a bathing suit, he was wearing his underpants which were still wet from his swim in the stream. They clung to his thin, muscular body, revealing every change in position and size of his private parts. If he itched there, it was not beyond him to scratch himself in front of the passing Frannie for whom it was impossible to avert either her eyes or her annoyance. Albert never again put on the clothes he had taken off. He pranced about the compound nearly naked, wearing not much more than his inability to speak our language.

By contrast, Geoff Thomason was well covered at all times, wearing long pants, socks, shoes, and a long-sleeved shirt that he kept buttoned up the front almost to the collar. Instead of parading back and forth like Albert, Thomason let his eyes patrol for him. He sat in front of his cabin writing in a notebook. When he glanced up to survey the compound for straying campers, his eyes alone moved, not his head, as if by retaining the exact position of his attention to the open notebook on his lap he would regain the exact thought that he had interrupted.

Frannie continued to nurse Jeffie. She brought him a cool

drink and asked me to bring a candy bar or cookies for energy, which I did. But Jeffie wasn't hungry. He fell asleep while Frannie was massaging his paralyzed arm.

"You can't do anything about it," Frankie said to her. "Even Stone himself can't put him back the way he was."

"What do you mean Stone can't?" Frannie asked, holding a flaming match away from the tip of her cigarette until she finished her question. Then she lit up.

"There's a mathematical principle called commutation," Frankie was only too happy to explain. "What it means is that if you do a, b, c, and d, you can only undo it by doing d, c, b, and a. I think that's the principle you have to apply to Jeffie's arm. Someone has to reverse the process whereby Jeffie's arm was paralyzed. And I don't think anybody can. Not even Stone."

"Well, then why the fuck did that bastard do it to him in the first place?"

"Maybe he didn't know what he was doing," I intervened, remembering Stone's two attacks. "Remember, he was having an attack," I said, suddenly realizing that only I knew that it had been an attack because only I had seen the identical symptoms the day before when Stone had fallen into Colt's Point Stream.

"How do you know it was an attack?" Frannie asked me.

"Because he had one yesterday. I saw it from up on the bluff where I was hiding. Only there was something different, I can't say exactly what, something very different between the two attacks. And yet they were identical. He looked drunk and weak and helpless just like this morning. But there was something else. I'm trying to remember."

Later that day, after Frannie had decided to confront Stone, I realized what the difference had been between the two attacks. The first had run its course despite Stone's mighty effort to overcome it. But the second had been aborted by Stone. He had conquered his demons through the sheer force of his will.

III

"Let's have a nature project," Frannie announced to her boys. She wanted to preoccupy them while she went to Stone's cabin to lodge her protests and demands.

"A nature project," Frannie explained, "is what we're all out here in these *wonder*ful woods *for*. Really," she said, trying to convince herself as well as the boys. "Think of all we miss by living in the city. There are lessons to be learned in every leaf, every stone, every footprint, every noise."

The boys strained to hear one voice among the many that were singing the constant woodland chorus. From daybreak to night-fall there were chesty, full-throated soloists of every type and timbre — warblers, screechers, squealers, screamers, honkers, whistlers, whiners, bellowers, growlers, cluckers, grunters — all blending together against a background of ripple and rustle. At night the crickets took over with their steady percussion; there were fifty startling cries of *whip-poor-will* in a minute; a good ear heard the tireless whistle of a nighthawk's wings as it searched for burned-over land. Every night, right before dark, and then on into the night, I was able to pick out the nighthawk as it dived. It was not that I had particularly sharp hearing, but rather that I was somehow attuned to this creature and the lilting hum of its rapidly fluttering wings as it dived for a charred piece of earth on which to nest and breed. However, nothing as peculiar as the nighthawk nor as ordinary as the wind riffling the long, soft needles of the pines caught the attention of Frannie's boys. They were as lost in nature as they would have been in the sea. Nothing looked different, distinguishable, unique. It was all a runny wash of green and brown and blue, a drifting mix of sounds which became a single sound that disappeared as soon as their ears grew accustomed to it. But they were willing to venture into the woods for Frannie's sake and give nature a try.

"What do we do?" Sammy asked.

"Bring me something," Frannie said, her eyes sparkling at the clever decision she had made. "Yes, bring me something from the woods. I don't care what," she said, cheerfully pushing her boys off in the direction of the woods, "a leaf, a berry, a rock, a bug, a nest, you decide. Then we'll put each item on a piece of paper and write what it is right under it on the piece of paper and by the end of camp we'll have a whole big collection."

"I'll help you identify the things they bring back," Frankie said from behind her.

"Why aren't you with Jeffie?" she demanded. Frannie had asked Frankie to look after Jeffie while she gave the rest of the boys their nature assignment.

"It's okay. He's sleeping." Frankie tried to calm Frannie. "Besides, I told you there's nothing anybody can do."

"I'll do something."

"What are you going to do, Frances?"

"I'm going to see Stone."

"What do you mean you're going to see Stone?"

"I'm going to tell him that things aren't right. I'm going to ask him to fix Jeffie's arm. I'm going to find out what the hell is going on here, Francis!"

"I wouldn't if I were you."

"I know you wouldn't. You wouldn't stand up for Stoney yesterday either. You wouldn't quit your stupid teaching job and be a musician. You wouldn't do a lot of things, Francis. You wouldn't even fuck me when you had the goddamn chance."

I was embarrassed to overhear them, but they didn't seem to know I was there.

"I'm going," Frannie said. She may have thought Frankie would stop her, for she hesitated ever so slightly. But he was as eager as she was to bring Stone out in the open.

Frannie got as far as the door of Stone's cabin before she had a second thought about entering. But an inescapable magnetism drew her forward. What was this strange attraction? Afterward she told me everything she had felt and thought and said in such precise language and with such seemingly perfect recall that the experience in Stone's cabin sounded like a religious one. Like those who have witnessed a miraculous revelation, she relived her experience when she related it.

The door to Stone's cabin was not quite shut. From the crack

Frannie heard Stone's familiar voice. But it was neither loud nor deep.

"Six-one-two," the voice labored.

A few seconds later, "six-one-three."

Then, "six-one-four."

Then, "six-one-five."

Frannie's hand was on the doorknob. She gave the door a slight push.

"Six-one-eight." Stone's voice got louder and louder as the crack got wider and wider. "Six-one-nine."

Frannie was able to identify another sound. It was the sound a man makes when his body strains to perform a difficult feat. Sometimes this sound preceded the number. Sometimes it succeeded the number. Sometimes, as in the numbers six-one-three, -four and -five, the straining sound occurred along with the numbers, causing Stone to squeeze out the three digits with the greatest difficulty.

Finally Frannie could see in through the open doorway. There on the floor of the cabin was Dr. George Stone doing sit-ups. Each time Stone sat up he showed Frannie his massive shirtless back. His hands were clasped behind his head, his fingers hidden in his curls, and each time he sat up on the floor and leaned forward he would touch the elbow of his right arm to his left knee or his left elbow to his right knee, alternating that way while Frannie stood and watched. All she could see was his huge naked back and his tensed arms until he lay back on the floor, revealing a flash of white in the middle of a long, large smooth body, for Stone was wearing only an athletic supporter, nothing else, and when that part of his body was visible, Frannie could not take her eyes off the wonderful white bulge. So overwhelmed was she by the huge, naked, sweating, bulging sight of Stone so completely engrossed in what might have been the sacred repetitions of some pagan ritual, that Frannie could hardly speak. She remembered being aroused. She remembered the sensual images that came to her while she stood in the doorway and did not, could not, move. She imagined great smooth rifts in roseate mounds of earth, a fine fringe of delicate, wet hairs bent along the moist seams like the silken filaments inside voluptuous flowers. She imagined all the sand of a desert as one boundless, smooth stretch of undulating skin, her own footprints marring the flawless plain, and a faceless, dark-skinned figure poking his head up from the long cleft between twin tumescent dunes, a blazing white kaffiyeh belted about his bobbing head. She imagined earth colors, mounds, rifts and clefts and chasms, flashes of white — all surely inspired by the animal magnetism of the camp director.

Then Frannie heard her words burst out in a rush. What torture for an actress not to be able to control her speech!

"You've got to help Jeffie get his arm back . . ." Frannie blurted and gushed. ". . . it's broken, no, I mean, but if it if you did it only you can undo Jeffie's arm is . . ." and she felt as though her breasts were swelling, "who is so small boy so scared of you that if it was an accident okay but anyway," Jesus, "you can adjust make adjustments," Jesus, she thought, staring at the soft white pleated pouch between Stone's legs, "and we want you to fix it and start again and do again," and her head began to spin, and she needed oxygen, and her breasts were about to explode.

Frannie forced herself to turn away from Stone, the pulsating white pouch still alive in her eyes like a glowing white flame, and she ran as fast as she could, out the door, away from the flame, down the steps, back to her boys.

"Six-six-six," Stone groaned.

·

"Well what happened?" Frankie asked.

"I don't know. Nothing. I didn't really talk to him."

"You know, I was thinking," Frankie said excitedly, "that maybe Stone *can* do something about Jeffie's arm. It's not really science, so I don't know exactly how it works, but sometimes a chiropractor makes an adjustment on one part of the body in order to fix a completely different part of the body. There are chiropractors who will twist your neck in order to correct a problem in your toe. So while the principles of commutation pertain, the principles of chiropractic prevail. Isn't that what you wanted to hear?"

"Are you all right, Frannie?" I asked.

"Jesus," she said.

IV

Sammy ran full speed into Frannie's leg and grabbed on to it, partly to stop himself and partly to hold Frannie right there until the others arrived. The others came rushing up to us as fast as a group could, especially one that was holding close together for the sake of some special, fragile object at its center. The boys were all screaming at once so that their news was tantalizingly garbled. Homer, who was carrying the center of attention in his hands, had to pull his shoulders to the right or left or hunch them forward in order to keep whatever he was holding out of the excited reach of one and then another and another and another boy. The object was a small bird.

"Look what we found, Miss Frannie!" yelled Sammy.

"It's a baby bird!" cried Harry Jr.

"Who says it's a baby?"

"We found it on the ground."

"An animal could eat it up if we didn't save it."

"It is too a baby!"

"We're going to give it food."

"We have to find a box for it."

Each excited shout colored in more of the group's adventure. It also revealed each personality. One boy wanted Frannie to see. Another boy wanted to feed the bird. A third wanted to name it before doing anything else. Only Stoney was quiet.

"What kind is it?" Homer wanted to know.

It fell to Frankie, who was quickly on the scene, to make certain explanations, pronouncements, and decisions concerning the bird. It was not only his credentials that qualified Frankie, but the practical benefits of his education. By learning why and what, Frankie had come to know how and when and where. The practical application of all that he knew was truly remarkable, touching, it seemed, on everything that had a biological, chemical, physical, mathematical, or mechanical explanation. And what on earth didn't?

After carefully examining the bird, Frankie said to the group, "This is really odd. He's a skylark. What's a skylark doing such a long, long way from home? Well, unless we can mend his wing, he's never going to get back."

"A skylark?" Harry Jr. asked, betraying the fact that his familiarity with birds was limited to the American eagle, the Thanksgiving Day turkey, Donald Duck, and the pigeons of Central Park.

"Let's call him Seth!" said Ezra, whose brother was named Seth.

"How about Shelley?" Frannie said. "And I'll tell you why. There was a famous poet who wrote a very famous poem about a skylark," Frannie explained. "And that poet's name was Shelley. Percy Bysshe Shelley," she said carefully.

"But what's a skylark?" Harry Jr. persisted.

"A skylark," Frankie explained, "is a small bird, as you can see, usually about six inches in length, with a thin bill and these tiny streaks up and down his breast." Frankie pointed to each feature as he described it, indicating the streaks, and then the head markings, the medium-size tail feathers, the pinkish legs, the puffy body. Then he talked for a minute or two about the skylark's habit of walking along the ground looking for bugs and tiny seeds, almost never perching in trees or on bushes, and singing its sweet, long liquidy song only when soaring through the sky.

"What is amazing is how far this little bird has flown," Frankie said matter-of-factly. "Who knows his geography? Who knows where Canada is?" Ezra wanted to answer but didn't want to show off in front of the younger members of the group. Homer said Canada was in Europe somewhere. "Well, it's north of our own country, right above us on the map," Frankie said. "And it's divided into different areas called provinces. And one of the provinces that's farthest away from us, all the way across America and then up north into Canada, is a province called British Columbia, and that's where most skylarks in this part of the world live. On an island called Vancouver, in a province called

British Columbia, in a country called Canada. If that sounds far away, it is. This bird probably flew thousands of miles to get here. And look what he got for his trouble. Probably a racoon or something swatted him and caught his wing."

"Then why didn't the racoon eat him?" Homer asked. The question surprised Frankie, who was fixing up the box Homer had found in the kitchen. Frankie was filling it with scraps of paper, pine needles, and whatever other nest materials he could find. "Well, maybe that's not how it happened," he admitted.

"Or maybe Shelley could still fly to safety after the racoon got him but then later his wing got worse and worse," Ezra hypothesized.

"Maybe," Frankie conceded. He placed the bird carefully into the corner of the box where he had piled the shreds of paper and feathery pine needles. "I don't know if he's going to make it. We'll give him some bread crumbs and a little water," he said, holding out hope. "But that won't fix his wing," he concluded, allowing hope to fly away without the skylark.

Everyone was eager to help the poor bird so Frankie gave each boy a task. Homer had gotten the box. Sammy was to get a slice of bread. Ezra was to crumble the bread and put it in the box. Harry Jr. was to bring water from the stream.

"Stoney, why don't you keep watch?" Frannie suggested.

For the first hour the bird moved only when it trembled or tried to nestle deeper into the pile of shredded paper. A few inches away lay the untouched bread and water. Sometimes the bird looked as if it were falling asleep. Its eyes would close halfway and its puffed-up body would begin to tremble less frequently but more violently, the way a human being's whole body flinches when he feels himself falling during the first shallow stages of sleep.

"Why won't he eat something?"

"When's he going to move?"

"Maybe it's dead."

Then the most unlikely thing happened. There was a short whistling sound, and the boys scrambled around the cardboard box to see what the bird was going to do.

"Shhh," Frankie hushed everyone. Again the bird made a

143

sound. This time it had a definite lilt. It was not a death rattle as Frankie had feared. It was a note. A pure, sweet, modulated note.

The boys all stared directly at the bird's beak, waiting for another note, or for two and three notes to be whistled consecutively to make a little melody.

Once more the creature sang a shortened earthly version of its aerial song. And once more the group dared not breathe. Perhaps the beautiful notes were an overture, perhaps the crippled bird was about to eat, or drink, or — wonder of all wonders — to fly again.

But the bird never moved. As its song got stronger, its body seemed to grow weaker. And as the song the bird sang in the box became more like the one it usually sang in the sky, the boys grew tired and edgy. They were annoyed. They wanted a different sort of miracle. Homer stood up and pretended that his kicking the box as he walked away had been an accident. Harry Jr. said, "This bird is a cuckoo," and followed Homer back to their cabin. Ezra and Sammy had already begun to improvise a game involving handfuls of dirt and the flicking of pebbles with trusty forefinger, for they, too, had given up on the pathetic little bird. Stoney, however, sat quietly and patiently, staring at the bird's vibrating craw. Frankie sat patiently, too, moving the lid filled with water a little closer to the bird but scaring it with his big hand. And Frannie continued to be enraptured by the little Piaf her boys had brought her. As for me, I had rather bad news for Frankie.

"It's not a skylark, Frankie." I had waited for the boys to leave before correcting Frankie so as not to embarrass him.

"What do you mean?" He blushed.

"It's an honest mistake, Frankie. It looks an awful lot like a skylark. But it's a song sparrow," I said confidently, for Sister Victoria was a genius on the subject of birds, and I had picked up more from the hours I had spent on her porch than I could have ever learned from all the books Frankie had read.

"Are you sure?" Frankie asked. But he knew I was.

·

The sparrow's aerial song grew louder and louder, attracting Geoff Thomason.

"Why is it so happy?" Thomason asked. It was the question everyone had been asking. "Its wing is broken. It's crippled. There's no way that bird is ever going to fly again."

"Does it matter?" Frannie asked.

"The essence of a bird is flight," Thomason answered. "If you were to ask a hundred people, a thousand, a hundred thousand, they would all say the same thing: a bird is an animal that flies. That is what differentiates it from other animals. Without its wings a bird might as well not exist."

Thomason's voice was often so soft I had to strain to hear what he was saying, and his appearance was anything but compelling. But what he said was so convincing, so well thought out and phrased, so clearly heading in a direction you always secretly wanted to take that you had to go along with him right up to the dead end.

"This poor creature is crying for its lost soul," he told Frannie.

"Our sweetest songs are those that tell of saddest thought," she said, quoting Shelley's ode.

"Why don't you put the damned thing out of its misery?"

·

We decided to move the box inside the cabin where Jeffie was sleeping to keep the bird safe from predators and from anyone who might want to "put the damned thing out of its misery." I was making a feeble joke about the cabin's being an infirmary because of Jeffie's hurt arm and the sparrow's hurt wing when Stone threw open the door. He was dressed in a white shirt, white pants, and white shoes, but Frannie still saw him in his athletic supporter, the white straps and pouch evoking the flimsy costumes of ancient gods and heroes.

Stone walked to the box and reached in. He picked up the bird with his enormous hand and the long, sweet, liquidy song stopped. With his other hand he spread the injured wing, his fingers probing the delicate architecture of the wing, his thumb pressing against the sparrow's wildly beating heart.

145

"How is he?" Stone asked.

"His arm is paralyzed," Frannie said.

Stone pushed his forefinger under the bird's feathers where the wing joined the body. "Sometimes you have to suffer in order to become healthy again," he said, his attention focused on the silent sparrow in his hand. "Sometimes the adjustment is painful." His hand tightened around the body of the bird. "But it's the end result that counts." He twisted and pulled the injured wing with a quick motion. The sparrow screeched and tried to fly away. "Here," he said to Frannie, holding out the sparrow. And she took it.

·

Later that afternoon the bird was dead. Not peacefully deceased in its box, but with its feathers broken and plucked, its breast looking as if it had been crushed, its neck crudely sawed apart so that the head was connected by the slimmest threads of flesh.

I was the one who found the horribly mutilated sparrow. I had come from the kitchen looking for boys to help me prepare dinner when I saw Stoney sitting with his back to me. His right arm was moving rhythmically; his elbow moved back and forth and his arm was bent in such a way that I knew he was doing something on his lap. I dismissed my first thought because of his age. It had been a long time, but I didn't remember boys that young doing to themselves what it looked like Stoney was doing. And yet I couldn't dismiss the idea completely because of the strong feeling I had that I was intruding. Like a parent, I felt compelled to see what Stoney was up to but repelled by the prospect of what it might be.

Maybe I should have called out his name or cleared my throat to give him a chance to stop or change or disguise what he was doing, but I found myself taking especially quiet steps and holding my breath and taking all sorts of ridiculously subtle precautions so that I might surprise Stoney. He never heard me, or he pretended not to, and as I got closer and closer and saw more and more of his still rhythmically moving right arm and elbow, and then his forearm, and then his wrist, and then a finger of a fist, and another, and another — and then I saw what he had clenched inside his tiny fist, the horrible sight of it stopped me dead in my tracks. With a thin but not very sharp edge of a rock, Stoney was sawing the sparrow's head off at the neck.

I thought he might be having one of his fits and that I had better not disturb him until I was sure of what his reaction might be, the damage to the sparrow already having been done.

I walked around in front of him and squatted, trying to avert my eyes from the slaughter taking place on his lap. But wherever I looked I saw the bird's head dangling by strands of flesh and cartilage.

Stoney's face showed a disturbingly innocent intensity: eyes trained on his lap; knitted brow; tiny tip of the tongue running back and forth over tightened lips. It might have been the adorably preoccupied face of Tom Sawyer as he concentrated on running a sharp fishhook through a wriggling worm. The contrast between the cuteness on his face and the foul deed in his lap offended me. Finally I could not stand my silence and Stoney's indifference another moment.

"What are you doing?" I asked him, keeping my voice under control.

He stopped the sawing and looked up at me. "I'm see-see-seeing w-what hmmmakes him s-s-s-sing," Stoney said.

I had no answer. Stoney had nothing more to say. But I could tell from his statement that he was not having a seizure and so I stopped thinking I had to proceed with caution.

"Do you think it's fair, Stoney?" I asked, my voice rising slightly. "How do you think the other boys are going to feel when they find out that you killed the bird they were trying to nurse back to health?"

"I di-di-di-didn't," he said. This time he didn't look up at me.

" What do you mean?"

"I di-di-di-didn't k-k-kill it."

"Who killed it?"

He tried to tell me what had happened, but his stutter was so uncontrollable he could hardly get a word out. To help, I tried guessing the name of whoever might have killed the bird so that all Stoney had to do was shake his head yes or no.

"Did Stone do it?" I asked.

147

He shook his head no.

"Did Geoff Thomason do it?"

"Why don't you ask me," Geoff Thomason said. He had sneaked up and surprised me from behind.

·

There was a trial. Geoff Thomason was behind it and the boys were with him all the way. It took place that night, right after dinner, while everyone was assembled. Stone liked the idea and appointed himself judge and jury. Homer, Ezra, Sammy, and Harry Jr. sat at what Geoff Thomason called the plaintiff's table, for it was their bird that had been slaughtered and it was on their behalf that Thomason prosecuted Stoney.

Thomason's case was simple and persuasive: Stoney had found the bird on the ground, picked it up, and sawed off its head. Thomason explained how the bird had escaped the cabin and got almost fifty yards away to the base of the big oak where I had found Stoney and where Thomason had found the two of us. He described the desperate fluttering of the one good wing as the poor bird battled the shallow sides of the cardboard box and then as it managed to clear the sides but could not find the strength or rhythm to lift the helpless dead weight of its body off the ground, propelling itself instead for several painful and exhausting yards through the dirt and mud and brush until it could not move one more inch. The bird lay there, a victim of its own courage, until Stoney came along and murdered it.

"Isn't that right?" Thomason asked Stoney. But Stoney couldn't answer. He shook his head, but he could not say the word *no*.

"You killed that bird, didn't you?" Thomason insisted.

I remembered Stoney's chaotic reaction to pressure on the first morning of camp and expected to see it again. But I never had the chance. Stone walked behind Stoney and put his huge hands on the little boy's shoulders, applying a different kind of pressure.

"I don't think there's any question," Stone said. "The boy is guilty."

"I object," I wanted to cry out. But what good would it have done? Everyone agreed with Stone. I had expected the boys to

respond to the prospect of a six-week ordeal at Camp Freedom
by reverting to primitive, instinctive, even savage behavior. But
instead they became civilized. In only two days they had grown
up into a society of law-abiding citizens, a society held together
by the centripetal force of their fear. Frankie and Frannie belonged to that society, too. They had decided to stay at Camp
Freedom. They had decided to adjust. And that meant observing
the law of the land.

"I don't want to punish this boy," Stone said. "I want to heal
this boy so he will be strong enough to fight off his evil impulses.
We are all good by nature. We are all born true and good. But
something twists us. Something gets hold of us and makes us
weak." Stone raised his hands in front of his face and looked at
them as if they had just performed a miracle. "If he was good,
he can be good again," said the judge and jury and king and
chiropractor. "These hands will bring him back to the ideal
state of mental and physical health that is his birthright."

Stone raised Stoney to his feet and marched him toward the
cabin and the black leather and gleaming chrome inside. When
the door closed behind them, I closed a door on Camp Freedom.

NINE

The other counselors arrived almost two full days late. They should have arrived in two cars but rough riding destroyed one, and the reveling teenagers left it right where it died, the back seat littered with crushed beer cans and empty pints of vodka.

Thomason had put all the counselors in touch with one another in case they wanted to work out a plan for getting to Camp Freedom. Although it would have been easier for each counselor to map and follow his or her own most expedient route, the four Pennsylvanians and three New Jerseyans didn't mind the inconvenience of a mutual plan. It wouldn't have been too much to ask them to stop in the Sahara desert on their way to the North Pole. They were all young and eager and filled with the boundless energy of those who are on their own for the first time. None of them had been away from home before except in a strictly supervised situation. They all had been campers but never counselors. Two had spent a year in college, but their schools were so close to home that they hadn't had to move out on their own.

It was agreed that two cars were needed, one for each state, and that they would meet at a prescribed Howard Johnson's restaurant just off a certain exit on the New Jersey Turnpike. Then the two-car convoy would proceed directly to Camp Freedom.

But a few too many stops were made along the way, one to pick up beer, which led to another for more beer, and then to harder drink, and then to an all-night party at an all-night bar. By morning the counselors were too weary and too drunk to drive, so they decided to spend a few hours exploring the small antique of a town in which they found themselves. Still giddy from too much drink, too little food, and nonstop dancing, they bought cheap straw hats at a five-and-dime and paraded up the sleepy main street, provoking a fat, middle-aged policeman to ask for their identification. The hats, however, became badges of justified impropriety. "So what!" said the jauntily cocked hats when the policeman accused the group of being rowdy.

They were not bad youngsters, but somehow they got it into their heads to run from the fat policeman who did not have a horse or a car or a walkie-talkie. He did have a gun, which he purposely fired several feet over the counselors' floppy straw hats, giving the episode far greater importance than it ever should have had. The counselors ducked and fled, strategizing on the run.

"Circle around and meet us back at Faye's!" shouted one of the two drivers, and the others agreed to meet back at the all-night bar. To confuse the policeman, the Pennsylvanians ran one way and the New Jerseyans ran another. Then they circled back behind him. Once at Faye's, the two groups hurried into their respective cars and sped away, the policeman leaning forward, squinting, and jotting down one of the license plates.

I learned all this from Thomason who was with Stone when the director called the counselors on the carpet minutes after they came careening onto the campsite, all seven of them stuffed into one car, hanging out of open windows, singing at the top of their lungs, the driver blinded by his floppy straw hat each time it was hit accidentally from behind and pushed down over his eyes.

En route to the camp, the counselors stopped to congratulate each other on their cunning in evading the police.

"It's just too bad he got your license number," said the driver of the Pennsylvania car.

"What do you mean my license? He got yours. He was looking right at your car," said the driver of the New Jersey car. And the doubt that was raised caused everyone to panic.

They decided to change their plan and take a misleading route to Camp Freedom, to follow the byways instead of the highways, thereby throwing the police off their tricky trail. But the byways proved to be too difficult for the New Jersey car, and on a pitted, potholed stretch of no man's land the lumbering old Pontiac gave one last roar and then bucked and ground to an untimely demise.

"What else could we do but leave it there?" the driver of the New Jersey car explained to Stone.

So they all piled into the other car and pulled in at the very next beer stop to soothe their nagging headaches and come up with yet another plan.

This time they debated the merits of continuing on to Camp Freedom. Someone suggested that if the police were in fact after them, they might do better as a moving target than as a stationary one at Camp Freedom; but a wiser voice argued that they had no place else to go and sooner or later they would have to stop running anyway, so why not sooner, which would probably make the authorities go easier on them. Everyone saw the good sense of the latter argument. Over one more round they agreed to accept full responsibility for whatever laws or ordinances they may have broken, providing, of course, that the police caught up with them. If not, then so what. And that, too, called for a beer.

They were so pleased to be contrite and practical that they had a second and then a third round of beers and Bloody Marys; by the time they were done, when late afternoon came streaming through the westerly windows of the Kitty Kat Klub, they felt penitent and clever and, as they stumbled into the car, indestructible.

It was in that self-righteous and drunken condition that the counselors arrived at Camp Freedom. Their car nearly ran down a group of boys before skidding to a halt.

The seven tried to get out all at once, but they bumped into each other and fell back into their seats. Once again they tried to get out. Once again they bumped hats and heads. If the counselors hadn't looked so unkempt and sounded so obnoxious, the scene might have been as funny as a Volkswagen full of clowns. But the campers were too startled to laugh, and Stone was too furious.

When the counselors finally got out, leaving the four doors wide open and the headlights on, Stone marched them into his cabin, signaling for Thomason to join them. Stone asked the counselors where they had been and what they meant by their reckless and late arrival. The seven young men and women believed they were stone sober. The loud, boisterous, indignant blather that passed for an explanation of their whereabouts and general condition sounded as reasonable to them as the Declaration of Independence. They felt they had nothing to fear and everything to gain by telling their entire story. Every detail was another rivet in the ironclad case the counselors believed they were building to justify their tardy arrival: the revealing cut of Faye's dress; the hair on the mole on the chin of the hick who sold them their straw hats at the five-and-dime; the mailbox one of them threw up into; the swig of vodka they gave a disbelieving bum who happened to have been crossing a street where the old Pontiac was waiting for the light to change; the high-pitched anger of a bunch of hillbilly midgets whose hootenanny the Pontiac busted up; inane details such as these the agitated counselors deemed crucial to their account, and Stone and Thomason were bombarded with dozens of besotted references to irrelevant people, places, and things.

"Shut up! All of you!" Thomason quoted Stone as having shouted at the sloppy-mouthed, floppy-hatted counselors. They shut up at once.

"Do you know what you've done?" Stone asked calmly. The counselors' mood changed. The drunkenness they never would have admitted to was like the sea, buoying them one minute, swallowing them the next, and they surrendered themselves to swell or suction without a struggle.

"You have endangered the lives of little children," Stone finished.

Something like "Mnmrm," said a spokesman for the counselors, bowing his head so low that all Stone could see was the top of his floppy hat where a bright green price ticket was still pasted.

And then Stone exploded. "It was the only time I have ever seen him fly off the handle like that," Thomason told me afterward. "Normally he keeps the lid on, but not this time. You should know him by now, Gus. You know he never rants and raves. That voice of his makes him sound as if he's going to bite your head off anyway, he doesn't have to raise it."

"You have endangered children's lives," Stone stormed on the counselors' drunken sea. "You have dishonored a man who trusted you so much he gave you the most responsible jobs of your lives. You have involved the police — Jesus Christ, the police! I can't believe it! And you have insulted my intelligence by daring to stand here in front of me offering the stupidest excuses for your disgusting behavior anyone ever heard. You look bad, you smell bad, you sound stupid, and you can barely stand on your own feet. You demolished a car, alienated a whole town, involved the police, for Christ's sake, and you come tear-assing down into my camp — my camp, you sonofabitches — and you practically run over my campers, and now you have the nerve to stand here crying in your beer about how sorry and misunderstood and wonderful you all are!"

Thomason knew his voice could never capture the fire and brimstone of Stone's condemnation, but he did wave his arms during the retelling and, with his own much less vigorous voice, he shouted loudly and squeezed all forgiveness out of every one of Stone's words.

What happened next I myself witnessed. Stone herded the seven counselors outside. Two of the young men fell backward into a puddle, reminding me of my own terrifying first encounter with Stone.

"First," Stone said with an evil grin, "I will assign you to your cabins," which he did in a calmer voice.

The grin still on his face, Stone then picked out the biggest, strongest-looking counselor and grabbed him gently but firmly by the forearm. According to Thomason, it was no accident that the counselor Stone picked out also happened to have been the

most vocal when the seven were making their drunken explanations and excuses just a few minutes earlier.

"And now," Stone said, "let's see if I can sober you bastards
up."

Stone led the counselor through the crowd to the most feared
cabin. The two of them disappeared inside. For all we knew,
Stoney was still inside the cabin. He had never come out after
Stone took him there to "rehabilitate" him. That had been only
an hour earlier, right after Stoney's trial. We wanted to believe
that Stoney was resting inside the cabin after his ordeal. Now
someone else was being brought in for rehabilitation, and I
wondered whether the bodies were going to start piling up. It
was a black thought, and I didn't want to consider its implica-
tions, but I did wonder.

The vocal reactions of Stoney and the counselor to their adjustments dramatically illustrated the difference between man
and boy. Stoney's first scream had been a wretched, ringing, agonizing shriek that had never really stopped. It had turned into a
wail and then a bawl and then a yowl and then a screech, but
all without a break or breath of air, and the amazing persever-
ance of this running expression of his pain had left us breathing twice as hard for poor Stoney, panting for him, doing what
we miserable, unharmed witnesses could to ease his pain from
afar. But the sounds that came from the cabin when the counselor was being worked on were completely different.

There was not the steady wailing of a Stoney. There were
spaces. Between each manipulation of the counselor's body, there
was silence, which told me three things. It told me how many
adjustments the chiropractor made; it told me that there was
no echo of pain, that each torturous adjustment hurt only during the actual laying on of hands; and it told me that the counselor was trying to be brave.

In all, I counted seven screams. During the silence that followed the first and second, I thought the counselor had passed
out. But after the third silence, I learned how to interpret what
I heard. And even though the five middle screams seemed to
indicate less painful manipulations, there was a crescendo of

agony leading to the counselor's last, long, grisly, gurgling howl after which we all knew the silence would be lasting.

He was not dead. The bodies did not begin to pile up. The counselor walked out of the cabin on his own renewed power, Stone keeping several feet behind him so as not to steal the limelight from the star of his own show. As the counselor walked down the steps and through the crowd, looking like a new man, the campers gasped as if they had seen Frankenstein's monster.

The counselor's friends were too muddle-headed to fathom what had happened. When Stone had led the counselor into the cabin, they had no way of knowing what to expect. When the counselor came outside none of his friends knew whether to feel relief, anger, or pity. They waited to hear what the counselor might say.

"He's a fucking crazy asshole," he said. "We've got to get our asses the hell out of here."

II

The imposition of good is still an imposition. That was implicit in what Stone had done to the counselor and what the counselor chose to do in return. When everyone was sure the chiropractor would tie the counselor into a tight, wet knot, Stone did just the opposite. He applied all his skills to the counselor's alcohol-poisoned nervous system and — though the adjustments were painful — he succeeded in revitalizing the counselor's mind and body. Then, when everyone expected the counselor to be grateful, he was outraged.

From the moment he left the most feared cabin and whispered the epithet that became a famous joke among those of us who remained at Camp Freedom — "He's a fucking crazy asshole!" — the counselor spent all of his time arguing, plotting, and trying to recruit others to join him in his escape from Freedom to freedom. The counselor pressured everyone, his friends, the campers, Frankie, Frannie, even me.

"I'm an old man, leave me out of it."

"This fucking crazy asshole is going to kill you — all of you — I don't care if you're ten or a hundred and ten!" he shouted at me, angry that I didn't share his desperate analysis of the situation, and angrier still that I didn't seem to care about my own safety as much as he cared about it. He was someone who thrived on philanthropy.

"I gotta help get these people out of here! If you don't want to come with us, will you at least help us?"

I later found out that he had asked the same of Frankie and Frannie and three of his own friends who had decided that there was no reason to leave and even less reason to call leaving an escape.

"What would I have to do?" I asked, careful to keep my tone noncommital.

"Create a diversion, that's all. When we decide on a time, I'll let you know, and then you can do something to draw attention away from us. It'll be easy for you. You can have a small fire in the kitchen, a pot can boil over, the stove can throw a spark, a bottle of soda can explode."

"I don't know. I don't think so," I said.

"Jesus fucking Christ!" the counselor said in disbelief. "You really don't think anything's wrong here, do you?" He laughed. It was a mocking laugh directed at all of humanity's complacency rather than at me alone. What he did not know, of course — what no one at Camp Freedom knew and some may have only half suspected — was that each of us would have to make his own escape.

That night I reflected on my decision not to join or help the counselor. Although I had not volunteered to be Camp Freedom's cook, I recognized that my services, no matter how meager, were desperately needed. That was why I would not make an escape along with the counselor. I could not abandon the little boys who depended on me for their meals. I could not leave behind the semblance of order I had created out of the chaos of supplies that had greeted me in the kitchen and expect anyone else to take over in my absence. "Do you understand?" I thought, intending the question for the counselor, but surprising myself by asking it aloud, to no one at all, to the darkness.

Out of the darkness came the familiar form of a grinning monster whose eyes never closed. It was the face of the car the drunken counselors had arrived in, and, though someone had switched off its yellow eyes, the sight of the car illuminated another thought: the counselor had a getaway car. He did not have to rely on speed of foot, stamina, guile; he had only to leap behind the wheel of his getaway car and zoom away. But then who was to be left behind? The counselor would have jammed as many as possible into the back, the front, onto the floor, into the trunk if need be, strapped to the roof and hood like slain deer if time allowed, and he would have been satisfied that he had done all he could. But I could not be satisfied knowing so many would still be left behind. Who would decide who stayed or escaped?

I could not go to sleep. For two hours I walked and walked, skirting the sodden banks of the stream, brushing the leafy edge of the forest, circling and threading the cabins and scattered gear of the compound. There were bats and balls, a volley ball net, wooden stakes and rubber horseshoes, folding chairs, a table, several black plastic bags of garbage. There were also objects I could not identify in the darkness.

I knew that others were awake, too. Until it was quite late, I could hear Frannie whispering to her kids. The continuous, one-sided whispering led me to believe she was telling the boys a story. And then another one. And another. Until finally the light of sleep glowed brighter than the light of imagination and made the night safe to enter.

The whispering in the counselor's cabin was much different. It was two-sided and heated, until, like heated butter, the whispering began to crackle. Three of his own friends would not cooperate. The four who wanted to escape were alone in their desperation. And they were afraid. And I understood perfectly what they were afraid of.

Stone. He was up. No one could see him, but everyone felt his presence. His all-seeing eyes were hidden in the leaves of the trees, in the brush, in the clods of earth. His image was everywhere: there, behind the wheel of the counselor's car! No, there, by the oak where I had found Stoney decapitating the sparrow. There in the kitchen! At a window! On the footbridge spanning the stream! Behind me! In front! In that cabin! That one! In his own cabin, his face pressed to the filmy window, his eyes wide open, unwilling to close until no one was left awake.

We all believed that Stone was the last to go to sleep. That was why the counselor dared not steal into his car in the dead of night and speed out of the compound as fast as the dirt road allowed. The counselor dared not try it because he felt that he was being watched by Stone and that retaliation would be swift and fatal. We all felt that way to a degree, although most of us did not have anything quite as specific as an escape in mind. We convinced ourselves that the feeling we had of Stone's constant surveillance was a kind of watchfulness instead, and we took comfort from this irrational notion that we were being guarded and protected from outside danger.

III

In the morning the counselor was the first one up, and he woke five others, leading them to the kitchen. I, too, was awakened and invited to be part of the counselor's assemblage.

"Did you sleep well?" the counselor asked sarcastically of me, Frankie, Frannie, a counselor named Michael Estabrook, and the two young women counselors. We were the ones who had refused to join him and the other three counselors in an escape.

"Well?" the counselor asked, the word sounding like the tapping of a foot.

"What do you want from us?" Frannie said through a false yawn, although it had started out as a real yawn before evaporating in midbreath. Rather than give it up, Frannie carried the yawn through to a transparent conclusion, but her point was made all the more convincingly by her unconvincing yawn; she wanted the counselor to know that he was boring them with his constant complaints and annoying attempts to enlist their help in his desperate dream of escape.

"How can you all just stand around like you were still sleeping? Don't you care that you've just spent the night in a filthy pigsty? Don't you care that these poor little kids haven't got a decent place to sleep or wash or go to the fuckin' toilet?"

"We straightened up our bunk the first day," Frankie said, putting forth his words as tentatively as a peace offering. "We swept the floor and fixed up bedrolls and sleeping bags and . . ."

"Shut up, Francis," Frannie said. "He doesn't want to hear about what we did or what he might have to do in order to survive in a place like this and even make things a little comfortable for us and the kids too until we all get used to the situation and into a routine . . ."

"Or into a hospital with snake bite or dysentery or a goddamned broken back from that fuckin' crazy asshole out there and his goddamned torture chamber." The counselor interrupted Frannie as rudely as she had interrupted Frankie. "Have any of you seen what he's got in there? Did you see that fuckin' table?" he asked Frannie, using the fact that he had been on Stone's chiropractic table to discredit everything Frannie had said or might say. "Well, I have! I was *on* that goddamned table. You know what happens? The fuckin' middle drops out and your stomach and your back are just hanging there over nothing and that fuckin' crazy asshole hits down on you so hard that it feels like your goddamned spine just caved in and you can't even breathe because all the wind's knocked out of you and you swear you can hear your bones cracking and your muscles ripping, and that's okay with you, huh? And you, too? All of you?" The counselor tried to slap sense into everyone with his slashing tirade.

"Listen," he continued, suddenly trying to calm himself. "It's not going to help to get upset. There's no point in shouting."

"There's no point because you're full of shit," Estabrook said. He was a well-built young man who was always more aware of the presence of women than of men in a room. Even while he challenged the counselor with whom he had been co-leader of last night's drunken revels, Michael Estabrook was shooting little glances at the three women to see how they were responding to him.

"Do you remember what you were like when Stone took you into his cabin last night?" Estabrook asked, flexing a muscle or two for Frannie, his froggy voice as contritely sober as a reformed drunk's. "You could barely stand up. None of us could. We were dead drunk last night, soaked through, all of us. And you and me, we were the worst."

The counselor resented being coupled in any way with his antagonist. "Bullshit, Mike," the counselor said, dismissing Estabrook with a flippant wave of his hand.

"No, don't shut me up, I'm going to finish. You and me were really polluted last night. Really hopeless. And then this Stone took you inside and he threw you around a little or whatever he did to you in there and when you came out you were okay. I mean you were not just sober, you were in good shape. Whatever he did in there that you call a torture chamber, it was pretty fuckin' good I think. I think you came out a lot better than you went in. And now this morning I feel like shit and you're prancing around okay all because of the same guy you keep calling a fuckin' crazy asshole. Maybe you're the fuckin' crazy asshole."

He stood there defiantly. He knew he was stronger than the counselor, but not smarter, and he basked in the glory of his verbal victory. The revolutionary sensed that he had lost his edge, and, rather than make a last stand, he turned on his heels and left the kitchen. When Estabrook looked to see if the three women were stealing glances at him, he found them staring at the door the counselor had just slammed.

IV

All day the four counselors who agreed that Camp Freedom was a "goddamned hellhole" run by a "crazy fuckin' maniac" worried about imminent disaster and planned their escape. Whenever they could do so without being seen or without appearing conspiratorial, they stood off by themselves and whispered worried fragments of thoughts, eyes darting all about the compound for a surprise attack by Stone or for the "ass-kissing" Thomason to put the quartet's suspicious behavior on report. Their desperation increased as the day's events reinforced their worst fears. Almost as soon as the counselor had slammed the kitchen door on us, losing that battle but still flying the flags of his crusade, there was an uproar outside that attracted everyone. Thomason and Sammy were causing the commotion while Stone was taking his sweet time stepping in to solve the problem.

Geoff Thomason was screaming at Sammy. The screaming was so nasty and excruciating that Sammy kept covering his face and moving backward as if to avoid being physically struck by Thomason's words. In Thomason's right hand, dangling from the forefinger, was a soaking-wet sheet. Sammy's pajamas, too, were soaking wet.

"What am I going to do with you?" Thomason screamed over and over again, his voice reaching hysterical levels of exasperation, frustration, and blind anger. "Wet! Wet! Every morning wet! Are the other boys wet?!" Thomason grabbed at the nearest camper with his free hand, caught one, and pulled the shocked little boy in front of him so he could thrust the dry example at Sammy, pull him back, thrust him at Sammy again, menacing the shivering, back-pedaling bed-wetter for several yards before letting go. "Yesterday! and then I told you! And now today again! Wet! Wet!" Thomason continued to scream, sounding more and more like a parent, like a woman, like Sammy's mother. He ordered him to strip off his wet clothes, "Get them off! I said get them off!" And his scream made Sammy shake.

"What happened?" Frannie asked Homer.

"He caught Sammy carrying his sheet down to the stream. He was going to wash it out like yesterday when he got caught and Mr. Thomason started to go crazy. Remember yesterday how mad he got?"

Thomason shouted again and again, "Get them off! Get them

off!" and Sammy was so intimidated that he stripped off his clothes until he stood stark naked in front of everyone.

"Now run! Run! I said run! Around the cabins! Twenty times! Run your little ass off, you bed-wetting sonofabitch!"

Sammy's scrawny white body scooted away and began twenty laps around the compound, always within earshot of Thomason's derisive screaming.

"You're nine years old, Sammy! You're not a goddamned little baby! Nine-year-old boys don't pee in their pants! Nine-year-old boys get up and go to the bathroom if they have to pee! Or else they have to run around the camp! Run! Faster, Sammy!"

The other boys watched Thomason snap Sammy's pajama bottoms like a horse trainer's whip while his naked pony pranced around and around. Somehow Thomason had gotten them to count off the laps, and each time Sammy passed a certain large tree thirty-two voices called out as one.

"SIX!"

"SEVEN!"

"EIGHT!"

By the tenth lap Sammy could hardly breathe. He was running on adrenaline, fear, and shame. His throat was trying to close up. His heart batted against his rib cage. His breaths burned in his chest and throat and then turned to ashes in his mouth.

"SIXTEEN!"

"Run! Run, Sammy! Maybe this'll teach you. How do you like running like this in front of all your friends?!"

"SEVENTEEN!"

"There's no excuse, Sammy. No excuse! I don't care if you've got a goddamned hole in your bladder the size of my fist — there's never any excuse! You have to overcome!"

"EIGHTEEN!"

"You have to wake yourself up! Concentrate! Use your brain! When you feel it all hot and wet, it's too late! You can't wait that long. You've got to feel it before it happens, before the pee leaks out!"

"NINETEEN!"

"You've got to feel it when it's not there!" Thomason screamed, cracking the pajama-bottom whip with the thumbless fist of his right hand.

At twenty, the crowd cheered and Sammy stumbled and fell despite his determination to keep running for the rest of his life. Some of the boys picked him up and carried him to Thomason.

The crowd belonged to Thomason. Whatever he might have asked, the boys would have done, and Thomason felt a surge of this frightening power. Perhaps he should ask the boys to carry Sammy down to the edge of the woods and throw him into one of the ditches — the one for peeing. "What justice," Thomason mused. "What irony!" But as the frenzy of the crowd increased, Thomason grew uneasy, and he looked past the eager eyes and over the bobbing heads of the fanatic tribe of boys for the totem pole that was Dr. George Stone.

Stone walked through the crowd, parting the throng with each thrust of his powerful legs. The boys stopped their odd combination of cheering and chanting which had begun when Sammy passed the big tree for the twentieth time.

"You can see the problem," Thomason said to Stone. "He wets his bed. He did it yesterday, and today, and he'll do it again tomorrow unless he's made to realize how demeaning it is. How all of his peers are secretly laughing at him. How disgusting it is to sleep in your own vile waste."

"It's an inflamed nerve," Stone said. "In the lumbar region. We've been working on it. It flares up," he explained, putting a huge hand on Sammy's naked shoulder. "His mother has been bringing him to my office for regular adjustments."

"I'd sooner take my chances with the mob," the counselor whispered to his co-conspirators.

"Come on, Sammy," Stone said, rescuing the still trembling, still breathless, quietly sobbing little boy by leading him out of Thomason's crowd toward a leather-and-chrome salvation.

This stunning crystallization of Stone's purely physical approach to life's flare-ups compared with Thomason's psychological approach inspired the first of those late-night kitchen conversations between Thomason and myself. It also reinforced the conspirators' resolve, for there was no way poor Sammy could have won; if Thomason didn't break his spirit, Stone would break his back. And if that hadn't been enough to spur on the conspirators, Homer provided the motivation at lunchtime.

Once again Homer was not able to eat his meal. This was the third in a row that he could not keep down. As usual, he took one or two obligatory bites, started to sputter, gagged, and then threw up the few forkfuls in a pink puddle of mucous and blood. Except for this violent reaction to anything he tried to eat — eggs, cheese, salmon, peanut butter, soup — Homer seemed fine. No symptoms other than weakness and easy fatigue plagued him and they were the result of his not eating.

It was Frannie who had brought Homer's condition to my attention. She thought I might cook him something special, a blander, more digestible meal. But Homer threw up spoonfuls of cream of wheat, soft-boiled egg, and tea with powdered milk.

"Should we ask Stone?" Frannie wondered.

"You ain't getting *me* on that table!" Homer swore, and he ran out of the kitchen.

At lunch, the counselor happened to be seated at Homer's table. He witnessed what had become a matter of course for Frannie and me. Homer nibbled at his sandwich, sputtered like a cold engine, and then threw up more than he had taken in. Frannie wiped the boy's mouth, pushed his ruined plate away, said, "We'll try again later," roughed Homer's hair affectionately, and sent him from the table with a pat on the backside and the proviso that he stay in camp and not wander off on his own.

"What the hell was that all about?" the counselor asked Frannie when he judged that Homer couldn't hear.

"He threw up, that's all."

"What do you mean, that's all?"

"I mean that Homer has a problem. He can't keep any food down."

"Don't you think that that could be serious?"

"I think it's nerves."

"Nerves?"

"He's a very nervous kid."

"So he throws up all his food?"

"Look, you don't know Homer. He goes around acting like nothing bothers him. He's got a lot to prove. The other day Stone got on him for being late and I think it really upset him. Hey, grownups get ulcers, don't they? So Homer throws up. It'll pass."

But the counselor noticed that Homer threw up again an hour later, and an hour after that. Every time the counselor happened to see Homer, the boy looked paler, weaker, less and less like the energetic ringleader he still tried to be.

Miserable living conditions. Physical and mental torture. Sickness. Fear. This is what the counselor saw as he surveyed Camp Freedom. But why couldn't everyone see? Why were the others so willing to defend and rationalize and offer hope?

He went off by himself and took a walk around the edge of the woods. He climbed my bluff and settled on a ridge near my lookout. There he sat, looking down on the distant activities of the campers. Only one activity appeared typical of camp life. Michael Estabrook and Ezra were tossing a ball back and forth. Estabrook stopped, walked to Ezra, and showed him something — the correct way to throw a curve ball perhaps — and then walked back. Ezra was wearing a baseball glove, Estabrook was not, but there was more of a sting in Ezra's gloved hand when Estabrook threw the ball to him than there was in the well-built counselor's bare hand when Ezra returned the throw.

Estabrook began mixing up his throws. Some were grounders to Ezra's left or right, others were little looping tosses, still others were high fly balls Ezra had to shade his eyes to catch. The counselor could see Ezra's confidence grow each time he successfully fielded one of Estabrook's throws.

"Maybe I should stick it out a few more days," the counselor dared to think, "maybe I should give it a chance. I'm as tough as Estabrook. As any of them." He started down the bluff.

One of the looping tosses was just out of Ezra's fully extended reach. The ball bounced behind him, struck a stone, and shot off into the woods. Ezra followed the ball into a stand of white pines. With his gloved hand he pushed aside the needles.

Halfway down the bluff, the counselor noticed that a small but concerned crowd was gathering at the edge of the wood where just a few moments ago Ezra had chased Estabrook's errant throw. Estabrook was searching the stand of pines and calling Ezra's name. Apparently the boy had never come out of the woods. At most, only a few minutes could have passed. When Ezra took off after the ball, Estabrook took the opportunity to run to the stream for a few gulps of cold water. While he was there, Ezra disappeared. The boy was nowhere to be found. Estabrook's shouts went unanswered. Whoever poked his nose into this or that opening in the woods found nothing. Not a trace. Not a clue.

Stone put Thomason in charge of a search party. Thomason hooked his camera bag over one shoulder and took Estabrook, Frankie, and the counselor and his co-conspirators on a photographic safari until it grew too dark to take pictures or look for Ezra. The party was gone for several hours and had no luck at all. Even Frankie was stumped. Never had he felt so helpless. Science failed him. The deeper into the woods Thomason led him, the more he felt like one of his own stupid students, in over his head, ill-equipped to grasp the simplest concepts, bewildered by every aspect, every force, every pattern of the unfamiliar world that surrounded him. To compensate, Frankie provided a running commentary on the flora and fauna of every spore and spoor, volunteering references to alluvial deposits, aeolian activity, soil variations, Wisconsin glaciation, lithology, morphology, and assorted other geological, biological, and ecological tidbits. Some of his information would have been delicious if not for the search party's bitter mission. Frankie pointed out edible, inedible, and medicinal shoots, leaves, stalks, berries, flowers, and mushrooms. When one of the co-conspirators mistook a northern pine snake for something worse, Frankie coaxed him down from the small tree he had climbed with assurances that there were only two poisonous snakes in all of New Jersey and that any fool could see that this wasn't a rattler or a copperhead. Most disconcerting was when Frankie recited geology as though it were poetry.

"We are walking the Kirkwood Formation," he marveled. "Ten, fifteen, twenty million years ago, in the Miocene Age, that great middle of the Tertiary, giving rise to the Cohansy Sand beneath our feet," he exulted, stooping to scoop up in his hands "the pulverized gravel, silt, and clay" in which Ezra had left no footprints.

While Frankie was reciting geology, Thomason was taking photographs of everyone and everything, finding subjects and compositions where the others saw none. Barely pausing to sight, frame, focus, and adjust the f-stop, Thomason shot on the move and in spurts, sometimes cocking, triggering, recocking, and triggering again as rapidly as if he were in a shooting gallery. He used four rolls of film, thirty-six shots per role.

I realized when I watched Thomason pack his various lenses to take with him on the search that a fascinating parallel could be drawn between the photographer and the chiropractor: both in their own ways paralyzed whatever confronted them. One with his hands, the other with his camera.

They came out of the woods at different points. Frankie had inadvertently camouflaged himself with the many samples he had taken of leaves, bark, flowers, rock, soil, arrowheads, and fossils. There was something sticking out of every pocket, something tucked into his hatband, hooked onto his belt, tied to his legs and body with wiry vines. The conspirators came out of the woods naked by comparison. Though more resolved than ever to escape the torture and black magic of Camp Freedom, their defenses had been stripped away by the unyielding forest, leaving them vulnerable and thankful to be back in civilization. Estabrook came out of the woods reluctantly, constantly looking back over his shoulder. He would always be the last to give up the search for Ezra, just as Thomason would always be the first.

"What happened? Where is he?" I asked the leader of the search party.

"We didn't find a trace of him, Gus," was Thomason's automatic answer to my question. "But maybe this did," he added, indicating his Nikon as he freed the high-power lens from the camera by detaching the bayonet fitting.

"What do you mean?" I asked him.

"Maybe one of the shots will show something, a clue we missed, a stone we left unturned, some disturbance or irregularity in the total pattern that emerges when you can look at the woods with perspective, Gus."

I watched Thomason transfer the four rolls of exposed film from one bag to another.

"Perspective, Gus. That's the secret."

V

Stone officially called off the search on account of darkness, suggesting that Ezra would probably show up by himself, that boys were always wandering off, getting everyone upset, and then showing up again with the simplest of explanations. He said this partly to calm the counselors and campers and partly to persuade himself that he was neither legally nor morally responsible for Ezra's disappearance. Estabrook, however, did feel responsible, and he refused to give up the search. Convinced that Ezra must have met his mysterious fate within twenty yards of the clearing, Estabrook kept scouring the edge of the woods. "The boy wouldn't have, he couldn't have gone farther into the woods to look for that damned ball in the short amount of time it took me to run over to the stream and get a drink," he thought aloud. By talking to himself, Estabrook not only reinforced his efforts, but he kept himself company during the darker and darker night that fell like a black shroud over Ezra's absence.

It took the campers longer than usual to settle down that night. Although no one knew for certain what had happened to Ezra, each boy worried in his own way. Each boy's most frightening demon snatched Ezra away from Camp Freedom and cruelly slaughtered him. Snakes slithered in and out of his

empty eye sockets. A huge dark figure repeatedly bashed in
Ezra's skull with the limb of a dead tree, causing red-and-white
goo to spurt out of the open wounds. Leeches sucked out all
his blood. He drowned. He suffocated. He was thrown off a
high ridge and tumbled down an endless slope that was covered
with jagged rocks and broken bottles. His flesh was torn from
his bones by the snapping, growling, dripping jaws of ferocious
dogs. He was hanged, shot, knifed, run over, beheaded, set ablaze,
strangled, lashed, and eaten by bats, rats, sharks, and spiders.

The boys knew that these were only waking nightmares and
that something about them was unreal, impossible, foolish to
worry about. But they could not hide their worry.

"Miss Frannie," Sammy said pathetically, his tears glistening
even in the darkness of the cabin, "please, I don't know how . . ."
he sniffed, ". . . I can't . . . can't . . ." and the sobs came pouring
out. Burying his head in Frannie's lap to stem the tears, Sammy
tried again to ask for help. But his voice was muffled and no
one could understand a word.

"I'll wake you up," Frankie said. "I'll wake you up in the
middle of the night and catch you before you do it."

"I'm hungry," Homer said, absolutely unwilling to accept the
fact that he had not been able to keep down his last four meals.

"I'll take you to Gus," Frannie said quickly. She was as eager
to get out of the tense gloom of the cabin as she was to help
nourish Homer.

"Anybody want anything?" she asked.

Jeffie wanted an apple, peeled and cut into eight sections the
way his mother always prepared it for him.

"What should we have, Harry?" Frankie asked the little boy
who was sitting in a corner by himself. Harry had kept to himself more than the other boys in the group; Stoney's tape recorder
seemed to be all the companionship he needed. But Harry had
always been talkative, constantly chattering into the microphone,
and now he was quiet. Too quiet.

"Last call, Harry," Frannie warned, her hand on the door.

"What's the matter with Harry?" Jeffie shuddered. Sammy
stopped worrying about wetting. Homer, who had already gone

outside to wait for Frannie, came back inside the hut when he heard that something might be wrong with Harry.

"He was playing with Stoney's tape recorder," Jeffie told Frannie in the manner of a tattletale.

Frannie stooped down to look Harry in the eyes. "What is it, Harry? What's the matter?" she whispered. Behind her back she heard the boys crowding in closer. Frannie pried Harry's fingers off of Stoney's tape recorder. "Is it something you heard on here?" she asked, rewinding the tape to the beginning. A click signaled that the tape was completely rewound. Frannie pressed the play button.

"This is Harry Mix, Jr., coming to you live from Camp Freedom in New Jersey over station STA. That stands for Stoney Alcock whose tape recorder this belongs to. I mean this is his tape recorder. Stoney is still not around. We don't know exactly where he is but we think he's in Dr. Stone's cabin being punished on account of Stoney killed the baby bird we found."

"Hey, can I say somethin'?"

"Gimme that back!"

"I want to — "

"I'm talkin', ain't I? Let it alone. Andnowwehavetotakearealfast breakforbreakfastnyaaa!"

"Homer threw up again after lunch. Oh this is station STA again. Homer threw up after lunch. I said that already. Frannie told us we were going to be in *The Sound of Music* show and we could be the Trapped family."

"Hey, Harry, I'm gettin' that tape recorder next. You can't have it all the time. It ain't yours anyway."

"Stoney said I could play with it."

"Stoney ain't here, is he?"

"So what!"

"So nothing!"

"There'll be a slight change in this evening's program, ladies and gentlemen, because Harry Mix, Jr., son of world-famous disk jockey Harry Mix, Sr., doesn't feel too good. I'll be okay though. Don't worry. The show must go on."

"HOOO-HOOO-AWOOOOOO!"

"That's a wolf or something out in the woods. Ezra got lost in the woods and now they're out looking for him."

"HOOO-AWOOOOOO!"

"I don't know if that means the wolf smells him or if he found him already and he's eating him."

"AWOOOOOO!"

"I don't even know if it's a wolf."

"I want to dedicate this . . . to dedicate this next . . . this next . . ."

"Miss Frannie, please, I don't know how . . . I can't . . . can't . . ."

". . . to my mother . . . to . . . who can't be with us tonight . . . who can't . . . she can't wake up . . ."

"Smfray to we-heh muh-uh-uh-uh beh-heh."

"No one can understand you, Sammy."

"Shhh."

"What's the matter?"

"Mfray. Fray to weh muh beh."

"I'll wake you up."

"What the hell are you talking about? What the hell do you mean you'll wake him up? And stop playing with all that shit, Francis. Get that shit out of here, will you? You and your god-damned leaves and birds and — It's all right, I'm all right, Jeffie."

"I'll wake you up in the middle of the night and catch you before you do it."

"I'm hungry. Can I get something? I promise I'll eat it. I won't throw up this time."

"You can't promise a thing like that."

"I'll take you over to Gus."

"You can't promise you won't throw up. Something's the matter with your stomach. Let me hear your stomach promise you won't throw up."

"Anybody want anything? We're going."

"Could I have an apple? Could I have an apple peeled in a curl in one curl and cut up into eight pieces the way Mommy cuts it up for me? Daddy bites into the whole apple with the skin on and everything and there's blood where he bites into it because he has bad gums. He shouldn't bite into it like that my mommy says. My mommy says it's bad for his gums. She should peel it in one curl and cut it up into eight little pieces for him like she does it for me."

"What should we have, Harry? Hey, Harry?"

"What does the Frankie and Harry Show want? Last call, Harry."

"What's the matter with Harry?"

"He's just staring."

"Snap your fingers."

"He was playing with Stoney's tape recorder."

"I'm gettin' the tape recorder next."

"What is it, Harry? What's the matter? Is it something you heard on here?"

VI

The all-important diversion the counselor was still looking for arrived with a bang at one in the morning. It came as a complete surprise, although the counselor himself had been indirectly responsible.

Frannie and Frankie had finally gotten everyone including themselves to bed. Last conscious thoughts were of Ezra's mysterious disappearance, Homer's steadfast refusal to acknowledge his inability to eat, Stoney's continued absence, Jeffie's increased use of baby talk, Harry Jr.'s sudden trancelike loss of speech, and Sammy's nightlong fear of wetting his bed. Two or three times every hour he would wake himself to take a preventive leak out behind the cabins.

"Ezra! Is that you!" shouted Estabrook, pouncing upon the scene and causing Sammy to wet a pajama leg.

"It's me."

"Oh, it's you," Estabrook said, finding the boy's face with his flashlight.

"I thought you were Ezra."

"I was just g-going to the ba-bathroom," Sammy apologized.

173

"Then do it," Estabrook said, turning his flashlight toward the woods.

Estabrook was as determined as ever to be the one to find Ezra. He went over the same ground again and again.

"He went in here," Estabrook thought aloud, aiming his flashlight through the pines and crossing the threshold of the forest.

"He could have gone this way," he hypothesized, veering a few feet to the left only to find that route impassable. The underbrush was too thick and wiry to cut through, especially in the dark, although it was not dark in Estabrook's mind. It was still midafternoon, the sun shining down brilliantly on the field where he and Ezra were tossing the ball.

"The ball. He had been chasing the ball. Could it have rolled through here? Never. Too thick. Much too thick. I can hardly move my foot." Estabrook narrated his efforts, repeating almost exactly the very words and steps he had used the last time he tried going in to the left, and the time before that, and before that.

After retracing his steps, Estabrook tried the middle passage. Again he met with resistance, this time having to circumvent a huge tree firmly planted in his path. In effect, going straight in through the middle meant going left or right at the tree, and since Estabrook had already explored the left approach, he turned right. Five or six times before he had come to this same tree and the same conclusion. Each time his right turn took him to a dead end of felled trunks and crisscrossing branches. But this time Estabrook was able to take a few steps beyond the obstruction he expected. And a few steps more after that. And another few steps. And another. It was as if he had accidentally stepped on the right stone or touched the proper twig to open a secret panel in the forestal wall and then slipped through to the other side where he had a clear and seemingly endless passage into the center of the wood.

"Holy shit!" he said.

Estabrook was excited but cautious. How easy it would be for this passage to come to nothing, to lead back to the clearing, for Estabrook to follow it and never cross paths with the boy whose

disappearance he had somehow caused. But Estabrook felt that
the same forces which had thrown him and Ezra together and
then had driven the two of them apart would eventually reunite
them. To Estabrook, who specialized in five track and field events
including the hammer and the discus, there was more justice in
a fieldhouse than in a courthouse. He was not to blame for
Ezra's disappearance, but he did feel linked to it. He did feel
that he was destined to be there when Ezra reappeared. Although
he couldn't even say what color shirt Ezra had been wearing
when he vanished, the fact that he had been the last person to
see Ezra alive assured Estabrook that he would be the first person
to spot him.

Estabrook seemed to be leaving the camp far behind. Each
tiny, tentative step felt like a boundless leap. Tangent branches
parted for him. The forest cooperated and obliged every whim
of his body and gait. It seemed to draw him in and on and
helped him along a path that opened and widened as he moved
forward. He followed this path bravely. He was not afraid of
anything or anyone that might come between him and Ezra.
Then he heard something.

He froze and listened. His heart pumped berserkly. His eyes
strained to break night's code. Though he was frozen where he
stood, his mind flew through the woods at superhuman speed,
cutting through the trees like a runaway chain saw, soaring over
the forest in smaller and smaller circles until only a bull's eye
remained — and there would sit Ezra, nibbling blood-red berries,
tossing the ball with one hand, waiting for Estabrook.

At last a small, boyish figure came into the circle of his flashlight's beam. Estabrook watched him thread his way through a
dense stand of pine trees.

"Ezra!" he called out.

The small figure stopped and disappeared behind the trees.

"Ezra!" Estabrook shouted again, taking a step in the direction
of the shadowy figure he could no longer see.

Estabrook could not wait. He charged down into the pines
as though he were after a ghost and the only way to catch it was
by rushing in and tackling the ghost before it had a chance to

dematerialize. But when he got into the middle of the dense stand, he found no sign of Ezra.

"Ezra! It's me! Mike! Come on out!"

"Shut up!" came the answer.

Somewhere in front of Estabrook there was the figure of a young boy darting in and out of the trees, showing a flash of flesh and a streak of a T-shirt and then fading into the black night, while somewhere behind him was the angry owner of a voice that had faded in like a distant station to "shut up" the devout searcher. Estabrook was caught between a voice that wanted to be heard and a figure that did not want to be seen.

"Ehhhhzraaaaaaaah!" he screamed. "Ehhhhzraaaaaaaah!"

There was a rustle of needles. Estabrook wheeled around and swam through waves of soft pine. Beyond the stand crouched the figure of the boy.

"Ezra!" Estabrook whispered as he inched forward. "You're all right, you're safe," he kept whispering, trying to calm the skittish camper the way a bronco-buster tries to steady an unbroken stallion while sneaking close enough to get a rope on him. "Easy . . . easy . . ." Estabrook whispered, moving ever so slowly toward the figure of the boy crouching in the bushes. He must be so scared, Estabrook thought to himself.

As he drew closer he could see more and more of the hidden figure. Whatever didn't look like Ezra, Estabrook attributed to the illusory play of moonlight, the density of the forest, and his fatigue.

". . . so scared, so scared . . ." he said out loud, still whispering, still trying to steady the jittery stallion hiding in the bushes, hiding inside Ezra.

"YaaaaaaaaHOO!" All of a sudden the figure of the boy leaped from the bushes and flung himself upon the startled bronco-buster. The figure's thin arms and small body had disproportionate strength, and that strength coupled with the surprise of the attack easily knocked Estabrook down into the rough underbrush. The small figure moved as quickly and purposefully as an animal. He put one knee on Estabrook's neck, pinning the strapping counselor to the ground. With his left hand, in another surprising move, the small figure grabbed Estabrook between his legs and squeezed just hard enough to let his prisoner know how foolish it would be to struggle.

"Marcus!" the small figure called out, and a second small figure, virtually identical to the first in physiognomy and in dress, jumped out of the dark and squatted down at Estabrook's head. Estabrook could see his face clearly and the prisoner wondered how he ever could have thought for even a second that either of these two ugly creatures was his poor, lost Ezra.

The face that Estabrook saw was as small as Ezra's, but it looked as though it had shrunk to that size. The features were small as a boy's, too, but as weathered and old as the forest. There was a spot of blood in one of the eyes, like a spot in an egg, and the pupil turned way out. The nose was a wrinkled road map of busted blood vessels. The smiling lips were thin and dripping with the gritty juice of a foul-smelling plug of chewing tobacco. What passed for teeth was an unmatched set of corn niblets. It was impossible to tell the color of the niblets in the dark except to say that they smelled brown.

There was something about the smiling face that scared Estabrook, but also made him feel pity. There was something recognizable, too. Far back in the deepest, trickiest recesses of Estabrook's memory — that part of his memory that frequently surprised him with colorful bits of obscure information — he remembered the smile and the chaw in the cheek and the high-pitched voice that had screeched, "Ya hoo!"

VII

Marcus and Marcus Kristal had been dancing with their clan when Estabrook and the other counselors in the Pennsylvania car came weaving across the Kristal property on their reckless way to Camp Freedom. The car grazed a stack of three wooden boxes on top of which was a child's record player. The Kristals, all of whom I knew very well, were having their daily hootenanny. But theirs was never an ordinary hoot of square-dancing, clog-dancing soloists, and family sings. The matriarch and patriarch of the Kristal clan were former circus performers, and that heritage was in the blood and in the dancing of every Kristal who lived in the pinelands.

Maizie Sparks had been a tumbler, and her common-law husband, Gustave Kristal, had been a high-wire walker. They formed their bond when they were both thirteen years old and disenchanted with their circus lives. Their families had come from Eastern Europe and had reacted to the freedom of their first American tour with Dionysian abandon.

Maizie and Gustave, however, could not stand what this exaggerated feeling of freedom was doing to their families. It was as if all their relatives were using the American tour as an excuse to run wild. And when the managers of the circus — Gustave's father and uncle — announced that they had decided to stay in America indefinitely, Gustave and Maizie began plotting their escape together. Their basic plan was to run away and live in Atlantic City. But they needed train fare to Atlantic City first, which they could save only from their meager allowances. They promised each other that as soon as they had saved enough for two one-way tickets, no matter how long it might take to save the money, they would make their move.

"We learnt our first important lesson about life, Gus," Gustave told me one day while we were going through his old scrapbooks. "What happened was that we was traveling west. And every time we was about to come up with enough money to get us back to Atlantic City, the circus moved on to the next town and the fare would be that much higher. Our savings grew, but Atlantic City kept getting farther and farther away. That was our first lesson, that you can't get ahead of the game. Your dream is always one more town away. Just out of reach. But then we learned another important lesson, too."

The other important lesson was that life was a cycle. One day you were down, but the next day you were up. When the circus traveled as far west as it could, it turned around and headed back east, making the train fare to Atlantic City less and less expensive with each arrival in a new town.

"But there was more to that lesson than meets the eye, Gus.

Me and Maizie had enough money to get to Atlantic City when we hit New Mexico. But the longer we put it off, the more our savings piled up and the less of that savings we wanted to use for ticket money. Greed got us, Gus. Pure greed. And the fact of the matter is we didn't leave the circus until we was all the way back in New Jersey. And we never did get to Atlantic City. We been right here for sixty-two years. We took our dough and bought this land. We slipped away in the middle of the night while the folks was doing everything they could think of to have a good time, and we footed it all the way from Montclair — you know where that is? We walked, and ran, and hitched for two miles on the back of a dray cart, and wound up right here where we's sittin', Gus. A man comes over to us and says do we want to pick cranberries for fifty cents a day and we said sure we do. And in two months we seen the percentages of having our own bogs and setting up house right in the pines here, and so that's what we done. We ain't ever even been to Atlantic City on a visit. 'Cept for coming across to America and that one time over in Californ', we ain't never seen no ocean again neither. That's what Atlantic City was all about."

I suppose Gustave and Maizie were the only kids ever to run away *from* the circus. But they still had circus in their blood. And they kept their talents alive through practice and through their children who were quick and happy to learn their parents' skills. Then in the forties hard times fell on the Kristal Euro-American Circus. Gustave's father died of too much booze. Gustave's uncle had no head for finances and ran the circus too far into the red for anyone to ever bring it back out. In addition, the majority of the performers had compromised their talent and skill with too much drinking and carousing. When the faded red-and-white tent finally folded for the last time, ten of the Dionysian offspring were able to find Gustave and Maizie who by then had built up a thriving cranberry farm.

"Could I turn them away, Gus? In one little girl's face I seen my mother's eyes and my wife's smile — that's how mixed up and outter control it all got. But could I say no to them eyes and that smile?"

179

The new arrivals moved in, helped work the farm, and raised families.

"Sure they's lacking in certain ways. You can't find too many Kristals or Sparkses who can add too good or write their name down, but we's family, Gus. We's more family than most. Look at us. We all got that same kinda look. And we's all small like Maizie's mother. She wasn't no dwarf or midget, but she was only four and half feet high, if that, and so was her sister, and Maizie's sister, too, and come to think of it we Kristals was a smallish bunch usselves. So we's all kinda small, and we all have that certain look, and we's all the fiercest kin you'll ever find anywheres, Gus."

And they all cartwheeled and low-wire walked and built human pyramids and even integrated quite comical pratfalls into a typical Kristal hootenanny — all to the lively old circus tunes squawking out of the record player which the Pennsylvania car eventually knocked over and broke. Marcus and Marcus, twin sons of a half brother and sister, set out immediately for revenge. They were both called Marcus because they were identical in every other respect, and so it made perfect sense to the parents to give them identical names. "Who cares which one comes when you call 'em?" their mother always said with a laugh. "One's as bad as the other."

The two Marcus Kristals had strong feelings for revenge. They had stalked the Pennsylvania car's tracks up to the point at which it had turned right at the last of the intersections, indicating it was headed for the circle at Colt's Point Stream. So they took a shortcut through the forest which they loved. Like jungle monkeys, Marcus and Marcus leaped, swung, and scampered their way through the dense heart of the woods until they arrived at the edge of the circle a day and a half later. They were exhausted and starving when finally they spotted Estabrook poking around at the edge of the woods, but the two brothers were able to draw enormous strength from their seething hatred of "them hat heads" as Marcus called the floppy-hatted counselors in the Pennsylvania car. The other Marcus showed two crooked rows of niblets and laughed like a mule at his brother's wit.

Still, now that they had Michael Estabrook pinned to the

forest floor by his neck and balls, what were they going to do with him? How were they going to make him pay for his part in breaking up their hoot? And it was not just that one interrupted hoot Estabrook had to pay for, it was the next hoot, too, and the one after that, and every hoot thereafter until they could get the music to play again.

"Whar's yer hat, hat head?" the smiling Marcus asked as though Estabrook's life depended on the answer. The Marcus who had him pinned laughed with his whole body, causing Estabrook to gag and wince from the inadvertant pressure applied to his personal parts.

"What're we going to do with him, Marcus?" asked the laughing Marcus when he settled down again. These were not evil hillbillies. They were inbred, defective boys in the bodies of men. They were strong and athletic and fiercely loyal, but they were completely unresourceful.

"Well . . . we best ketch th'other hat heads, too, don't we?" Marcus said triumphantly, not caring that they were two against many and had no plan of attack.

"Oh yeah," Marcus agreed. "Yeah!" he repeated as though he had seen the light of the Lord. And he got up off Estabrook who breathed out for the first time in five minutes it seemed.

Estabrook stayed on the ground assessing his situation. The high-pitched voices of his captors told him who they were. Suddenly he was able to review his drunken trip to Camp Freedom as a sober observer. There was the careening car, the stack of wooden boxes beneath the record player, and then, among all the dancers and acrobats, there were the twins, their feet held in each other's hands to form a human wagon wheel that rolled back and forth in time to the music.

A subhuman wagon wheel, Estabrook silently corrected himself as he watched the two Marcuses scratch their heads, each hoping the other would suggest what to do next.

They're cute, Estabrook thought, in a sad sort of way. The only danger may be that they don't know their own strength. But I don't think they'll hurt me.

Estabrook decided to make a run for it. He would ask their permission to stand up and then, as he was getting to his feet, bowl one or both of them over and start running as fast as he could. He judged he was three or four hundred feet into the woods and that his track runner's stride would get him back to camp in plenty of time to alert the others that Marcus and his twin brother were on the way. But Estabrook underestimated the twins' arcrobatic ability and overestimated the distance he had gone into the forest.

"Can I get up? Please?" he asked the twins.

"We gotch yer, y'know."

"I know you do," Estabrook said obsequiously.

"Whar's yer hat?" the other Marcus said, and his brother gave out with his best mule laugh when he heard the word *hat*.

This is it, Estabrook thought, and he sprang to his feet and threw a powerful shoulder block into the chest of the Marcus who was laughing. The stunned Kristal let out something like the "oomph" you read in the comic strips and went sprawling backward into the soft needles of a huge white pine. But he recovered.

Instinctively Marcus grabbed hold of the branches to stop his fall and then pulled himself free of the pine. He threw himself onto the back of Estabrook's leg, immediately attaching himself like a spider monkey. Through sheer strength, Estabrook was able to take three or four more steps, and through even greater strength and determination, Marcus was able to climb up Estabrook's back and put his arm around Estabrook's throat. By that time Marcus's brother had snapped out of his daze and was sprinting toward the monstrous shadow staggering through the branches. Marcus stopped a few feet short of the mark, sprang into the air like a midget wrestler, and kicked Estabrook in the forehead. The three of them came thundering out of the woods like an avalanche. They had been no more than ten or fifteen yards from the exact spot at the edge of the woods where Ezra was last seen, and now they tumbled into the clearing, fighting like wild dogs.

"Don't worry!" a familiar voice said, and then a loud, sharp, cracking sound stopped everyone's heart for a moment. It stopped Marcus's heart forever.

VIII

The familiar voice was Thomason's. The gun was Thomason's, too. But it was Stone who had had it in his hand when one of the Marcus brothers stiffened and slumped and the other one fought desperately to free himself from the dead body on top of him. Estabrook played dead, but he did so knowing that his life had been saved. Although he may have miscalculated how far into the woods he had gone, he knew that now he was safely back in the arena of civilization and that no one was about to shoot a man who specializes in five track and field events, a man who one day might carry his nation's banner in the Olympic parade.

Marcus, however, had no such feelings of security. A Kristal had been killed. Marcus just didn't know which one. He paused for two or three seconds to see if it were he or his brother who was still breathing, and then he tried everything he could to get out of the way of the next bullet. When he couldn't free himself from his dead brother and Estabrook's dead weight, Marcus decided that his best chance was to use Estabrook as a shield. And so he latched on to the huge possum who had hunted him and now would protect him. Trying to drag Estabrook with him, on top of him, Marcus crawled and clawed toward the woods. If he could get back into the woods, he could escape everything but a lucky shot in the dark.

There were five more bullets left in the chambers of the gun, and Stone fired every one of them. The first struck a mud puddle and Marcus actually heard the tiny splash under the noisier explosion of the gun blast. The second bullet struck Marcus's dead brother, making his body jump. The third bullet caught Marcus's leg and woke the counselor who woke his co-conspirators. So prepared were they for their plan of escape that the conspirators were able to dash around in the dark like bats, shimmying into their jeans, hurrying into their shoes, grabbing their possessions, and silently cutting across the compound toward their getaway car. This was exactly the way they had planned it, if and when they could find someone to create a diversion.

As the conspirators ran across the open field, keeping as low to the ground as possible, they glanced at the perimeter of the circle and saw Stone's massive figure pointing the gun and firing the fourth bullet. It hit Marcus in the shoulder, forcing him to let go of Estabrook who popped up like a downed boxer anxious to show everyone he's not hurt.

Now Marcus had two wounds to lick — his ankle and his shoulder — and they kept him from running or crawling. He was at Stone's mercy. And Thomason's.

By now everyone was awake and had come outside to see what was happening. No one could understand why Stone was shooting, or what would happen if he stopped, or the meaning of the lifeless body lying only a few feet away from Stone's current target.

"Keep back!" Estabrook said when Frannie looked as though she were going to run right up to Stone and grab his gun.

"What's going on?" she demanded, her fearlessness motivated by a maternal instinct to defend her boys from stray bullets.

"That fuckin' runt tried to kill me! Him and his brother!" Estabrook boasted, certain he had justified the fact that he would not let Frannie pass.

Because of the darkness, the smallness of the figure on the ground, and the distance between them, Frankie thought Marcus was one of the campers.

"Gus! He's gone crazy!" Frankie cried to me. "He's killing the kids! Where's Jeffie? Where is everyone? Does Frances know where everyone is?! It must be Stoney! Where the hell did he put Stoney?!" Frankie ran off in the direction of Stone's cabin and the last I could see of him in the patchy darkness was his red-and-white striped pajamas as they disappeared behind Stone's door.

Estabrook continued to hold the crowd back single-handedly, jabbering the whole time. "He's got him. Don't worry. Stone's got everything under control. Don't worry. Go back to bed. I'm all right. They didn't hurt me. Go on back to bed."

Geoff Thomason talked steadily to Marcus, speaking as though the gun were in his hand, not Stone's, as though he held the power of life and death over the trapped and cringing prisoner.

"This gun is registered with the New York City Police Department," Thomason said. "We are perfectly within our rights to use it to defend these young children from any clear and present danger. If you think we're afraid to use it, you'd better look at your partner over there."

In a tone of voice as pungent and deadly as the scent of burnt powder playing in the breeze, Thomason barraged Marcus with accusations and insults.

"Who are you? Or should I say what are you? A thief? A hobo? A child molester? What are you doing here? Why are you skulking around in the dead of night? There can be very few acceptable explanations."

The more Thomason carried on in this vein and tone, the more Marcus winced and whimpered like a dog being scolded with a rolled newspaper.

"Are you and your friend thieves in the night? Were you hiding in the forest waiting for us to fall asleep so you could sneak into our camp and loot our supplies? Were you after our money? The gold and silver in our teeth? Were you going to steal our food?

"Or were you and your friend on the prowl for something so awful, so unspeakable that a bullet through the head would be better than you deserve?"

"You already got one, didn't you?" Estabrook cried out in anguish. "You already got Ezra!" he sobbed.

The surviving brother's eyes jumped back and forth between Stone and Thomason. The gun-bore and Thomason's mouth merged into a single menacing black hole. Marcus feared it would suck him in and shoot him out.

A thousand volts of pain shot through his ankle as Marcus used his powerful hind legs to spring at his tormentor.

The sound of a shot. And then another. And another. All heads turned and saw the backfiring getaway car screech in reverse, stop, churn up red-lit smoke and dirt, and then take off against the black night like something from outer space, only the tail lights visible as the car rose higher and higher along the one-lane dirt road that led through the forest to two-way streets, shop-lined avenues, broad, busy thoroughfares, and state-run highways. The conspirators had made their escape. They had taken advantage of one diversion and provided another one themselves: in the noisy confusion of their getaway, a second Marcus Kristal was shot to death.

IX

"Stoney? Is that you, Stoney?"

Frankie touched the bunched blankets at the foot of the thick sleeping bag Stone had left half unzipped. Gently, Frankie squeezed the bundle, probing for Stoney.

"Wake up," he whispered.

He found a corner of a blanket and tugged at it, hoping to unravel more and more of the bundle until he reached Stoney. He continued to pull the corner gently, afraid of jarring Stoney should the boy be in pain.

"Stoney," Frankie whispered again. "Wake up. It's Francis."

The movement startled Frankie. He jumped back. Stoney's head appeared. A tiny breeze caused by Stoney's movement coaxed a downy feather from his mussed red hair and it wafted into the night. He was warm. He was happy. He was not in pain. He had been peacefully asleep in Dr. George Stone's sleeping bag.

TEN

Over the next several days Camp Freedom became the opposite of what its name promised. It became a prison camp, with Stone as the warden and Thomason, Albert, and Estabrook as guards.

The immediate cause for the new tone of severity in Stone's already authoritative regime was still sprawled on the ground come morning. The two Marcus Kristals had to become symbols. They had to be thought of as enemies of the camp. Their murders had to be considered acts of heroism. Stone could not allow the killings to be misinterpreted.

Shortly after sunrise, Albert and Estabrook herded the campers into the prison yard. When everyone had been assembled, Stone came out of his cabin. Right behind him marched Stoney, making his first appearance as Stone's convert and aide-de-camp. The boys from Stoney's cabin were glad to see him. They were surprised that the feeling didn't seem to be mutual. Stoney ignored their words of welcome and tried to be as straight and stiff as the flagstaff he carried.

"Good morning," Stone said confidently. As prearranged, Stoney planted the American flag on Marcus Kristal's chest and held it there with one hand.

"Quite a lot of excitement last night," Stone acknowledged. "But now you know. Nothing is sacred. No one is safe. Even here, at a summer camp, at a place where children and adults have come together for a precious few weeks of learning, growth, and enjoyment, even in this sanctuary, danger can and will strike."

Stone paused to give his words greater meaning.

"What a lesson we have learned," he continued. "We have learned that even if you take care of your mind and body, filth and evil will try to strike at you." He indicated the Kristal brothers with a wave of his hand, refusing to dignify them with a nod or glance. "These evil creatures tried to strike at the healthy mind and body of Camp Freedom."

Stoney stood a little taller when everyone's eyes naturally traveled from the dead body of Marcus Kristal, up the flagstaff, to the little red-haired boy standing at unblinking attention.

"But the mind and body can take care of themselves." Stone smiled. "Just as the body can heal and defend itself without pills, injections, transfusions, or surgery, Camp Freedom can heal and defend itself without outside interference. And there is the proof!" Again Stone indicated the dead bodies with his hand. "These scum would have stopped at nothing. They would have committed sins you and I cannot even imagine. But the greatness of Camp Freedom was able to withstand their attack. We should be proud, boys."

Stone deftly built his case. Playing the campers like a good lawyer plays the jury, Stone resurrected the Kristals with his lurid descriptions of how they'd creep through the forest, eating insects and toads, how they'd do things to each other that little boys shouldn't know about, and how they'd wait until dark to kidnap little boys and humiliate them and then, if the little boys refused to do what the Kristals wanted, how they would torture them and kill them, which was probably what they did to Ezra.

"I pray," Stone chanted in his best evangelical style, "that a pack of wolves tore Ezra's flesh apart, that a bear squeezed the life's blood out of him, or that a hunter's bullet found Ezra's brain rather than think that vermin like these two got him."

Stone was brilliant. Harmless corpses terrified the boys. But

Stone's most brilliant stroke was yet to come. He ended his invective by calling for a fitting disposal of the bodies. The muscle of decent men, he claimed, was far too precious to waste on the digging of graves for such despicable creatures as the Kristals. A watery grave implied honor and was therefore out of the question. Cremation was ideal because the vermin would be consumed by hellish fire, but it was dangerous without a proper furnace. That left Stone only one alternative.

"They came crawling out of the scum and slime and rot of the forest; let them spend eternity there!"

Albert and Estabrook came forward. Stoney removed the American flag from the dead man's chest and stood it on the ground next to Stone.

"We pledge allegiance," Stone saluted, "to the flag," and the campers could not help but join in loudly and happily, "of the United States of America," Camp Freedom pledged as the Frenchman and the athlete each dragged a Marcus Kristal to the forest, "and to the republic for which it stands, one nation, under God, indivisible, with liberty and justice for all!" One of the boys said "invisible" instead of "indivisible."

II

"Why isn't he afraid that those boys who escaped will notify the police and bring them down here?" I asked Thomason on his first visit to the kitchen after the shootings.

"What do you mean 'escaped'?" he said disbelievingly. "I love you, Gus. You old folks think everything's black or everything's white. Those boys just couldn't hack it. They didn't escape. They quit, Gus."

"You mean any of us could quit any time we want?" I asked coyly.

"Who's to stop you, Gus?" he answered just as coyly. "And why should those boys call the police down on us? What did we do? You heard him out there this morning, those midgets were looking for trouble. It was us or them. It was the kids or them,

Gus. Who knows what the hell those dwarfs would have done!"

"I know those brothers, Thomason. They're not like that. They wouldn't hurt anyone."

"Then what were they doing sneaking around here in the middle of the night like jackals? I love you, Gus — you've got a soft spot for everyone. Only it's in your head."

"I'm telling you, I know them and they're harmless."

"We know you know them. Stoney told us you were talking about them at lunch. We'd like you to stop talking about them. What's done is done, Gus. Don't make it worse than it is. Everyone's satisfied except you. Doesn't that make you stop and think?"

"You know what makes me stop and think . . ."

"What?"

"What a smart guy like you is doing going around apologizing for that psychotic."

He left without a smile, but I knew I had gotten to him.

III

After the shootings, Stone imposed new rules. One required everyone at camp to have a daily chiropractic adjustment. No one was excused. Early in the morning the boys would line up outside the cabin and one by one enter the torture chamber of "that fuckin' crazy asshole," the epithet that hung around longer than the young man who originated it. When the boys went in, they felt fit and limber; when they came out, they were stiff and stooped, shuffling like men ten times their age. But within an hour they felt better than ever and were willing to forgive and forget.

The adults had their manipulations while the boys had lunch. Thomason, of course, had been devoted to Stone for a long time and waxed poetic on the subject of chiropractic. Estabrook regarded spinal manipulation as just a fancy way of saying physical therapy, which, as a member of the track team, he believed in wholeheartedly. The rest of us had our doubts. And our fears. We knew how strong Stone's belief was in the daily adjustments.

We also knew that there was at least one gun at Camp Freedom, and that Stone was not afraid to use it. And so we inched into his cabin and put our tense bodies into his hands.

The process took only a few minutes. The patient would lean face forward against the huge black-leather-and-chrome table, Stone would depress a foot pedal, the vertical table would descend slowly until it and the patient were perfectly horizontal, then Stone would probe with his safecracker's fingertips until he found an irregularity, a blockage, the beginning of a malfunction, a tiny short circuit in the neural network, something only he could feel. That found, Stone would release the center of the table, leaving no support beneath the patient's back, and proceed to lull the patient into a false security. His fingers would move gently over the irregular area until they were perfectly in place, and during this painless, rather pleasant few moments, the patient would be fooled into relaxing his or her muscles for the fraction of an instant Stone needed to strike like lightning, sharply twisting and jerking the vertebrae, while the patient cried out in sudden pain.

Each patient was given a different adjustment. Sammy's was designed to stop him from bed-wetting. Stoney's was supposed to cure his stuttering and prevent his seizures. Eventually Frankie's round-shoulderedness would disappear thanks to a regimen of adjustments that would make standing straight feel as natural and comfortable to him as slouching. And Homer's stomach problems began to show signs of improvement after only two sessions.

Stone's adjustments seemed to hurt anyone whose problem was psychological. Jeffie regressed more quickly into infantile behavior. Harry Jr. steadily declined from the cat's having gotten his tongue to catalepsy to catatonia. And one of the female counselors, Sandy Chalkers, suffered grave psychological consequences at the hands of Stone. Her first adjustment brought on a hysterical menstrual period which threw the young woman into an inconsolable state of depression. A sufferer of acute menstrual symptoms normally, this altered cycle dampened her spirits beyond any monthly moodiness she could remember.

Too embarrassed to protest and too scared to resist, she pressed her pelvis against Stone's table every lunchtime and let him pervert her nature and her sanity.

To those of us who felt fit as a fiddle, Stone would say, "You're right, but the fiddle needs tuning," and he'd pluck at a spinal cord and loosen a muscle until even a Stradivarius would let out an ugly screech.

IV

In time people get used to anything. Even to their own abnormal behavior.

Jeffie got used to the speech, logic, and fears of the three-year-old he had become. If he had been fearful when I first found him outside the kitchen window, now he was paranoiac, averting every glance, clinging to anyone who'd let him, talking like a baby in hopes of being comforted and protected.

Harry Jr. had something far more extreme to get used to. At first the boy just shut up and sat very still, swaying slightly, his face blank, his eyes staring at something no one else could see or understand. In the next phase, Harry became rigid. His body locked itself into a seated position. If someone had pushed him over onto his side, his body would have remained seated, bent at the waist, legs folded, hands in his lap, eyes still burning into his private horror. One of the boys pulled Harry's arm out of his lap and, when he let go, watched in dumbfounded amazement as the arm snapped back to its former position. Then, in the third phase, the frozen Harry Jr. thawed and took on a flexibility that enabled him to be molded into any pose. He still didn't speak or move, but he took food, slept soundly, and looked as though he understood everything that was going on around him. Technically he may have passed into schizophrenic catatonia, but I prefer to think that his eyes finally got used to the dark scene they were doomed to watch forever.

Sammy overcame his bed-wetting by fighting off sleep twenty times a night. I'd hear him stumbling around in the dark and think of my third wife who had fought so hard against death during the last six months of her confinement. To keep herself from crying, she insisted upon wearing mascara, knowing how foolish she'd look with black tears streaking down her cheeks. And to keep herself from dying, she refused to go to sleep, fearing that if she closed her eyes for even a few seconds she might never open them again. In her weakest hour, with disease tightening its fatal grip on every vital organ, she had to be given sedatives to force her to sleep. That's how Sammy coped with his fear of bed-wetting — by not allowing himself to sleep. Every few minutes his fear sounded an alarm which roused him from his bed and made him thread his way through the darkness to the edge of the woods where he would try to pee in the prescribed ditch. Even if he didn't have to pee when he woke himself, by the time he got to the ditch the cold, the fear, or the bare foot he always managed to put on the muddy lip of the ditch sent a shiver down his spine and into his bladder. Twenty times a night fear would stream, trickle, or dribble from his exhausted body.

Homer, too, had come to terms with his strange, enervating sickness. After two chiropractic adjustments, he was able to keep down small bits of food, although it may have been a coincidence, since I had been experimenting with smaller and blander portions for him. I had given Homer a cracker soaked in grape juice and he was able to swallow that mush without throwing it up. No one knew whether it was my concoction or Stone's adjustments that caused the improvement. But since Stone took credit for it, everyone believed him, including Homer. Homer became Stone's favorite example of the miracles his hands could perform, and he allowed himself to be trotted out every time Stone felt the need to reassert the moral, physical, and spiritual efficacy of chiropractic. Thankful for Stone's partial cure — Homer still courted horribly convulsive heaving if he dared swallow two soaked crackers instead of one — the independent, adventurous boy became slightly more subdued and conservative.

Stoney operated as a spy for Stone, but his cover was enslavement to Stone. Everyone thought Stoney's life was in constant danger, that Stone had his hands dug into the boy's spine and was ready to twist him into a grotesquely knotted corpse at the slightest sign of Stoney's emancipation. Stoney lived in Stone's hut — "In his sleeping bag, for God's sake!" Frankie told us. He was given more adjustments than anyone else, two or three a day. And he was charged with several small but honorable tasks, such as carrying the flag, helping wake the campers in the morning, and blowing the whistle — four long blasts — for breakfast, lunch, and dinner. His stolid obedience saddened those who cared about Stoney. They assumed he had no choice, and that although his tasks amounted to privileges, he was being forced to do them against his will.

"Poor Stoney."

"How can we help you, Stoney?"

"Let's sneak into the kitchen and get some cookies for Stoney."

"Come back to our hut, Stoney. Stay with us."

"Sneak out when it gets dark. We'll hide you."

"Don't be afraid to talk, Stoney. Did he do something to your mouth? Don't be afraid of him, Stoney."

They never realized, never suspected, never dreamed that Stoney enjoyed sleeping in the same bag with Stone. The red-headed devil of that very first hour of Camp Freedom had traded his soul for a healthy body. The madly stuttering fits of inhuman rage that had seized Stoney and blinded him with blazing whiteness and set his brain on fire had not occurred since Stone took matters into his hands. In the back of every mind there was hope and doubt about Stone's miraculous powers. Everyone wanted to believe that Stone had cured Stoney, for only that was adequate payment for Stoney's enslavement. And when Stone announced one dinner hour that Stoney would lead the saying of grace, every eye focused on the red-headed angel at the head table, and every ear strained to hear proof of Stoney's martyrdom — the miracle of a seizure-free, stutter-free thanksgiving.

There was an eerie silence as every camper watched and listened and put himself in Stoney's place. They anticipated his transformation and saw themselves, too, passing from bed-wetting, baby-talking, lost, bewildered children into confident, able-bodied young men. Although their reward would not be nearly so great as Stoney's — the conquest over seizure and stutter — the campers sat in suspended time and space, not one of them daring to breathe, waiting for the justification of their surrender to Stone to come streaming gracefully out of Stoney's mouth, just a few simple words, a short blessing over the tasteless hotch-potch of canned vegetables I had prepared for dinner.

Stoney bowed his head. Every other head moved forward, cocked to pick up Stoney's precious words of gratitude. As the boy opened his mouth to speak, our hearts stopped. We were about to hear our future, and naturally we were transfixed and terrified by the prospect. Could we speak without stuttering? Had Stone healed us? The woods were silent. Night was still hiding behind the setting sun. The fullness of grace weighed heavily on Stoney's hunched shoulders as an aura of ritual blessedness fell like a shining rain over his table, splashing off in dazzling starbursts upon the startled heads of the congregation.

He mouthed grace. Not a word. Not a sound. As Stoney's lips moved, the smooth delivery of his prayer was as silent as a stone.

V

"What about Stoney?" I asked Thomason during one of our candlelit talks.

"What about him?" Thomason played dumb, snooping through boxes, barrels, and bags for something to satisfy his midnight appetite.

I offered him a cracker which was not particularly good tasting but was packaged to stay fresh for a long time, and that was a treat. Thomason's hands were full of the overripe fruit he was considering when I held out the cracker. He leaned toward me and opened his mouth. Instinctively, I put the cracker into his mouth and held on to my end so that he didn't have to eat the whole cracker at once. He bit off a piece, smiled approvingly, and opened his mouth for the rest, which I promptly placed on his tongue.

"Why has Stoney deserted us?" I asked.

"You insist on creating sides, don't you, Gus? But we're all in this together. Stoney has seen the light, that's all. He has decided to swim with the waves instead of against them."

"I think he's been brainwashed, Thomason. And I think you have, too. Although I suspect that you brainwashed yourself."

"I love you, Gus. You old-timers really believe in psychological warfare, brainwashing, mass hypnosis, thought suggestion."

"He became a different boy overnight. Why? How?"

"Through chiropractic," Thomason answered quickly. But I sensed that he was not convinced.

"We've all been to the chiropractor," I said ironically. "How is it that we haven't changed overnight? Except for Sandy Chalkers, of course, who's so depressed she's ready to drown herself in those 'waves' of yours. And Jeffie, who doesn't say anything without crying or whining. And Harry, who doesn't say anything, period."

"Maybe he doesn't have anything to say."

"And what do you have to say?"

"Stoney was given a chance. Not a choice. A chance. And he took it."

"That's because he had no choice."

"There's never a choice between right and wrong, good and evil, health and disease, life and death. Who in his right mind has ever chosen or would ever choose to do wrong, to sin, to fall ill, to die? All the momentous choices are figments of our imagination. The most important choice any of us ever makes is chocolate or vanilla." The glow of assurance back-lit Thomason's eyes. "As for Stoney, he was given the chance to speak without stuttering and to live without the threat of those terrible seizures."

"And you believe that chiropractic can cure those problems?"

"I believe that a few days ago Dr. George Stone, chiropractor, fell on his face in front of all of us, and through the sheer force of his will that man stood up and conquered a disease no medical doctor in America would have touched. He had a blockage in his brain, Gus, a temporary shutdown of blood and oxygen, a breakdown of memory, speech, perception, and coordination. To everyone else he might have looked and acted like a drunk, reeling and slurring and unable to focus his eyes, but to Stone, those eternal few minutes of disorientation and lack of control were a living death." Thomason's eyes lit up a little more, as though he had just turned a three-way bulb to a higher level of brightness. "But he conquered it, Gus. You saw him do it. And so did Stoney. And what must Stoney have thought? Surely there is a kindred spirit, surely Stoney found in Stone a fellow sufferer, and vice versa. And while Stone may never have experienced the excruciating pain Stoney had to bear, surely he understands the misery and frustration of having your own brain, your mind, your very thoughts, Gus, held hostage by an invisible, unpredictable enemy. And then," his eyes burned brighter and brighter, "for Stoney to see Stone overcome his enemy! To see that a man can create peace and harmony and health out of chaos and disease! To know that with Stone as an inspiration, he, too, might one day vanquish his nemesis!"

"Very poetic, Thomason," I kidded him. But he took it as a slap, and his stung cheek reddened in the candlelight as he stared at me with glowing coals for eyes.

"Let me tell you about poetry," he snarled. "Stoney's father is a poet. But what the hell has any poet ever conquered, Gus? A poet thrives on indomitable misery. James Alleman Alcock is no example for his son. He can't even think in terms of Stoney's getting better. He can only think in metaphors, similes, images, conceits. While the pain of those damned seizures blinds Stoney, it illuminates his father's world. The pathetic poet wants to peek through the cracks in his son's brain, not seal them up. He wants to achieve grace through the suffering of his flesh and blood, but it's Stoney who must suffer, not the poet. It's Stoney's flesh and blood — and it will be Stoney's grace, Gus. He will stop stuttering. He will be free of his seizures. And it will be because of Stone. Because of his special knowledge, and his strong example, and the genius of his — "

"His what, Thomason? His madness? His cold-bloodedness? His murderous cruelty?"

"— his hands! The genius of his hands!"

VI

In the middle of everything — forced marches to the chiropractor's torture chamber, oppressive surveillance, a rapidly diminishing larder of edible foods, hysterical and real disease, a haunted forest that seemed to be closing in on us at the same rate hope was running out — amidst the old squalor and inadequacies of Camp Freedom and the new woe and despair of our prison camp, Frannie decided to mount her production of *The Sound of Music*.

"That's what I was hired for and that's what I'm going to do," she declared to Frankie, the musical director. Then she told Geoff Thomason of her plan. At first he shrugged it off, believing that she'd never manage even a third-rate amateur production because of the absence of a proper stage, lights, a piano, girl campers to play some of the roles, the absence also of costumes, sets, and, above all, enthusiasm.

"Go ahead," Thomason said, "that's what you were hired for." Then, realizing what a boost to the morale of the camp her production could provide, he added enthusiastically, "Yes, by all means, *The Sound of Music!*"

"Then you won't stop us?" Frannie asked with fresh excitement.

"Why should anyone stop you? In fact, let me know if I can help fill the hills with the sound of music. I don't promise to climb every mountain for you, but I'll do what I can."

Frannie went right to work. She cast Homer as Captain von Trapp. Sammy was persuaded to take the part of Maria. The roles of Friedrich and Kurt were combined into one, and Frannie promised herself Jeffie would be able to deliver the two boys' lines and sing their songs. Harry was to be another von Trapp child, and Stoney, too, if he consented, but they would only be on stage to flesh out the family, not to speak.

198

To fill the remaining parts, Frannie decided to hold auditions. Almost everyone showed up at the designated hour, but hardly anyone was capable of delivering an expressive syllable or well-rounded note. The tiny voices choked, cracked, and giggled. The boys who were asked to read speeches obviously meant for girls were too embarrassed. Those who were willing to sing had the benefit of Frankie's accompaniment on a recorder which along with two tambourines and a harmonica were the only musical instruments available. Frankie played each tune exactly as it was played on the original cast album, modulating, bending, inflecting, and coloring every single note in the precise way the original performers sang and played during those performances which were taped and edited for the record album. Frankie's smooth and dazzling recreations combined with the melodious sound of the recorder still could not make the auditioners sound good.

But Frannie was undaunted. She rewrote large chunks of the show, simplifying speeches, combining characters, cutting unnecessary scenes, streamlining everything she could without compromising, or distorting the unabashedly sentimental messages of *The Sound of Music.*

When she had cast her players, untalented, undisciplined, and unenthusiastic as they might have been, Frannie called everyone together. "Congratulations," she began. "I am happy that all of you were chosen to be in *The Sound of Music.* Being in this show makes you all actors, and being an actor makes you special. That's why actors are always up on a platform, on a stage, and everyone else is down below, looking up to them. Actors are up on the stage because they show how wonderful it is — or how terrible it is — to be a human being. If the show is sad and ends up with people suffering or dying, then the audience sees the bad parts of life and thanks the actors for showing them the bad parts so that they can try to understand or avoid sadness in their own lives. If the show is happy — like *The Sound of Music* — then the audience thanks the actors for showing them how to live the right way, how to be brave and honest and full of love." Ignoring the fact that much of what she was saying was either incomprehensible or uninteresting to

199

her assembled cast, Frannie continued her directorial pep talk, for she believed that it was style rather than content, form rather than matter, fury rather than significance that moved people. As an actress, she knew instinctively that if she strutted across a stage with her chest held high and her eyes flashing and her arm upraised she would project honor, courage, and dignity, even if the words she spoke were gibberish. "How many of you know the story of *The Sound of Music*?" No one raised his hand, though several had known the more popular songs from the show — "Do Re Mi," "Edelweiss," "Climb Every Mountain," "My Favorite Things," and, of course, the title song. "This is a story of a family living at a time . . ." and Frannie proceeded to tell her children all about the von Trapp children, about the loss of their dear mother, the military strictness of their father, the arrival of Maria, and the tuneful happiness Maria brought not only to the children but to every member of the von Trapp household. Frannie touched also on the sad confusion in Maria's own life, how her deep desire to devote herself exclusively to God was shaken by her love for the Captain, and how the sisters of Nonnberg Abbey and her own conscience helped her resolve the dilemma. Finally, Frannie told of the historic background, the imminent takeover of Austria by Hitler's army, and the three possible reactions to that takeover as represented by the defiant Captain, by Rolf, the turncoat postboy, and by Max Detweiler, the compromising entrepreneur.

When Frannie finished the story of the von Trapps, I wondered how many of the campers had realized that they had just heard their own story, that they, too, had been separated from loving mothers, and that Stone was in many ways a surrogate father, every bit as strict and militaristic as the Captain.

VII

"What I want to know is why Stone wasn't worried about those boys beating it out of here. Why didn't he ground them by confiscating the keys to their car or removing some essential part of the engine? We all knew they were planning to escape, didn't we, and that their only hope was that car."

"Did I ever tell you about Robert Newton? Thomason answered, biting into a brittle cracker. "Robert was on line in front of me for a physical when we were called by the United States Army." Between Thomason's bright eyes and the ethereal glow of the candlelight, his story about Robert took on a ghostly light of its own. "It was during one of the biggest call-ups of the Vietnam war. The doctors were counting eyes, not examining them. That's how desperately the army needed men. And the men knew it. Most of them responded with honor. Ninety-six out of a hundred guys would have killed on the spot just to get the chance to kill in Vietnam. The ninety-seventh guy was a coward. The ninety-eighth guy was a religious fanatic. Ninety-nine was a commie. And one hundred was Robert." Thomason looked unashamedly pleased with the taste his rhetoric left in his mouth. Or was it the second bite of the cracker?

"Robert talked the whole time. I never said a word. But he kept talking and talking as though he were hoping that sooner or later he'd come out with a good explanation for why he felt so unpatriotic at such a crucial moment in his country's history. He wasn't against the war. He wasn't a coward. He wasn't a religious or political fanatic. But he *was* a fanatic." Thomason rubbed his hands together to get rid of the cracker crumbs. "I know that, Gus, because when we got to the doctor who sticks his finger up your ass Robert revealed his reason for not wanting to be inducted. Still clutching the two notes from the two doctors describing the two ailments he hoped would excuse him, he said, 'I feel like a goddamned fucking animal. No name, no clothes, no personality, no individuality, just two arms, two legs, two eyes, red blood — ' and then the doctor broke in and said, 'Drop your drawers, boy, and bend over,' and Robert said, 'Wait a minute. Here. Let me show you these letters. I got them from my doctors. I didn't know who to show them to.' The army doctor took Robert's letters and laughed at the first one. 'Allergies? Well, you ain't allergic to rice paddies, are you, boy?' And then he read the second letter and didn't understand a word of it.

'What does this mean, boy? Put it in your own words.' The army doctor was annoyed. Robert was discouraged. He had put most of his hope in the first letter, the one describing severe allergies and asthmatic symptoms. Robert had told me that the allergy doctor was a friend of the family's and had agonized over the wording he used in the letter. He wanted to give Robert the most dramatic excuse he could without lying. Robert's other doctor, however, wrote his letter begrudgingly. He tossed it at Robert with disgust and warned him that there was no way a congenital bone deformity of the knee — the letter used more technical jargon — would keep Robert out of the army. Now here was Robert having to rely on his unreliable knees for a rejection. 'It means,' Robert finally said, 'that I can't do a deep knee bend.' As stupid as that sounded to everyone else in line, the army doctor responded with great concern. 'Let me see,' he asked, gesturing toward the floor with his clipboard. Robert squatted down, his knees cracking out of joint, and he stayed there. 'Now get up,' the army doctor said kindly. And Robert grabbed the army doctor's hand, forcing the startled examiner to help the incapacitated inductee to his shaky feet. 'I'm sorry, I'm sorry,' the army doctor said, stamping his rejection on Robert's papers, apologizing again and again, and then putting his heavy arm around Robert's naked shoulders while he gave the boy final instructions.'' Thomason's hands became more agitated. I thought I saw them tremble. It was an angry trembling.

"That's when I noticed that Robert was shaking. It looked like he had gone into shock. The army doctor could feel the shivering through Robert's thick shoulders, but he misinterpreted what the shivering meant. He believed Robert felt disappointed. Humiliated. 'Not all of us can be in the army, son,' he said. He said 'son' instead of 'boy.' 'But we can all do our part. There's other work that needs doing, son. The country's got to be strong, too. It's not just the army that needs good men.' But Robert didn't hear a word the doctor was saying. He was too busy suppressing his jubilation.'' Thomason did not try to conceal the contempt he felt for Robert. "All I wanted to do was yell out that Robert was a traitor. That the reason he was shaking like a leaf was not because he couldn't serve his country, but because he was so terrified that the doctor would change his mind — and Robert's classification — or that someone in the administrative office, where Robert had to go next, would overrule the doctor's rejection and give Robert a rank and job that required no deep knee bending." Thomason was livid. The light in his eyes flickered angrily. "But I couldn't say a word. I was afraid of jeopardizing my own chances of being accepted by the army. I dared not call attention to myself. I had to try to slip through unobtrusively. Otherwise I would have told the doctor that Robert was a man without a country, a man without the simple love of a son for his motherland."

Then suddenly Thomason's anger subsided. He cocked his head and stared at me as though he expected me to have already figured out what he was about to say. "That's why Dr. Stone didn't try to stop anyone from leaving," he said unnecessarily. "Like the army doctor, it never occurred to him that anyone would choose not to stay. Not to serve. Not to dedicate his body and soul to a cause so much more noble than the future of one selfish individual."

Thomason stood up and opened the door. "But he doesn't feel that way any more, Gus." He winked. "In case you or anyone else has any bright ideas, Dr. Stone isn't as naive as he was a few days ago. Those counselors taught him a lesson."

"What about you?"

"Thanks for the crackers."

"Did you get through? Did you make it to Vietnam? Is that where that happened?" I asked, barely glancing at Thomason's thumbless right hand on the doorknob. He knew exactly what I was referring to. And by the time he could say "No," that hand had pulled the door to the kitchen closed behind him so that four fingers were virtually all that remained to be seen of Geoff Thomason.

VIII

The next night, during what had become our regular midnight discussion, Thomason told me never to ask about his hand.

"It's none of your business," he said, but I sensed that he wanted me to continue to pry and pursue and back him into a corner so that he could unburden himself. There could be no doubt that whatever had happened to Thomason's hand had plagued him ever since. The slightest reference to it caused an immediate flush, a tensing around his mouth and eyes, a squirming in his chair or a shifting from foot to foot. But beneath this first flush of uneasiness and his angry reluctance to discuss the matter, I thought I detected a person who was eager to be found out, who was tired of hiding the truth from strangers and from himself, who wanted to be pushed just hard enough so that the awful explanation would come spurting out like a blast of bad air he had kept locked in his lungs far too long.

"I wear a wig," I said suddenly, hoping the revelation of a personal embarrassment might make him confide in me. "I'm wearing it right now."

"That mess is a wig?" Thomason couldn't believe it. He wanted to laugh.

"A full wig. Top to bottom. One hundred percent human hair. Some other human's, not mine."

"I don't believe it."

"Why not?"

"It's ridiculous."

"What's so ridiculous about it?"

"You're an old man, that's why. Why do you need a wig? Who the hell are you trying to impress? And Jesus, Gus, if it is a wig, why does it look so bad?"

"I got it to please my last wife," I said as seriously as I could, not wanting the wig to become a joke. "She thought it made me look distinguished. Of all the women I have ever known, and the several I have married, my last wife was the only one who thought there was something distinguished about me. She was the one who talked me into a wig. It was the only thing she ever asked of me, and I couldn't refuse her. You see, when I met Patricia, she was a nun. It's true. Sister Patricia. I met her in an army hospital overseas when I was getting patched up, and she fell in love with me. You don't have to believe it if you don't want to," I said to Thomason's shocked face, "but she quit the sisters to become my wife. She divorced the church to marry a bald-headed buzzard almost three times her age. I was everything she had ever dreamed of and searched for, she said. I was the answer to her prayers — and they were the real McCoy, those prayers, not just some teenage prattle about Mr. Right. She proved how devoted she was, too. Patricia worshiped me. She washed me, fed me, slept at my feet, took care of me from the minute my eyes opened in the morning until they closed at night. She was even willing to do the kinds of things I never thought you learned at a convent. And all she ever asked in return was for me to wear a wig. Because it befitted a man of my stature, she insisted. She even had it picked out. It was snowy white with thick waves that came all the way down the sides and back. I looked like a judge or a king. Now it's a mess, like the rest of me. It's been too long between shampoos, and the tape's lost its stickiness so it shifts around — you may not see it, but I can feel it shifting — and it's yellow from too much sun, and thin and frayed and worn all the way through to the cap in spots. But nobody notices. Maybe people just think it's the mange. It sure looked good back then though. Patricia used to say I looked just like she had always pictured God."

Our candle was about to burn out.

"How bald are you, Gus?"

"I'm as bald as you can get. Every hair — gone!"

"Did it just fall out?" Thomason asked, nervously touching his own curly mop.

"I was fourteen."

"What happened?" he asked, trying to peek under the wig at my ill-fated scalp.

"It got burned off. Every last hair. Burned off."

"How?"

"What difference does it make?" I said mysteriously.

"I don't believe you."

"You can believe me, Thomason. Under this mess of yellow knots, there's the most pitiful head you ever saw." I leaned forward and half squinted and half winked through the last few flickers of candlelight. "I'll show you, if you tell me about your thumb."

IX

He didn't tell me about his thumb that night. He was too furious, reacting as if he'd been the butt of a practical joke, and he stormed out of the kitchen leaving me with a sharp warning.

"Don't push me, Gus. You push me and I'll have you taking off that wig in front of everybody tomorrow morning at flag salute."

But he wanted to be pushed, especially by someone who would sympathize with his embarrassment, someone who covered up his own embarrassment with a wig.

Thomason covered up his embarrassment with his art. Whatever he photographed or wrote was presented as unflawed even if that misrepresented an imperfect, flawed subject. He had done that with his brochure for Camp Freedom, eliminating from pictures and text anything that did not serve the ultimate purpose of the brochure — to persuade parents to place their children in Dr. Stone's hands.

"Elimination is illumination. Get rid of the darkness and there shall be light," Thomason philosophized. "Do you remember what Michelangelo said when he was asked how he went about carving a masterpiece out of a block of marble? 'The figure is in the stone to begin with,' he answered. 'I just chip away at everything that is not the figure.' "

How, I wondered, could I get Thomason to chip away at the figure itself?

ELEVEN

On the sixth day of camp, at brilliant high noon, a sports car came roaring down the one-lane dirt road as easily as if it had been on tracks, the high-gloss finish of the sleek model throwing off bursts of sunlight.

The sports car stopped in the middle of the compound. Without turning off the motor, the driver got out and began scanning the several groups of boys scattered about the area. One group was ankle deep in the soft ooze along the banks of Colt's Point; they were slopping in the mud like pigs, rolling in it, painting their faces, wrestling each other to the shifting slippery ground. Another group was challenging the rickety footbridge; each boy would stride defiantly over the bridge until he reached the center where he had to decide whether the creaking slats beneath his feet would hold, knowing that once he was across he had to return via the same creaking slats. On the other side of the compound another group was filling in a waste ditch before digging a new one. Estabrook was leading the largest group in a series of calisthenics; the sweating, exhausted boys could not follow Estabrook's perfectly executed push-ups, sit-ups, and jumping jacks, but that did not seem to bother the drill instructor.

The driver of the sports car appeared to be looking for someone in particular, his boy I assumed, but settled for the familiar face of Geoff Thomason who had been watching a rehearsal of *The Sound of Music.* He turned off the ignition and walked over to Thomason, Frannie, Frankie, and the rest of the cast who were in front of one of the cabins.

"Harry Mix!" he said impatiently. "Harry Jr.'s father. Where's Harry Jr.? I've been trying to find this place for two days. It's an emergency. Where's my boy?"

Thomason was speechless. We all were. The few moments of silence must have seemed like an eternity to Harry Mix, Sr. Once again he scanned the compound.

"Hey! Get the hell away from there!" he yelled at the muddy boys who had chased each other onto the trunk of the shiny sports car.

"Where's my boy, Thomason?" Harry Sr. demanded after his second look around the compound proved as fruitless as the first.

"Tell him!" Frankie suddenly shouted. The words just shot out of his mouth. No one could believe what Frankie had said or the tone of voice in which he had said it. Clearly he had had enough. He had suffered his own silence and everyone else's for too long, and now he was about to tell the outside world that Camp Freedom was a lie! That it was a nightmare!

Harry Sr. wheeled around and in two steps was upon Frankie.

"Tell me what?!" he ordered, grabbing Frankie by the shirt. Harry Sr. was dressed for Palm Springs, not the pinelands, and his pastel clothes, well-groomed hair, and artificial-looking suntan undermined the urgency and despair he tried to convey.

"Your boy is in that cabin, there. He's sick. He hasn't talked to anyone in two days. He's in a trance," Frankie said. "All these boys need help. Stone's a madman. He's been twisting their little backbones. He's been working extra hard on Harry. He killed two men from the woods who never hurt anyone. We're trapped here. Thomason's just as bad. He fooled you. Does this look like the brochure he showed you?" Frankie blurted out every detail he could think of. "There's no electricity, no phone, no proper food, no supervision, just leeches, mouse turds, torture chambers, one boy disappeared in the woods, another boy can't stop throwing up, your boy's in a trance, he's been shocked by something, he just snapped one night, you've got to do something, you've got to help him, you've got to help all of them."

All Harry Sr. heard was that his son was in a trance, that he hadn't spoken to anyone in two days, that Stone had been working extra hard on the boy.

Stone had appeared at the door to the torture chamber, the cabin with the chiropractic table inside, where he had been preparing for his lunchtime appointments. The chiropractor moved toward the trouble very slowly, clenching his fist like a gunfighter in a bad movie, and my heart pounded for poor Frankie. But then I saw something in Stone's eyes that I had never seen there before. "Look," I wanted to scream out to Thomason. "Look at him! He's been defeated. He can't cure poor little Harry!"

Harry Sr. rushed into the cabin and came out again quickly, his son in his arms, his eyes squinting at the harsh light, his nose and mouth screwed up in disgust, for no one had bothered to clean Harry Jr. who reeked of his own messes. Holding his son in extended arms so that the limp body of his boy would not dirty his stylish pastel clothes, Harry Sr. carried him in the direction of his car. When the boy became too heavy he gently lowered him to the ground.

Albert was fawning over the car, petting its fender as though it were alive. Then he put his head in through the driver's window and began speaking a fast and furious French. But Harry Sr. never noticed, or he surely would have chased the Frenchman away. He was too concerned with solving the immediate problem of getting Harry Jr. ready for the long ride home.

"Do you have any clothes for the boy? Where are his clothes? Will someone please help us?" Harry Sr. searched for a sympathetic face in the crowd that had begun to gather, but no one was willing to challenge Stone by helping Harry Sr. and his son. Everyone waited for Stone to speak. Everyone but Frankie.

"His clothes are in the cabin," Frankie volunteered. "I'll go get them." He had already gone beyond the point of no return.

Stone could kill him only once.

"Harry! Talk to me, Harry!" the boy's father pleaded.

"He can't talk," one of the boys said indifferently.

Harry Sr. appealed to Thomason, "My wife . . . Harry's mother
. . . she . . . she . . ." and then turned his troubled and tearful eyes
down toward his son's expressionless face, "she went away, Harry,
she went away," and hugged Harry Jr. to his grieving bosom.
"She's dead, Harry. Mommy's dead," he cried into his limp son's
shoulder.

Frankie had come out of the cabin with clean clothes for
Harry Jr. in time to hear Harry Sr. tell his son that Mommy
was dead. Frankie was not surprised.

The crowd grew more and more anxious. The boys were
waiting for Stone to make his move. They expected him to
handle anything that might interrupt the natural order of the
camp, the healthful flow of life's current from nerve to nerve,
from director to camper. But Stone did nothing.

"He was very close to his mother," Harry Sr. explained, putting clean clothes on his rag-doll son. "I know he couldn't have
known two days ago when she died, but I'd swear this not talking and not moving is all a reaction to her death. Somehow he
did know. Maybe she told him. Maybe there's a spiritual bond
between them. They were so close. I've got to get him home.
Maybe if he sees her he'll snap out of it?"

"He needs a doctor," Frankie interrupted, "a real doctor."

Thomason rocked forward on his feet and verbally sprang at
Frankie. "He needs a doctor?" he screamed in feigned amazement that anyone would dare think such a thing. "He *has* a
doctor! He *has* a doctor!"

Harry Sr. never stopped dressing Harry Jr.

"His doctor is too modest to speak out at a time like this,
but no doctor in the world can do more for Harry than he can,"
Thomason shouted into Frankie's face. Then he stood over
Harry Sr. and repeated, "No doctor in the world can do more
for Harry than Dr. Stone can! Don't you understand? It's a short
circuit. It's a misalignment. This boy will be walking and talking in no time at all. Who else can find the one secret break in

the millions of crisscrossing circuits? Who else can you trust to put things right so that Harry can heal himself? They'll give him drugs and shock therapy and God only knows what else. They'll fill him full of their poisons, stick him like a voodoo doll, wring out his brain like a sponge. You've got to save him!"

Harry Sr. picked up his son, pressing him to his sweat-stained pastel shirt, and started walking toward his sports car. Geoff Thomason shouted after him, continuing his harangue on the subject of Stone's magical hands, the miracle of chiropractic, the virtue of natural health and healing, the dangerous practices of the AMA, the importance of discipline, the desperate need in this country for leadership, and back again to Stone, to the miracle of his hands and the certain disaster Harry Sr. courted by taking his son out of those hands. Who knows how loud and long Thomason would have gone on had he not glanced back over his shoulder and found that Stone was not there.

Harry Sr. continued walking toward his car. Thomason stood staring at the ghost of Stone while some of the bolder campers took advantage of Thomason's daze and followed Harry Jr. and his father to the sports car. They, too, wanted to be taken away, like Harry Jr., lovingly cradled in their fathers' arms, gently strapped into the front seat of a sleek sports car, and driven home.

As the somber crowd drew nearer the car it became apparent that Albert was not leaning into an empty vehicle. Hiding in the back seat, pressed against the black upholstery, terrified by the leering Frenchman wearing nothing but underpants and then by the dozen pairs of small eyes, a beautiful young woman tried desperately to be invisible. Her coloring and the color of her clothing were anything but inconspicuous, for contrasted against the black leather were her long white skirt, flimsy white halter, and powdery white Oriental skin. Disappearing against the black upholstery were the shiny black strands of silk flowing from her fair scalp to within an electric inch of her delicate white shoulders.

The boys gazed at her as if upon a miracle. From the expressions on their faces their Lady of the Sports Car might well have been aglow, her phosphorescent visage floating up through the roof of the sports car, hovering overhead like the face of a madonna drawn upon the moon.

Albert, however, saw Our Lady of the Sports Car quite differently. He insulted her honor in his best street French. Though she did not understand French, his meaning was all too clear: he punctuated his alien wooing by vibrating his tongue and noisily sucking imaginary body parts.

"Get out of there!" Harry Sr. yelled. Albert jerked himself out of the window, smashing his head into the top of the frame.

"Get away from my car, you filthy, disgusting, degenerate idiot!" Harry Sr. screamed. "You miserable, disgusting pig," he yelled, opening the door to the passenger side. Carefully he positioned Harry Jr. in the front bucket seat, reclining the backrest so the boy would be as comfortable as possible. The car was very small, the back seat not nearly spacious enough for Harry Jr. to lie across. But Harry Sr. would have wanted him in front anyway, so he could keep an eye on his son, and so that his girlfriend remained out of sight. When Harry's wife died, the beautiful woman with luminous skin and black silken hair had gone from mistress to girlfriend, but she had not yet gone from back seat to front.

Harry moved his son's arms, legs, torso, and head into a normal passenger's position. But Harry Jr. did not look like a normal passenger. However natural his pose might have appeared, there was an unnatural deadness within that made Harry Jr. resemble a mannequin. One half expected to see a wire protrude from a fingertip, a strut break out of the torso, a plastic lid slide smoothly down the hard bubble of an eye when the boy's head was tilted back.

"Good-by, Harry," said one of the boys.

Harry Sr. closed the passenger door and waded through the campers to get around to the driver's side. "You boys stay here!" he said, slipping behind the wheel and putting his key into the ignition. "This is where you boys are supposed to be! Your fathers and mothers know where you are! If there's a problem, they'll come for you just like I came for Harry. Go back and play! What were you doing?"

"We were singing a song," Frankie said softly, suddenly aware that his heroic condemnation of Camp Freedom had fallen on deaf ears.

The car started. Harry Sr. revved the engine, hoping the noise and vibrations would make the boys back away from his car. "Get back," he warned.

To still the awful noise, Frankie put his recorder to his lips and began to play the song Frannie's cast had been rehearsing. The sweet reedy melody swallowed the roar of the sports car's engine like a snake gracefully slithering, striking, and devouring something much larger than itself.

Frankie did not have the effect of a pied piper. Instead the boys stared even more intently at the woman in the back, at her pale hand resting on her lap. When at last her hand moved, their hearts skipped crazily. Her long, delicate fingers reached into her straw bag. She brought out a small, white, circular plastic case and had some difficulty opening it. There was a reddish color on the inside of one section of the case and a soft pink pad on the inside of the other section. The pad was not attached, and she lifted it out of the plastic cover, dabbed it into the reddish color, and then pressed the pad to her cheek, leaving a rose blush on the face of the moon.

"Get out of the way! Move back! You can't come with us! There's no room!" Harry Sr. pleaded.

Angry revving of the car's powerful engine backed the boys away, but they never stopped staring at their pale Lady. Tears filled their eyes but did not fall. This was a parting that required courage, and each boy, in his own way, had found enough.

Slowly the sports car moved back and forward, trying to turn around, Harry Sr. yelling out the window the whole time for the boys to get out of the way.

"Good-by, Harry! shouted Frannie, suddenly coming to life. She ran toward the car and rounded up her boys. "Let's send him off in style," she urged them, speaking in a voice they recognized as the one she used when she wanted them to sing. Frannie joined Frankie at the bridge of the song.

Finally the sports car was headed in the right direction. One by one, the boys joined Frannie and Frankie in song, but they barely knew the words and were even less sure of the tune, making Frannie a virtual soloist. Though it had been Frankie's idea to wield this simple, soaring melody against the sorrowful circumstances that had visited Camp Freedom, it was now Frannie's coarse but confident voice that articulated the spirit of those who were never to leave.

The sports car accelerated and the boys in front had to leap out of the way. One boy refused to get out of the way and Harry Sr. had to bring the sports car to a sudden stop, throwing Harry Jr. into the well-padded dash. His body, still in the pose that his father had molded, looked corpselike hanging over the strained seat belt.

The sports car backed up quickly, nearly hit Albert who cursed it in French, stopped, veered to the right while accelerating forward again, by-passed Homer, the boy who had stood in its way, and sped off toward the one-lane dirt road.

Homer gave the finger to the car. Sammy felt his bladder overflow two or three drops and then shut itself off automatically. Jeffie waved good-by to the moon.

II

I watched their faces through the shadows of flames Estabrook's bonfire threw. They didn't need me any more. Maybe they never needed me. I could go. I could wait until the last spark of fire let night fall and make off into the woods without any problem — except for Stone's henchmen.

Following the murders of the Kristal brothers, Stone had warned us that he had "people" out in the woods, hired thugs pretending to be pineys.

"In this world," Stone had said, "you have to make certain concessions to evil. You have to fight fire with fire. If an action interrupts the natural flow of good health within a system — whether that system is the human body or the human condition — then we are forced to react. I have been forced to use agents, cunning and brave, to infiltrate the enemy's camp. They're hiding in the woods right now, keeping guard. They are licensed by me to use whatever means they deem necessary to correct disturbances in the system. They will be there day and night to protect us. To prevent this" — he had nodded his head contemptuously at the Kristal corpses — "to keep jackals like them out of Camp Freedom. And to keep all of us safely in."

Double agents: protecting us and imprisoning us. Maybe real, maybe not. Still I had to leave. But not without saying good-by to the campers, or without one last midnight conversation with Geoff Thomason. I still had to show him my bald head. He still had to tell me about his missing thumb.

III

Estabrook's bonfire was at its greatest height and intensity. Good scout that he was, he had cleared the ground for a diameter of at least three meters and shaped his tinder, kindling, and fuel into a huge tepee ready for lighting. Then he had lit a curl of birchbark which flared almost at once, spreading flame crazily throughout the latticework of tiny dried twigs beneath the larger branches and limbs. Thick gray smoke escaped from the skin of a hissing green limb. Sparks lived and died in the draft. Dead wood exploded. Now the blaze was three times the size of the original tepee, which was crumbling within the red-and-yellow cyclone of flames it had ignited.

The campers and counselors were huddled around the bonfire, but there was no closeness. Thomason made a few announcements. He read from a single sheet of paper in the flickering light. When the director arrived, Thomason hurried through the remaining announcements and shut up, turning the evening over to Stone.

"Now this is what camp is all about, isn't it, boys?" the director said. He stood dangerously close to the fire, and the flickering made his face look as though it were twitching. It reminded me of the way his face looked when he was fighting off one of his seizures.

Estabrook meanwhile kept feeding more and more large dead

limbs into the voracious blaze. The flames were now well over Stone's head as he slowly circled the collapsing tepee in the manner of a witch doctor engaged in some pagan dance. Everyone expected him to launch into another of his passionate lectures on the great art and science of chiropractic. But instead he spoke of marshmallows and campfire songs.

"Why don't you lead the boys in something, Frances? And why don't you and Albert bring some marshmallows and sharp sticks," he said to me.

Turning away from the huge fire made the night seem blacker than it was. While Albert groped through the fringe of the woods for sharp sticks to use for toasting marshmallows, I went into the kitchen and collected a dozen bags of the soft white confection. Behind us I heard Frannie valiantly trying to lead the boys in a famous song. But the only other coherent sound was Frankie's accompaniment on the recorder. The few campers who attempted to sing along were off key.

On the way back to the blazing campfire I decided to disguise my good-bys by telling a story.

"You try putting a marshmallow in a fire this size and your whole arm'll go up. Why don't I tell a story while it dies down," I half asked, half announced. Thomason or Stone could have stopped me from telling my tale, but neither of them said a word.

Frannie asked, "What kind of story, Gus?"

"Just a story. A good-night story."

"Is it scary?" Jeffie wanted to know.

Only Jeffie showed childish awe in my presence. He still remembered our first moments together when I had heard him whimpering outside the kitchen window and lifted him up and brought him inside and tried to protect him from Stone. Now, in his regressive behavior, Jeffie tended to look up to everyone, to think of everyone as his protector, but there had been something special in the way he asked me if my story was scary; he expected me to change it for him, to take out all the scary parts, to love him as much as he loved me. Because I loved him, I couldn't lie.

"All stories are scary," I said solemnly.

IV

"When I was small, smaller than you," I began, listening to my own ancient voice as though I were as much in the dark as my audience, an old man told me about a thing he remembered hearing that had happened on this very spot." I drove my forefinger into the dirt for emphasis.

"It happened before New Jersey was called New Jersey, that long ago. An Indian of these parts staked out an area of this very land," I spread my fingers and arms for emphasis, "and called his new nation Wee-Kwaw-Hik."

Fingers of flame came loose in the fire's failing attempts to reach the moon. The roar of its efforts almost drowned out my storytelling voice, but I managed to outshout the fire and still maintain the folksy style necessary to make my harrowing tale palatable.

"In those days the bones of an animal could conjure a magic as thick as smoke. And bones were what that wild but not so crazy Indian used to stake out his claim. Big clean bones; the femurs and tibias of deer. He stuck them every few feet into the ground, making a sort of fence.

"Other Indians in the region were scared off by the bone fence, feeling the naked whiteness in their own bones. But one of them, the Indian's father, dared to trespass. When the Indian saw his father striding defiantly toward him, he drew an arrow, stretched his bow against it, and released. The old Indian fell to the ground, his son's arrow in his heart. Almost immediately, two of the father's friends ran into the son's nation with raised, menacing tomahawks. These two the Indian also stopped in their tracks. It had been foolhardy of them not to think that he who had constructed an entire border of bone would have neglected to keep at the ready whatever ammunition might be necessary to protect his new nation.

"Later that day other Indians nosed around under cover of the grove of pines, and when they ventured too far out into the open — zing — they were shot for their trouble. Eventually, toward dusk, the Indian police arrived; a band of good hunters, good marksmen, fierce, unafraid braves came to subdue the

Indian and reclaim his nation. But the Indian outfought the police.

"When the old man described the battle, it seemed that there were fifty of the one wild Indian and only one of the many braves who had come to avenge a son's killing of his father. To Indians, elders were sacred. If a father told his son to lop off his finger or his arm or his leg, the son would obey.

"Against all odds, the Indian fought his fight. Instead of swarming in and taking their losses and guaranteeing a victory, the braves attacked in small, hesitant groups and allowed themselves to be kept at a distance — and thus at a disadvantage. From a distance, the wild Indian was able to pick off the braves one by one. He had succeeded in reversing the odds and in holding his enemies at bay by dashing to just the right vantage, to just the right cover, to snipe here and ambush there as if some sixth sense whispered all the right moves. Some say the greatest generals have such a sense, that they can feel the presence of an enemy bristle up the backs of their necks, that they always find themselves in the right place at the right time. I think such a sixth sense does exist but isn't peculiar to crazed Indians or to decorated generals. I think that all sorts of people find themselves at the right place at the right time. Some of them are with us tonight, sitting around this fire. You can tell that they hear the whispering. Sometimes you can see them walking the soil of an ancient nation as if they were the first to have claimed it. Well, they can have it, if they're strong enough. The wild Indian tried and went up in puffs of smoke that said: Let this be a lesson to you.

"When the braves finally couldn't help but overcome him — 'Lawd,' the old man would say, 'they was so many of 'em; they was two new ones for every one he'd zing; some of 'em was bound to git theyselves through; hell, odds don't stay turned forever' — the wild Indian was captured by accident.

"Two braves who were good climbers tried to reach the wild Indian by stealing quietly through the treetops. Their plan was to start outside the circle a short way down Colt's Point in the glen of blooming sycamores, work their way around the pines, if possible, and zero in on the great oaks that still guard Wee-

Kwaw-Hik's western frontier. The lead brave got all the way
into the oaks, but he lost his quiver. The second brave knew
he'd never make it past the pines, but he had a full quiver and
half a good idea. Though he couldn't set his sight on the wild
Indian, the second brave saw a clear path of flight to the fat
trunk of the oak where the lead brave was out on a limb, poised
but no longer armed for the kill. The second brave took long,
deliberate aim and let fly, thinking to send his leader an arrow.
But the arrow caught the lead brave by surprise. It didn't hit
him, but the whir of its flight and the thwack of its bite upset
his balance and he fell more than thirty feet onto the wild
Indian. The wild Indian broke the brave's fall; the fall broke
the wild Indian's hip and leg and his will, and, of course, his
hold on the new nation.

" 'Sorrowful,' the old man would cluck and sigh. 'Seems like
more happens by accident than on purpose. Makes you wonder
if our best-laid plans ain't just the accidental falling together of
pieces that happen to fit.' But the capture, that sure didn't fit.
And not the verdict either.

"Nothing like this had ever happened in Indian memory, a
brave killing his own father. So they tied him to a tree —
maybe the one those squirrels are playing in right now," I said,
pointing back over my shoulder in the direction of the big oak
for emphasis. "And they set fire to the stakes at his feet." Each
boy sat with a stick in his hand, a marshmallow stuck onto the
end like the pierced heart of the wild Indian's father. "And they
whooped and hollered like Indians." The twitching shadows of
flame on Stone's face melted into sweating flesh and darting
eyes. "And their eyes and throats were filled with the awful sight
and stink of him melting and crackling and turning into smoke
and ash, save his bones." Good-by, boys.

V

"He just stood there, Gus."

"What else could he do? What did *you* do? Frankie was the
only one who did anything."

"And never paid for it," Thomason said.

"He failed. Dr. George Stone failed, and he knew it. He tried to bring Harry back and couldn't. It got out of hand, Thomason. Why do you think Stone looked so defeated? Beneath all the mumbo jumbo, he's a logical man. What can be more logical than the nervous system? He believes in chiropractic with all his heart, you know that. That's why he was so defeated. He realized that his art, his science, his very life was not all powerful."

"He should have done something. Anything."

"He did. He gave the boy back to his father."

"Who I suppose is beating him right now until the poor little bastard finally walks and talks for his old man."

"You hate parents, don't you? The idea of parents. You and Stone had it all figured out — you did anyway — this camp, his physical manipulations, your psychological and photographic manipulations, a brave new world where kids are not indulged by their parents but are molded into men."

"You mean where they are not victims of their parents' indulgence."

"And I mean 'molded,' like Harry Jr."

"Yes, I hate them. They're the ones responsible for every flaw, every weakness, every inability, every handicap. They're the ones who should be laughed at, or excluded, not me!"

"I think you give parents too much credit."

"What do you know, old man? What can you even remember about your parents?"

"I remember my father vividly. He was a follower of a little-known branch of a mystical religion. His long beard always smelled of my mother. He would quote obscure philosophers like Pico della Mirandola, who I thought was a flower. He made me wear a black suit and a black hat and grow my hair according to the unstylish precepts of his religion. I remember seeing myself in a glass storefront at no more than fourteen years of age. I looked like Toulouse-Lautrec. Then suddenly my father grew old. In just a few months he went from young and strong to old and frail. His beard was filled with cracker crumbs. No longer did he have the physical strength to make me do as he wanted, but he made me submit to his intelligence. And he loved to argue. Arguing gave him the chance to rhapsodize about the aim and worth of his beliefs. And he ranted grandly, the crumbs flying from his beard like sparks, and the hot sap of worship flowing through his veins, threatening to split apart the tips of his fingers and spray pods and spores and seeds of every kind throughout the room in an epiphany of his oneness with God and Nature and Magic. I argued that I didn't want to wear the black suit and black hat. But I lost the argument because I had no other clothes. There was only one thing to do; I took the hot liquid wax that had collected beneath his rows of holy candles and burned all the hair from my head. That was my devotion. The pain was my rapture."

"You're lying!"

"Let me loosen the tape."

"You're lying!"

"Look for yourself!"

"If you're telling the truth, then you know what a fiend your father was."

"Did he do this?! Here! Look! He didn't do it! I did it! I burned my hair off!"

"But he made you."

"I made me."

"He was responsible! You didn't know what you were doing! He should have known better than to leave you with no other choice. He shouldn't have left. They should have waited another five minutes, that's all. Five minutes more and they would have known!"

"Would five minutes have made any difference really?"

"They would have found her! Yes, it would have made a difference. All the difference in the world. She died, Gus! She died!"

"Who?"

"And if they had waited five minutes more they would have found her."

"Who died?"

"They were going on a belated honeymoon — that's what he told me, Gus. He took a perverted delight in making sure I knew that they hadn't been able to take a honeymoon when they were first married because she was already a month pregnant and he had to work two jobs to get the 'three of us' started. He never let me forget that instead of spending their wedding gifts on an unforgettable honeymoon, they had to use that money to buy supplies for my untimely arrival. He listed every item in a nasty tone of voice making it painfully clear that my carriage had replaced their limousine, that my crib had replaced their heart-shaped bed, that my formula had replaced their champagne cocktails. But two years later he had established himself in business and was able to quit his second job and take her on a belated cruise to Bermuda. We lived in a big apartment house exactly four floors below my grandmother.

"My grandmother was going to take care of me for the week they were away. She was going to stay in our apartment since all the baby's things were there. But, as usual, she was late. They called her up and asked her where she was, what she was doing, and she told them not to worry, she'd be right down. But they did worry. They had a boat to catch, and they were haunted by the vision of a gangplank's being hoisted as their liner pulled away without them, the foot or two of water widening into a channel, a river, and then a swollen sea heaving between them and the paradise of their belated honeymoon in Bermuda. They had phoned ahead for a taxi, urging that it be on time, and they heard it pull up in front of the building, an insistant honking announcing its arrival. They looked out the front window and saw the driver leaning on the horn. Then they watched him get out and open the trunk. Then they watched him pace back and forth the length of his cab, reaching in through the window every sixteen paces or so to give the horn another two or three blasts, the last one always the longest and angriest. Again they phoned my grandmother. 'I've got one hand on the doorknob,' she said. She was on her way, but precious seconds were passing. My father looked at his watch; the driver honked; my mother imagined thousands of cars jamming the highway; the ship sounded its thunderous departing whistle; my father's watch ticked louder than the honking, louder than the whistle, louder than the traffic, louder than the panic. 'You'll be right down?

Okay! We're going to go then. The cab's outside and we're going
to miss the damned boat. Don't forget there's a lambchop for
you thawing on the stove, and Geoffrey's in his high chair, just
give him — okay okay, I know you know. Don't forget, it's the
Pompano Beach Hotel — I'm coming! — We have to go! See
you in a week!' And they left. Oh, they kissed me good-by
and told me to be good and promised to bring me back a present
from Bermuda. But they left me. I was only fourteen months
old, but I swear I heard her tell her mother that they were
leaving, that they'd see her in a week. And then they left me. In
my highchair. Waiting for my grandmother who had one hand
on the doorknob, don't worry. She was just a quick elevator
ride away. A ride she had taken a thousand times before. Except
this time she never made it. As she pushed the down button for
the elevator, she had a massive heart attack and died on the floor
in front of the elevator doors which opened, buzzed, and closed
again. By the time the police were able to get all the information together and figure out where my grandmother was heading
with her overnight bag, I had been left completely alone for
three days."

"And you've never forgiven your mother and father since."

"I cried."

"Or your grandmother, for that matter."

"All babies cry. But I howled until I had no voice left and I
could hardly catch my breath."

"And you've never forgiven Harry's parents either, have you?
Or Stoney's?"

"And I sat there in my own pee and in my own diarrhea, my
legs burning hot, burning cold . . ."

"Or Sammy's parents?"

"And as my body emptied itself out all over itself and my lungs
ached for a breath of air between convulsive gasps and hiccups,
I felt an incredible hunger and an incredible thirst create a new
person inside of me who made me suck the air desperately and
flail my arms wildly and shut my eyes to keep out the burning
salt tears . . ."

"You've never forgiven any parent for what you yourself did,

Thomason. For what all the children do to themselves."

"... and, Gus! God! Gus! God Almighty, Gus! I ate it ... I ate it, Gus!"

"Is my hair on straight? I'm going," Gus said.

"I ate my own thumb!"

PART III

Kingdom Come

TWELVE

Jus' Gus, the chief cook, the one lone observer, left Camp Freedom at top speed, although there was no one around to stop him except Geoff Thomason. The old man ran right out of his wig, catching it on a branch, never stopping for fear of becoming an easy target for Stone's thugs, if they were out there. But the idea that they might be out there was enough. The idea that there were human beings with powers Gus could neither see nor combat began to work on the old man's brain. Once he had gotten himself back to his familiar hideout where he felt safely protected by the cover of brush and rock, he was afraid to move a muscle.

In the morning, when Gus's absence was discovered, Dr. George Stone announced that he would personally track Gus down — if his agents hadn't already done the job — and make the old buzzard pay for leaving the camp with no cook. The gun that had killed the Kristals in his hand, Stone spent the better part of the morning searching the woods. At high noon a shot rang out from deep in the pines, and everyone froze.

Stone returned, the gun still in his hand, his other hand hidden behind his back.

"Well, it's over. I had to do it."

No one moved. Campers and counselors stopped what they

were doing and looked at Stone from their scattered positions.

"How do we know?" Thomason, of all people, challenged Stone.

"Because I've got proof!" Stone shouted. He spotted Thomason in front of one of the cabins and walked toward him. "I've got the kind of proof Gus himself would have appreciated!" he called out as he continued walking toward Thomason.

"I shot him!" Stone shouted, thrusting his hand out from behind his back. "And I scalped him!" The familiar mop of gray-and-yellow hair was clutched in his fist. He held it up and waved it like a flag over a conquered nation.

II

Things began to fall apart at Camp Freedom. Or they began to fall together, accidentally, as the old man in Gus's campfire story had concluded.

Two fathers, an aunt, and a chauffeur came to pick up their charges and, like Harry Mix, they would take no other campers with them. One of the boys begged his visiting parents to take him home, but they fought back tears and refused, assuring their son that he'd get used to being away if he gave it more time. Frances spent a whole day helping her boys write letters home which she asked Albert to post that evening, and the next morning she found the letters torn and scattered in one of the trenches the boys used as a toilet. The campers were treated more violently during their chiropractic sessions, and the adjustments which once seemed to benefit them now seemed to be weakening them as a wide assortment of stiff necks, back aches, and painful joints developed. It was announced that there would not be a performance of *The Sound of Music*. A scabby black dog limped out of the woods, an illegible message tied to its neck with a piece of rope. The scribblings had been made on the back side of a circular that advertised remarkable savings on canned goods; the indecipherable markings became an ink-blot test.

Everyone "read" the message in his or her own way. Estabrook was sure it was a ransom note from the kidnapper who held Ezra, or possibly from Ezra himself. Albert was convinced it was written in French by someone with a very poor command of the language. Though he never voiced his belief, Thomason felt that it was a message from Gus urging him to chip away at the figure of Stone. Francis approached the message scientifically. With the magnifying glass of his Swiss Army knife, he analyzed the age of the paper and the markings, concluding that the message had been freshly penned in ballpoint by a purposeful hand. Francis set himself the thrilling task of deciphering what he decided had to be an exotic code. Stone, of course, attributed the "ridiculous chicken scratching" to "those illiterate retards of the woods who keep threatening us with the contagion of their evil diseases, their rotten teeth, hunched backs, crossed eyes, dwarfism and who knows what else. The two we killed in self-defense were just two cankers on the fetid, oozing body of the devil!" He even insisted, though Francis corrected him, that the note had been written in the blood of some poor sacrificial animal.

"It was written with a ballpoint," Francis contradicted Stone, flush with the confidence of someone who had defied the authorities once and gotten away with it. Once.

Frances worried about her friend's boldness, and that no doubt colored her interpretation of the message, which was by far the most curious and the most frightening.

Frances read it as a prophecy. She ignored what was written and reacted to the fact that the message existed at all, and that it had emanated from the forbidden wood, and that it had been delivered by blackest death on four scabby legs.

Frances was not sure what danger the message foretold, but she felt it was sexual. As she waited her turn to try deciphering the message, she began to imagine herself being sexually attacked. In her fantasy she was in her cabin at the darkest moment of the night and heard someone panting. She opened her eyes and saw only blackness. The panting continued. It got closer and hotter and suddenly she could smell the breath of her invisible attacker. She felt him upon her, his hot breath inhumanly foul, his tiny fists batting against her shoulders and neck. Though he was fully

stretched out over her, he was half her size. And then she realized he was the black night incarnate, a piece of it forcing itself
into her. She reached down to grab at his weapon and felt the
long, thin, hairy organ of the dog spurt all over her thighs.

After she had seen the message, held it in her own hands, and
felt its vibrations commingle with her own irrepressible stirrings,
her imaginings became more frightfully real. Images that she
had actually seen were extended and exaggerated into hideous
scenes of sexual menace. Albert's penis, which Frances could not
avoid seeing at various times flopping or stretching or peeking
out of his disgusting underpants, now came at her in terrifying
slow motion. It saluted. It was greasy and veinous and tied off at
the tip like a swollen red sausage. Then suddenly it was rooted
in the bulging flash of white Frances had seen between Stone's
legs when she had watched him doing sit-ups. The same swollen
weapon that had belonged to Albert and Stone attached itself to
Estabrook, too, and Marcus Kristal, and Gus, and even to Stoney.

Instead of being attacked by Geoff Thomason, Frances attacked
him. He, too, had come in the night and forced himself upon
her, succeeding in guiding his weapon through her forbidden
wood and deep, deep into her gut. But when he tried to get away,
she held him with internal muscles and would not let go. As
Thomason struggled, Frances tightened and squeezed until she
could feel vestigial teeth digging into his weapon. But Thomason
would not give up. He pulled and strained and grunted, drool
slopping into his curly beard, and finally was able to pull away,
reeling backward across the cabin and against the wall. There
he lay, cradling his raw and ragged right arm, blood flowing freely
from its ravaged hand, the thumb still imprisoned inside Frances.

She did not fantasize about Francis at all.

III

Officer John Kim arrived on a motorcycle, the escaped counselor
in the sidecar.

Kim was an American-born Japanese who was proud to wear

the blue uniform of the Pennsylvania Police Department. He had his hat under his arm, his gloves strapped to his shoulder by an epaulet, and one hand on his gun handle for effect.

The counselor led Kim around the grounds, pointing out offenses. But it soon became apparent that if there were to be any charges brought they would have to be trumped up. The camp may have been in disarray, but the counselor could not point to any real evidence of wrongdoing. When Kim and the counselor got to Stone's cabin which housed the dread chiropractic table, Stone smugly invited Officer Kim inside.

"Would you like an adjustment, Officer?"

"Then you'll see what I'm talking about," the counselor said quickly, his voice and manner straining under the frustration of not being able to convince the law that the law had been broken.

"It hurts, of course, in the beginning," Stone said smoothly, "but it feels good in the end, Officer."

"He almost broke my back. This place is like a prison camp," the counselor argued.

"I'm surprised you felt any pain at all," Stone addressed the panicking counselor. "You were so drunk when you drove down here I thought you were numb."

Kim glared at the counselor as though he were grilling him.

"Do you know, Officer, that a chiropractic adjustment can even help detoxify a person who has an unlawful amount of alcohol in his bloodstream?" Stone added for good measure.

The counselor could feel Kim's trust drain out of his own body and start filling up Stone's body.

"I don't guess you're interested in pressing charges," the young officer asked the counselor.

"*I'll* press charges!" It was Francis. Francis knew that his chances of getting Officer John Kim to make an arrest were no better than the counselor's, but he wanted to seize the dramatic opportunity of the moment to exercise his courage to speak out. He felt sanctified by the truth and as invulnerable as one who has been a witness to the truth.

"I'll press charges against the devil! He has terrorized, threatened, and tortured our little boys in the name of discipline, therapy, and moral rectitude. I have seen the devil's thumbprint on every pressure point. I have seen the blood drain from a little boy's face because he was sure leeches were sucking that blood out through his leg. I've seen a boy vanish, snatched by the devil's hand and pulled into a maze of woods. I've seen our little boys lose the use of a limb, speech, movement and, worst of all, I have seen them lose faith. They deserted. They went over to the other side. They mutilated a skylark. They threw malingerers from their own ranks into the leech-infested stream or the bogey-infested woods or the fly-infested toilet trenches. They saw two young men lying dead, murdered, right where I'm standing, but our little boys raised a flag in honor of murder and won't ever say a word about it. If I accuse the devil of murder, I'll be all alone."

"Did you say murder?" Kim asked, his Japanese eyes wideening.

"This sacred wood is littered with the corpses of the enemy," Francis said. "And a few months from now, or a few years, our two corpses will be just another headline, two more dead bodies found in the Jersey pinelands, and people will nod knowingly and blame it on the mob."

"Jersey!?" Kim said, suddenly startled. "This isn't Jersey, is it?" he asked the counselor angrily. "We didn't cross into Jersey, did we? I thought we were still in Pennsylvania. I don't have any goddamned jurisdiction in Jersey, for Chrissakes!"

IV

"Francis?"

Frances whispered his name in the middle of the night.

"Francis?"

"Is that you?" Francis awoke.

"I'm scared."

"Don't."

"I'm scared. I've had a premonition. Something awful is going to happen."

"Something awful always happens. Remember what Gus said? 'All stories are scary.' "

"The policeman wouldn't save us."

"It wasn't his jurisdiction. It's ours. We have to save ourselves. We have to make sure we get what's rightfully ours." He put his hand under her chin and turned her face so that they were staring into each other's eyes.

"And what is rightfully ours?" she said, recalling the Seminar Training Exercise called The Catechism.

"Attention." Francis answered quickly.

"What else?"

"Respect."

"What else?"

"A demilitarized zone."

"How is it measured?"

"By an arm's length."

"Whose arm?"

"The other person's."

"What if they trespass into the DMZ?"

"Stand my ground."

"What else?"

"Stare them down. Stare them back. Stare them into kingdom come."

He kissed her, their lips finding each other in the dark like magnets.

V

Geneva Diego arrived in a panel truck emblazoned with the famous logo of a national TV network. The same symbol — an eagle's eye and beak — was sewn onto a patch on Geneva Diego's hunter-green blazer, and she seemed prouder of that breast than of her other one. Her permanent-waved hair was long and full, and below her corona of curls were two bright eyes and a brilliant red mouth. She and her two-man crew had come to Camp Freedom on the strength of an anonymous tip.

"Are you Stone?" she asked Estabrook.

"We're here to investigate a report that the kids are being mistreated," she said to Stone after Estabrook steered her to the director. Geneva Diego spoke like a policeman informing a suspect of his legal rights. "According to my source — and it looks like he's right — there's no supervision, no organization, lousy facilities, etcetera, etcetera. I'm from —"

"I know where you're from," Stone said. "We've got nothing to hide. I'll have someone show you around."

Stone asked Geoff Thomason to give Geneva Diego and her crew a tour of the camp. There was nothing to be ashamed of, the director thought. And if there was, Geoff Thomason would know how to present it to its best advantage.

But as Thomason showed Geneva Diego and her crew through the compound, he did not attempt to influence what the Eagle Eye camera saw and the mircrophone heard. He only wanted to make sure that nothing was missed.

"What's this all about?" the reporter asked when Thomason led her into the cabin Stone used to give his chiropractic adjustments. The guide explained.

"Domingo, make a note, this chiropractic stuff could be another segment," Geneva Diego said to her sound man as Thomason dropped the center out of the table to help demonstrate why the adjustments were so painful.

"Did you get that? Do that again," she said to her cameraman and Thomason.

Thomason continued to expose every detail of life at Camp Freedom to Geneva Diego's Eagle Eye. He showed her the stream and offered to submerge his naked arm to try to catch a leech for the camera; he showed her the reeking toilet trenches, the spot where Ezra had vanished, the field-mouse turds on the floors of the cabins; he pointed out the bizarre spectacle of Albert's prancing around with the older boys, his penis, which every so often peeked out of his filthy underpants, causing problems for the cameraman who usually edited as he taped.

"This is good stuff," Geneva Diego told herself every time the crew got another ugly detail on tape.

Then Thomason suggested that she interview the campers and also the people in charge.

Stoney balked at the camera and microphone and ran off.

Estabrook said something about an honest day's work for an honest dollar.

Sammy and Jeffie said they were supposed to be in a show called *The Sound of Music,* but that the show had been canceled.

"*The Sound of Music* is just too ambitious," Frances said. "Too many parts, too many sets, too many songs. We just haven't got the facilities. We need to start with something simpler."

Stone smiled and looked at the camera as though it were an audience of millions. "The time has come," he said, "for the American Medical Association to admit that chiropractic is the way of the future."

Thomason said that he could not add anything to what the others had said.

Then Homer ran in front of the camera. Instinctively, Geneva Diego shoved the microphone into Homer's face and the cameraman rolled the tape. The boy was so anxious to tell his story that he tripped over his own words. By telling everything at once, he told nothing very clearly. But he could not stop himself.

"This is good stuff," Geneva Diego said loudly enough for Domingo to overhear, making sure he was getting all of poor Homer's incoherent spitting and sputtering on the tape recorder.

Homer might have gone on for hours. But a group of boys appointed themselves to march up to him and shout him down. When Homer continued to scream out his incoherent story, the boys lifted him up onto their shoulders. No one made a move to stop the vigilantes, and the news crew followed them past the cabins toward the edge of the wood. Just before they reached the wood, the boys stopped and lifted Homer still higher. Together, the boys counted to three, swaying to and fro in rhythm, and at the count of three hurled Homer into a buzzing miasma of human waste.

"Got it!" the cameraman shouted gleefully, kneeling at the edge of the trench. "Just about out of tape, too!"

Francis had let the boys throw Homer into the trench. He had let them make a hero of Homer. Now he fished Homer out of the trench and held the filthy boy up to the camera.

"This is your story," Francis said. "The story of parents who

235

don't care, charlatans who care too much, and boys who only care about themselves."

"Should I tell him we're out of tape?" the cameraman whispered to Geneva Diego.

"Your story is about misguided men who have twisted the bodies and minds of little boys," Francis continued. "Homer was not speaking only for himself. He was speaking for all the boys of Camp Freedom. They're all in danger. They've all been forsaken and enslaved."

"I think you've got enough," Stone said to the cameraman, firmly squeezing his arm. The cameraman hurried back to the truck, Domingo and Geneva Diego quickly following.

As Domingo shifted into first gear, Geneva Diego stuck her wild curls out of the window. "I don't know when this segment is going to be on," she said to no one in particular. "Tomorrow, if it's a slow night. But probably Thursday or Friday. You know, a thing like this they can keep on the shelf until they really need it. They gotta run all the topical stuff first — what the president said, the latest junta, who died. They can put this on next year if they want, who'd know the difference? But figure Friday. Check tomorrow night and Thursday just in case. But figure Friday."

Thomason thought he heard "This is good stuff" as the Eagle's Eye disappeared along the dirt road.

THIRTEEN

Frances's premonition of danger came to pass.

It was just before daybreak. Sandy Chalkers was squatting over a trench in the disappearing darkness, tending her hysterical menstruation in the privacy of predawn. Fifteen minutes later the trenches would be teeming with defecating, urinating, expectorating little boys.

When she had stopped the flow of her own blood, Sandy Chalkers accidentally discovered the blood of someone else. She swung her left leg back over the trench, but her foot landed on soft ground. Her knee buckled and she went sprawling onto the sandy strip of ground between the narrow trench and the shrubby fringe of the forest. Her hand felt something damp and sticky which she recognized immediately as blood. Though she was not hurt by the fall, the recognition of blood weakened her. She could not get up. Fumes from the trenches suddenly overwhelmed her. A bird wheeled and screeched. She passed out.

She thought she had been out for hours, but the blood was still wet and sticky when Sandy Chalkers regained consciousness. She was strong enough now to get to her feet.

"God God God God God God God God . . ." she panted when she saw the body through the thick underbrush and the heavy low limbs of the pines.

Had Sandy Chalkers seen the full extent of the damage done, her hysterical screams would have awakened everyone. But she saw only a few spots of flesh and blood through the underbrush and branches, and that confused her more than it frightened her. Whimpering rather than screaming, she jogged back to the compound and entered the first cabin she came to.

"Hey! What's going on?!" Estabrook shouted, grabbing for a sheet, a towel, his pants, anything to hide his morning erection from the wide-eyed intruder shaking him awake.

"It's one of us I think!" Sandy Chalkers blurted between heavy breaths, pointing toward the woods. Estabrook sprang to his feet unashamedly and followed her down to the edge of the woods, crazily hopping into his pants while trying to keep up with her, his mind racing far ahead of them both, imagining a battered but safe Ezra lying in the bush.

By now the sun was up. Everyone started down to the edge of the woods to visit the toilet trenches. When they got there they surrounded the trembling figure of Sandy Chalkers who was looking on as Estabrook tore away the stubborn vines and stalks that bound the body.

One could hear the rustle of leaves in a stand of oak farther into the wood. A deer appeared on the bluff and the crowd of nearly forty was so still the deer was not frightened away. It bent its neck gracefully and nibbled at a shrub; then it picked up its head and froze, neck still bent, large brown eyes watching Estabrook pull a body by its legs from a tangle of stalks, branches, vines, and torn clothing.

Frances looked at the body and grew faint. The tops of the trees spun against the brilliant sky. An invisible force kept butting her painlessly in the chest, driving out every bit of the air she fought frantically to breathe. Then the ground on which Frances stood turned to water and she sank. But she refused to lose consciousness.

The body had been attacked, perhaps by a beast, although the side of the head looked as if it had been clubbed, or bashed in with a large smooth stone. Such a blow, or repeated blows, would have been more than enough to knock out the victim and allow the monstrous attacker to commit the other far more hideous violations to the body.

Who or what could have done it? Who or what could have clawed and bitten and torn flesh away from bone? The flayed skin and hundreds of tiny red lacerations, many of them clotted but many of them still trickling jagged lines of blood, conjured up an attack by a beast or a madman.

Who or what?

The right thigh bone was broken, causing a large swollen mass that made the thigh look like it contained a football.

Who or what?

The most frantic part of the attack seemed to center and radiate outward from genitalia too mutilated to classify according to gender.

Who? What?

The face, however, told gender as well as surprise and disbelief.

"Let me," Frances insisted, trying to sit up.

"I'll do it," Stone overruled. He helped Estabrook remove the vines and weeds and leaves and needles from the body. Sometimes a peel of skin would come off along with the weed or leaf that was being removed. Carefully, Stone and Estabrook moved the body clear of the brush and onto the sandy tract of ground between the brush and the trenches.

The crowd gasped.

Francis opened his eyes.

"He's alive!" someone shouted.

Frances fought to her knees and moved closer to the mutilated body of her friend.

"Don't come closer!" Stone warned. "His nerves are all exposed. He needs to be treated."

Frances threw herself past Stone and crawled over to Francis whose eyes were closed again. Frances took his bloody hand in hers and wept freely for the first time in her life. It was as difficult to decipher the words she wept as it was to decipher the message that had been tied to the black dog's neck.

Who or what?

Fresh blood ran profusely.

239

Who or what?

It caught the hem of her nightshirt and spread into the absorbent fabric.

Then Geoff Thomason came forward, bent down, and whispered into her ear. Frances let Thomason console her. She let him ease her away from the body. She held on to Francis's bloody hand while Thomason lifted him slightly to inspect the source of the bleeding.

"Oh my God!" Frances cried.

"Get them out of here!" someone yelled, referring to the children, and Estabrook leaped into the crowd of spellbound campers to disperse them.

It was no longer a question of who or what. No beast could have done the awful deed.

"Don't!" Thomason stopped Stone. "Pull it out and you'll pull out all his guts along with it. He needs a hospital. Fast!"

Francis had been brutally raped with his own recorder. Worse, the instrument had been forced into him as far as humanly possible and then hammered in even farther. The inch or two of the recorder that was still visible appeared battered, as if by repeated blows, and it took little imagination to picture the other end buried deep in bone, tissue, and eddying pools of blood.

"Are you telling me what he needs?" Stone confronted Thomason. "Are you telling me what to do for him?"

Francis died while Thomason and Stone argued over the best treatment to save his life. He died while Frances clutched his bloody hand. She thought she heard a faint gurgling whistle emanate from his body, as though the Angel of Death had blown one last breath through Francis's recorder. George Stone was sure he heard the chattering laughter of demented pineys. Geoff Thomason heard the door slam as his parents left on their belated honeymoon.

II

Long after the others had dispersed, Geoff Thomason kept a vigil over Francis's body. Almost two hours passed. Then Thomason stood up and walked to his cabin. He came out with his camera bag and returned to his spot next to Francis.

It was a bright morning. As Thomason switched camera lenses, sunbursts bounced off his equipment. With nine struggling fingers, he removed the standard fifty-millimeter lens from his camera and put it on the ground, finding a soft tuft of grass on which to rest the lens that approximates normal human vision. Then he reached into his bag and removed a telephoto zoom lens ranging in power from eighty to two hundred millimeters. He attached the zoom lens to his camera, enabling himself not only to see four times more closely, but, he hoped, four times more clearly.

With the same instrument of deceit he had used to lure children and their parents to Camp Freedom, Geoff Thomason photographed the very pores of reality.

Click.

He would make amends.

Click.

He would capture the awful truth exactly.

Click.

He would neither crop nor superimpose these photos to make reality conform to his own distorted sense of the truth.

Click.

This time the whole truth would be told.

Click.

The truth was that he had taken his own thumb.

Click.

The truth was that Francis had taken his own life — whether it had been Stone or Albert or Estabrook or a piney or even Frances who had done the actual deed.

Click.

The truth was that the children, too, had taken their own course in life, and it was not separate from the course they would forever travel, for childhood is not ephemeral, it does not change or die, it is hard as stone, and upon it and around it, we construct the apparatus of adulthood.

Click.

When Stone saw Thomason photographing Francis's hideous

corpse, he knew he could not allow it. He also knew that it was pointless to try to get Thomason back into his camp; the poor misguided fool had become a nonbeliever. Thomason had argued about what to do for Francis like a member of the American Medical Association, and now he was taking pictures like a damned reporter, not like someone who creates brochures about everything that's decent and fundamental and holy. Stone felt a blessed synchronization of nerve and bone and muscle as he lifted his right arm, looked all the way down it to the sight on the gun barrel, and took careful aim at the back of Geoff Thomason's head.

Click.

Even in her shock, Frances automatically lit a cigarette. The cigarette dangled from her lips as she held a match to the tip. The lit match fell from a numb hand. Sparks flew from the explosion in the gun. A ray of sunlight burned through the fifty-millimeter lens.

FOURTEEN

It took fifty-one seconds for the fire to ignite. At precisely 8:16 A.M., a conflagration of incredible intensity and velocity materialized full blown and spread wildly for several miles in all directions. The fire burned brightly for four days and glowed for two more. Even after the firefighting forces had succeeded in drawing their lines and extinguishing the fizzling firestorms, the forest floor smoldered and crackled ominously.

When the area was deemed safe enough for outsiders, the TV news crew returned to Camp Freedom to report on the death and destruction of innocent people and invaluable forests. Finding no one left from the camp to interview, Geneva Diego settled for lingering shots of herself pointing out eerie black-and-white relics of the fire while delivering a maudlin monologue.

"This devastated wasteland you see all around me," she began, "used to be the site of one of the dozens of idyllic summer camps tucked away in the wooded hills and dales of New Jersey. Now it is gone, ravaged by a fiery holocaust. Yet somehow one can still hear the shouts of the swimmers, the giddyups of horseback riders, the crack of a bat, the splash of an oar, the trudge of tired feet on dirt trails, the singing of traditional campfire songs. But the warm and friendly glow of the campfire has been consumed by the hungry flames of a deadly inferno."

No one will ever know exactly what touched off the fire, not that that's unusual in an area as historically rich in mysteriously set fires as the Pine Barrens. One can never discount the theory that the fire started by chance. Soil conditions, fuel build-up in the soil, droughts — even partial ones — combustible litter on the forestal floor, the presence of oily and waxy shrubs such as sheep laurel and leatherleaf, can create or contribute to a spontaneous wildfire ignited by a bolt of lightning, a concentrated sunbeam, the magical and/or accidental generation of a single spark. But man's suspicious nature always favors a more diabolical explanation. And so there are pineys who will go to their graves believing that the fire was set to avenge the murders of two of their own, or that money was the motive — that someone wanted to collect the insurance on a failing business and was willing to defoliate thousands of acres along with the real target. There are cynics who suspect ecological sabotage by godless communists or deranged dissidents. Someone even reported a B-29 flying over the forests, but he wasn't sure if the plane was firebombing the pinelands or spraying chemicals that would put out the fire.

"Here is what remains of the cabins," Geneva Diego reported. "What had been roughly hewn Lincolnesque shelters for young boys learning to become men of self-reliance and character are now nothing more than brittle shells crumbling at the slightest touch."

The chrome of Dr. George Stone's chiropractic table stood intact. The leather was burned away, exposing the skeleton of the frame and mechanism. In the case of people and animals, it was bone that survived.

"Our cameras were not allowed into the area until the horrible disarray was put into some sort of order. Now one can't help but think of Dresden, Hiroshima, or Auschwitz when one sees the horrifying organization of dead bodies. Behind me is a row of small bodies that are no doubt the charred remains of the boys of Camp Freedom. But which boys are they? Who is John? Who is Tom? Which one is Billy?"

Neatly lined up now, most of the children were found scattered about. But three or four campers were found in one huge black ball of burned bodies held together by a bond of melted flesh. It was impossible to separate the bodies without destroying the individual campers. All had apparently run into the same cabin and found themselves trapped by blazing walls and swirling drafts of intense fire and smoke. They had probably huddled in desperation and hope, each one trying to burrow deeper into the huddle to protect himself from the raging menace. But in the end they could huddle no closer, burrow no deeper. Homer's father recognized his son's part of the ball by two crooked teeth in the boy's lower jaw. Jeffie's mother and father argued over charred flesh and bone, his mother insisting that they had found Jeffie's remains, his father insisting that no one could be sure it was Jeffie. Sammy's father made his wife wait outside the shell of the cabin while he tried to remove Sammy's ring without removing the boy's finger along with it. The fourth body, if there were four bodies, was immortalized as "the unrecognizable ash of my youth" in a private printing of poems by James Alleman Alcock.

"And there are the adults, too. The counselors, the instructors, the young men and women who gave their summers and their lives to teach and lead and love. So far an estimated twelve adult bodies have been found within a mile of the spot where I'm standing. One was found just ten feet away. Several were discovered deeper into the woods. Perhaps they were running for help only to be outrun by what authorities have called an unusually fast fire considering the absence of a strong wind."

But the fire had created its own wind. It had created its own rules. Drafts and eddies of air had thrown fireballs in all directions; fiery clouds of smoke had hovered over the treetops; it had appeared that the forests were being sucked up into a cyclone of flame while roaring red-and-black waves rolled downward, confounding the rules of normal fire behavior. In this unpredictable manner, lush terrain had been transformed suddenly into a ghostly lunar landscape.

"We're here now nearly five miles away from the heart of the fire in an area known as Red Lake. Incredibly, one entire side of the house you see behind me is blistered and blackened from the fallout of heat and smoke. The family that lives here refuses to be interviewed, but I saw some of the children earlier. They were shuffling and stooped over and they kept grabbing at their throats and stomachs."

Scientists will discover genetic mutations in the surviving Kristal line which they will trace back as far as technology allows. These mutations will be attributed to exposure to extreme thermal temperatures and radiation. A condition of retardation akin to Mongolism but uncharacteristic in its dwarfism will be called Red Lake Syndrome. The only known victims of Red Lake Syndrome will be "discovered" much the same as uncivilized tribes have been "discovered" in deepest darkest Africa, and, in a sensational piece of investigative reporting, the reporter will call the descendants of the Kristals "forgotten inhabitants of deepest darkest America."

Other pineys who were caught in the most extreme raging of the conflagration either died or suffered pain and disease that made them wish for death. Before she was allowed at the site of the fire, Geneva Diego visited a hospital where the burn victims were being attended. The doctor in charge talked to her at great length, off the record. However, his vivid descriptions of the bodies affected Geneva Diego's reports. When she delivered her melodramatic commentary, she pictured men, women, and children whose clothing had been burned from their naked black-and-pink bodies. Burns scarred their chests and legs and backs. Hair was scorched away, heads grotesquely inflated. Some victims were convulsing. Others hemorrhaged. Others could not keep from vomiting, could not even keep down the water given to them by weeping nurses. Gristly flesh hung in flaps and strips, or bubbled with tumors, or oozed a liquid that aggravated the burning pain. So cruel was this fire that it had torn all the way through flesh to deteriorate bone marrow and had still left its victims hopelessly alive. Survivors could expect ulcers, cancers, tuberculosis, cloudy and swollen livers and spleens, changes in their gonads and endocrine glands, disfiguration, discoloration, lifelong trauma.

"Perhaps the luckiest ones are dead," Geneva Diego would

have liked to say. She began the summation of her report by reading from hastily researched notes. "You won't always find the most witty and colorful pineland names on a gas station map. There are names like *One Eye Bush, Dead Dog Come Alive, Whistlin' Bridge Leap, No More Mule, Fiddler's Elbow,* and a hundred more that describe gullies, groves, swamps, bogs, disappearances, elopements, miracles, and other real or legendary occurrences." Putting away her piece of paper, Geneva Diego stared into the Eagle's Eye and suggested that "Today we might want to add a few more names — sad and terrible names like *No More Trees, No More Animals, No More People.*"

The beginning and end of Geneva Diego's report were recorded back to back to save time; they would be cut apart in the studio.

"We end where we began," she said. "Fish are now belly-up in that once refreshing stream, and the banks recede quickly into a terrible barrenness. This is the site . . . *was* the site . . . of Camp Freedom, where little boys came to experience the joy and wonder and responsibilities of living with nature. Perhaps one of those boys left this," Geneva Diego mused, stooping down to the ground to indicate a pile of stones. "This is a universal symbol for danger. Three stones piled one on top of the other. This is how one camper warns another that there is danger ahead. Maybe this is how a youngster from Camp Freedom tried to warn us that nature can be violent, too, and heartless, and that the responsibility can be overwhelming."

The camera moved in for a close-up of the three stones.

"All the area surrounding these stones has been destroyed by the fire. All you can see are the scorched limbs and trunks of once proud trees, the dead roots of ravaged underbrush, the charred and bloated remains of trapped, panicked wildlife: a true wasteland where only the warning of danger survives intact."

But it is not a wasteland. The songposts are gone, yet in the air a strange singing persists.

Seedlings survive. Cones that need heat to open have been forced by the solar temperatures of the fire. The highbush blueberry, largest and juiciest when borne on a young shoot, will soon poke through the black floor of the forest.

The pitch pines served as torches, maintaining the fire even while resisting its destruction. In the light of a pitch-pine torch, some animals preyed upon others, having been treated to an unexpected feast as smoke and heat flushed a thousand woodland creatures from their suffocating tunnels, holes, and hollows.

The animals will adapt. With the forest canopy gone, and the ground black, the laws of moisture, food, and cover will change, further altering the landscape and the habits of its wildlife. But the rough is gone. The forest is freer for the travel of its animals. There are fewer trunks, branches, stems, and twigs. There is less foliage, debris, and litter.

The warning of danger built of three indestructible stones was not all that remained. Transformation also survived.

"This is Geneva Diego for 'Eagle Eye News,'" she signed off. And then, more brightly to her crew, "Hey, that was good stuff!"